A
Christmas
Miracle
in the
Little Irish
Village

BOOKS BY MICHELLE VERNAL

THE LITTLE IRISH VILLAGE SERIES

Christmas in the Little Irish Village

New Beginnings in the Little Irish Village

ISABEL'S STORY

The Promise

The Letter

LIVERPOOL BRIDES SERIES

The Autumn Posy

The Winter Posy

The Spring Posy

The Summer Posy

THE GUESTHOUSE ON THE GREEN SERIES

O'Mara's

Moira-Lisa Smile

What goes on Tour

Rosi's Regrets

Christmas at O'Mara's

A Wedding at O'Mara's

Maureen's Song

The O'Maras in LaLa Land

Due in March

Michelle Vernal

A
Christmas
Miracle
in the
Little Irish
Village

bookouture

Published by Bookouture in 2023

An imprint of Storyfire Ltd.
Carmelite House
50 Victoria Embankment
London EC4Y 0DZ

www.bookouture.com

ISBN: 978-1-83790-818-9
eBook ISBN: 978-1-83790-817-2

For my family

May those who love us love us.
And those that don't love us,
May God turn their hearts.
And if He doesn't turn their hearts,
May he turn their ankles,
So we'll know them by their limping.

— IRISH BLESSING

PROLOGUE

The Village of Emerald Bay

This was what it must feel like to be a celebrity, Ava thought, leaning past her twin sister, Grace, to where the well-wishers were gathered outside the Shamrock Inn to see them off. The pub she'd always called home, which also served as a B&B, was a sturdy monument to their happy childhood. Today, with its window boxes filled with gardenias in deepening shades of pink, smartly painted blue door and gold signage, it was straight out of an Irish tourism brochure. She scanned the familiar faces hungrily, but the person she wanted to see most wasn't there. It was hard not to let her smile falter.

The excitement of their impending adventure was rippling off Grace like an electrical current. She was squeezed between herself and their dad behind the wheel, cases piled high in the back.

'Watch it with your hand there, Grace.' Liam Kelly flinched as she nearly slapped his cheek waving back at Mam and Nan.

You'd think it was the wilds of Timbuktu she and Grace were

heading to, not London, Ava thought, catching sight of Nan dabbing her eyes with her good lace handkerchief, the one reserved for solemn occasions like granddaughters leaving home. As for Mam, she could have been an Olympic flag bearer! Shannon, the oldest of the Kelly girls, had made the trip from Galway and, with an arm around their mam's shoulder, was on hand to pour the tea and butter the scones once her youngest sisters had gone. As for Imogen and Hannah, they'd FaceTimed from Dublin and Cork to wish the twins well on their journey first thing that morning.

What would travel have been like in the days before the internet? Ava had wondered as her sisters loomed out at her from their mam's iPad. Knowing she could push a button on her phone and see her family whenever homesickness twanged might be comforting, but it also tempered the adventurous days of old.

As dear old Mr Kenny, perched on his mobility scooter, sounded the horn his son had bought him as a safety measure, she winced. It was as though he was signalling the start of a race. It was a horn many an Emerald Bay pedestrian or motorist had cursed since its arrival last Christmas. His tooting earned a glare from Mrs Tattersall.

Meanwhile, Enda Dunne's retired farm dog, Shep, began barking and running about, eagerly joining in the cacophonous ruckus as he relived his sheep-herding glory days. Mrs Tattersall turned her attention to Enda. She didn't take kindly to being herded. Although with that Nessie Doyle perm special peeking out from under her headscarf, she did have a look of a sheep about her, Ava decided.

Liam Kelly took his cue, and with a final honk of his Hilux's horn, he pressed down on the accelerator. Sergeant Badger, who happened to be cruising up Main Street, had got wind the youngest Kelly girls were flying the nest today, so he chose to turn a blind eye to the illegally parked yellow wagon as it pulled away from the kerb and veered over to the opposite side of the road.

Ava twisted in her seat, craning her neck as she looked back to see if Shane had made a last-second appearance.

There was no sign of him, and she slumped back, feeling Grace's eyes boring into her.

'Right, Ava Kelly,' her twin bossed, taking charge in her usual manner. 'From this moment forth, Shane Egan, the fishy-arsed eejit, is to be cast from your mind. There's to be none of this long-distance love malarkey you're on about. London's a fresh start. Do you hear me?'

Ava dipped her head in acknowledgement, not surprised Grace had read her mind. She was right. Oh, she'd promised Shane they could make it work. Her in London, him in Emerald Bay, but they both knew they were words designed to patch over the facts.

She was leaving.

Of course, it wasn't just him she was leaving. Weren't all the shopkeepers on Main Street standing outside their businesses waving goodbye? Ava plastered the smile firmly back on her face as she gave the royal wave to Dermot Molloy, the local butcher, and Rita Quigley from Quigley's Quill bookshop.

'Dear God, what's that Eileen Carroll's after wearing? It looks like a knitted ski suit. Does she not know we've no Alps in Ireland?' Grace snorted.

'That or a giant Babygro,' Ava added, eager for the distraction the woollen shop owner and village gossip had provided.

Liam bit back a grin, adding that, sure, Eileen was sensibly dressed given the nip in the air and what that woman could do with a set of knitting needles was a wonder, but even he couldn't help a snigger after spying the sweatshirt Isla Mullins – who ran the Irish shop – had chosen to wear: 'I Left My Heart in Ireland'. 'Subtle she's not,' he muttered.

With flour on her cheeks, Carmel Brady waved out with

one hand and clutched her skirt to stop it from billowing up in the breeze with her other. Behind her, the Silver Spoon cafe tables were full of passing punters.

'I'm going to miss Carmel's apple shortcake, but don't be telling Nan I said that, Dad.' Grace waved back at the cafe owner.

Ava thought Shannon's best pal and owner of Emerald Bay's bespoke jewellery and art gallery, Mermaids, Freya Devlin, looked like a mermaid today. Her blue hair streamed behind her on the gusting wind, and Liam tooted for her benefit.

Then they passed under the Bon Voyage banner, fluttering under a watery blue sky the same shade as Ava's eyes. It signalled they were officially leaving Emerald Bay, the village where she knew everyone, for a city where they knew no one. That was the thing when you were a twin, though. You were never truly on your own.

Ava had to go. She had to know if the grass was greener, spread her wings, seek new horizons, all the clichés.

But why did wanting to see more of the world than Emerald Bay have to mean saying goodbye to the man she'd thought she'd be with forever?

1

***

London, one year later

Dating for introverts was tough, twenty-four-year-old Ava Kelly thought, trying to blend in with the wall. She could feel the solid bricks pressing against her back as she skulked under the red awning already adorned with fairy lights outside Carlito's Argentine Grillhouse. The festive season seemed to start earlier each year, she thought, catching sight of the chalkboard on the damp pavement. It urged expediency as the restaurant was now taking bookings for Christmas functions along with offering grass-fed steak to die for.

Carlito's – which had been her date Tyson's suggestion – was far enough from the Tottenham flat she shared with Grace to set her nerves jangling. Ava was unfamiliar with Argentine food and only knew a little about the South American country, but it was more than she knew about Tyson, and she'd like to visit it one day. Argentina conjured images of grasslands, cattle and cowboys, only they were called gauchos, and she'd read that they were a nation who adored red meat.

She wasn't big on beef, but she was a people-pleaser, so she'd messaged Tyson back to say Carlito's sounded grand.

Now here she was, delaying their first in-person meeting, and in a bid to stop herself biting her nails down to the quick, she decided there was nothing for it but to recite the Kelly girls' mantra:

'When it comes to men, remember these rules.
The Kelly girls don't date tools.
If he produces a toothpick, get out of there quick!
If he's got bad breath, it's the kiss of death.
A whiff of BO? Just say no.
If you're out for dinner, you'll know he's not a winner by the fish he decides to eat,
But most of all, if he's got Crocs on his feet, then sister, cross the street.'

She smiled to herself, but it faded fast as an uninvited question butted into her thoughts. *What if she'd got her outfit all wrong? What if, instead of channelling the boho vibe she loved, she looked ready for Bible class in her swishy prairie dress and boots?* The autumn floral shades and high neck set off her fiery colouring, and she'd thought it a wiser choice than Grace's suggestion.

Her sister insisted you couldn't go wrong with a little black dress. She'd offered to loan her hers, but given its length, Ava had replied that she wanted to avoid looking like she was up for more than dessert. She had, however, conceded to wear her hair in a topknot to appease Grace, who'd fussed about with hair-spray and stabbed her with bobby pins before declaring she was good to go and pushing her out the door.

The fluttering anxiety in her belly was unwelcome. Never mind that she wasn't much of a carnivore; she'd be unable to eat a thing the way she felt right now.

What was the time? Ava dug her phone from her coat pocket to see she was five minutes late. 'It's all your fault, Grace.'

She only realised she'd spoken aloud when a pigtailed little girl being tugged along by a woman – presumably her mother – stared openly back at her. It was true, though. Not the being-late part; the loitering-outside-a-restaurant part. If her sister hadn't egged her on to swipe right on Tyson in the first place, she would be at home watching *Coronation Street* with Binky, the neighbour's cat.

A suited man vaping sent up a cloud of steam as he strode past. People were always in such a hurry here. Their eyes never strayed from the path in front of them.

It wasn't too late to do an about-turn and head back to their gaff, she thought, eyeing the flow of people hunched inside their coats, throats muffled by scarfs, all so intent on getting to wherever they were going. When she'd first arrived in London, she used to call out a cheery hello to passers-by like she would at home, but she'd soon copped on that this was culchie behaviour. You didn't make eye contact with people you didn't know in the Big Smoke. It was an unwritten law.

Her phone springing into life made her jump, and she shook her head. It had been under forty minutes since Grace had seen her off, and she was already ringing to check on her.

She stabbed the green icon. 'What?'

'You're hanging about outside the restaurant, aren't you?' her twin panted down the phone.

Ava's gaze flicked to her left and right just in case Grace had followed her, but the coast was clear. 'I'm not,' she lied.

'You are.'

'Am not.' Ava pulled a face; Grace was all-seeing. 'I thought you were going to watch a film.'

'I'm walking and talking on my way to the cinema now.

Sure, you know yourself what you're like, Ava, which is why I'm checking up on you.'

'Well, there's no need to.'

There was every need. Ava chewed the inside of her cheek, wishing she'd suggested a quick drink instead of agreeing to meet Tyson for dinner. The thought of making polite small talk for the next few hours left her cold.

She didn't want a new relationship, but Grace was adamant the best way to get over a traumatic break-up was to get back on the proverbial horse and put herself out there. She'd been mooning for Shane long enough, she'd declared.

Ava's free hand was thrust inside her coat pocket and balled into a fist, her nails digging into her palms. It was all right for Grace. She and their older sisters, Hannah, Imogen and Shannon, were all Tinder pros, although Imo was officially off the market now that she'd hooked up with Ryan O'Malley. So, too, was the oldest of the five Kelly girls, Shannon, with her lovely American, James. Dad was keen on saying 'two down, three to go' whenever the subject of boyfriends came up. It was very annoying, so.

'Ava, are you listening?'

'Yes.'

'What did I just say then?'

'Er, a bus went past, and I didn't catch it.'

A sigh hissed in Ava's ear, and she held the phone away from her, scowling.

'I said, remember our mantra.'

'I've already chanted it.' Ava flashed back to the last time she and her sisters had all been together, and the topic of Ava venturing into the world of dating via an app had come up.

'I've already been there, done that, and I've no intention of going there again, thanks very much,' she'd informed them.

'Why, what was so bad about it?' Shannon had asked.

Ava had filled them in on Zac. His photograph had

reminded her of a brooding Jane Austen character, and she loved *Pride and Prejudice*.

'Mr Darcy,' Imogen had supplied. They all knew their baby sister's penchant for the character.

Ava had nodded. 'Yes, but Zac would have been more at home in a Stephen King novel.'

The Kelly girls had giggled.

'You must have read *Pride and Prejudice* a trillion times,' Shannon had added.

'It's the best romance novel of all time, that's why, and Zac was nothing like how I imagine Fitzwilliam Darcy.'

'Dark hair and eyes, sideburns, moody,' Hannah had piped up.

'You do realise you just described Shane Egan. Not helpful, Hannah.' Grace had glared at her.

Ava had ignored them. 'I could have got past the Mr Darcy thing, but not the tooth picking.' She'd had them in bits as she'd demonstrated Zac studying what he'd dislodged from his incisors with the toothpicks he'd carried in his shirt pocket.

'I bet you stayed for the duration of dinner with your tooth-pick man, too, Ava. Instead of making an excuse and getting out of there,' Imogen had said once she'd stopped laughing.

'She did,' Grace had replied for her sister.

Hannah had tsked. 'You're too nice.'

Shannon had been sympathetic because she'd have done the same.

Grace had grown serious then. 'It's time you let Shane go, Ava. Tell her, you lot. I've tried, but it's not getting through.' She'd glanced to the others for backup, and they'd nodded their agreement.

'The more dates you go on, the easier meeting up with someone new gets,' Imogen had reassured her.

'The key,' Hannah had advised, 'is a checklist.'

'She's right.' Imogen loved a list. 'If your date begins to tick too many boxes by the time the dessert menu's offered, it's time to fake an emergency and leave. Who's got a piece of paper and a pen?'

'In the drawer there – tear a sheet out of the notebook.' Ava had indicated her bedside table. A moment later, she'd leaned over Imogen's shoulder, watching as she wrote the headline, *Top No-Nos for a Potential Match*. She kickstarted the list by writing down no teeth picking, following it up with and underlining smelly breath and/or BO.

'A high level of personal hygiene is imperative, Ava,' Imogen had said, passing the paper to Grace before adding smugly, 'Nev is a walking, talking men's aftershave advertisement.'

Grace had scribbled that wearing Crocs to a restaurant was an instant red flag. It had happened to her, and needless to say, she'd hot-footed it out of there in her on-trend kitten heels. As for Hannah, her input – predictably given the person she'd like to meet most in the world was Greta Thunberg – was that if her dinner date ordered Atlantic cod, halibut, flounder, sole or orange roughy, it was time to get out of there, because she couldn't care for someone who didn't care for their planet. She'd then delivered a lecture on overfishing and eating endangered species.

Ava's lips curved as she remembered the argument that had ensued when Imogen retorted that she was partial to a nice piece of grilled halibut.

'C'mon now. Say it again with me,' Grace urged down the phone, making her sister blink as she pictured herself and her siblings, once they'd finished the list, standing in a circle, hands piled on top of one another like they were American cheerleaders. She dutifully recited the mantra for a second time, finishing with a giggle.

'Right so,' Grace bossed, getting back to business, 'I'll be checking my phone. If you need me to ring and give you an out, just text "H" for help. Got it?'

'Got it.'

'G'won then – go forth and have fun.'

Ava ended the call, slipping her phone back in her pocket, and sighed.

Modern dating wasn't for the faint-hearted; she would have been more at home in the days of gentleman callers and dance cards than apps, she thought, peeling herself off the wall.

She huffed into her hand to check her vigorous tooth-brushing session had seen off the remnants of chicken Caesar wrap she'd unwisely ordered for lunch. It had only dawned on her that the reason the croutons were so yummy was down to all the garlic salt they'd been baked in once she'd already scarfed half the wrap.

Then, running her tongue over her teeth to ensure she didn't have lipstick on them, Ava put her best foot forward and pushed the door to the restaurant open.

2

Carlito's was an assault on the senses. Ava hesitated at the entrance as her eyes, ears and nose tried to catch up. A tantalising smoky barbeque aroma greeted her. At the same time, laughter, the chink of cutlery and conversation were almost overridden by the pulse of a funky Latin beat. Her heart went out to the poor cows whose hides covered the chairs clustered around the tables and the wall spanning the entire right side of the restaurant. The urge to tug at the high neckline of her dress was strong as she scanned the diners for a glimpse of Tyson. God, how she hoped he hadn't posted a profile pic that was twenty years old.

It was a photograph that had seen her and Grace giggling drunkenly over Tinder, pausing with their wine glasses halfway to their lips and looking at one another with raised eyebrows. The word 'hottie' had hovered unsaid between them, but the saying about a photograph never lying was a lie, especially when it came to Tinder profile pics. Everybody knew that.

He was cute, and cute was as good a basis for a new relationship as any, Grace had urged. Ava thought it was a shallow comment, but Grace had argued that it was no different to catching the eye of a fella she liked the look of in a pub or club and striking up a conversation.

It was utterly different, in Ava's opinion. For one thing, she'd never be the one to instigate a conversation with a stranger in a pub, but she also knew her sister well enough to know there was no point in arguing with her. Hence, here she was in a vegan's nightmare, feeling like the neck of her autumnal prairie dress was strangling her.

'Buenas noches, madam. You have a reservation?'

Ava dragged her anxious gaze from the dining area to take stock of the waiter who'd materialised before her. He was as Argentinian as she was, but he looked the part. The word *snake-hipped* sprang to mind.

It was a description she'd read in a novel recently, and, liking it, she'd written it in her notebook. Ava loved words and had grand plans to write a book one of these days.

Swarthy, too, she decided, thinking about how she would write the waiter as a character. 'Er, I'm meeting someone. Tyson – Tyson, er...' Too late, she realised she didn't have his last name, and it was unlikely he'd booked the table under 'About Tyson'.

Snakehips raised a dark eyebrow, and Ava flushed at the thought that he now knew, or guessed, she was here for, all going well, a casual hook-up. Not that it was any of his business. But she had been raised in a small Irish village – casual hook-ups didn't happen in Emerald Bay, where everybody knew each other. Not to her, at any rate. She'd only ever been with Shane.

'Let me see.' He picked up the iPad from behind what resembled more of a pulpit than a pay station and frowned at the screen. He flicked through the bookings with his finger for a second or two before bestowing her with a smile that would reassure his mammy he'd been brushing twice daily. 'Here we are. Tyson Hiscock – a table for two at seven thirty.'

Janey Mack! Ava barely registered him asking if he could

take her coat because she was stuck on Hiscock. Ava Hiscock! She itched to call Grace and tell her she'd yet to meet Tyson, but there was no future for them.

'Your coat, madam?' Snakehips repeated.

'Oh, yes, sorry.' She retrieved her phone before sliding out of her coat, watching as he hung it on a cow horn protruding from the wall behind the pulpit and feeling oddly exposed standing there in just her dress.

'If you'd care to follow me, madam.'

Ava nodded. *Hiscock, Hiscock, Hiscock,* she repeated like one of her dad's scratched old CDs, trailing after Snakehips as he slithered into the heart of the dining area. She concluded there was no good way of saying the surname. Instead, she focused on the patrons sawing into slabs of steak.

So intently was she staring at a T-bone with blood oozing out the middle, she narrowly avoided rear-ending Snakehips as he paused alongside a table. She peeped around him in time to witness Tyson Hiscock give his reflection on the back of the dessert spoon a final once-over before putting it down as he registered the shadow that had fallen across the white tablecloth.

Snakehips pulled the chair opposite her date out, and with a faltering twitch of her lips in greeting, Ava sat down. Tyson's return smile was self-assured. He wasn't a newbie to this then, and deciding not to fixate on the surname or spoon gazing, she took a calming breath. She was here now and might as well make the most of it. Besides, he was just as cute as his profile picture, and dear God, the arms on him. The man was built.

'Hello there. I'm Ava.' She picked up the menu for something to do with her hands.

'Tyson – hi.' He gave her an approving smile.

Ava's eyes darted away from his round blue ones. They reminded her of a baby's – wide and a little blank. 'Sure, it's a gloomy night out there. It feels like we haven't seen the sun in forever.'

Tyson didn't respond to the weather chit-chat, saying, 'So, you're probably wondering why my Tinder profile doesn't tell you much about me?'

No, she'd assumed he was just wary of sharing too much online, as she was.

He took her silence as acquiescence. 'It's because I'm at a stage in my life where I'm sick of all the superficial shit, you know?'

This time, Ava nodded. She did know, and a spike of hope pierced her. She hated all that *look at me living my best life*, social-media crap, something that was a bone of contention with Grace, given her job title was Social Media Coordinator.

'I want to find a woman who sees past the brawn to the brain within.' He tapped the side of his head, presumably in case Ava was unsure where that part of his anatomy might live.

Her insides curled in on themselves.

'I might be a personal trainer and professional bodybuilder.' He paused and flexed his arm.

Ava watched, horrified, as a bicep popped up like a hillock.

'But I'm a deep thinker. You can squeeze it if you like?'

'Er, no thanks – you're grand.' Jaysus! She was about to dine with Popeye, and even though she knew she'd laugh about his offer one day, it was fair to say it wouldn't be with him. She'd been in his company for under three minutes, they hadn't even ordered a drink and it was blindingly obvious Tyson Hiscock wasn't a keeper. She may be better suited to speed dating.

Snakehips returned with impeccable timing to take their drinks order. Tyson relaxed his arm, picking up his phone and fiddling with it before passing it to Snakehips. 'Would you mind, mate?' Then he glanced at Ava. 'OK with you?' But he was already twisting in his seat and baring his teeth for the camera.

When the phone was handed back, Tyson inspected the photo with an approving nod.

Maybe she hadn't looked like a startled meerkat after all, Ava thought as Tyson flashed the photo her way before setting his phone back down.

'It's for my Insta, @TysonThebody.'

So much for being sick of all the superficial shit, Ava thought as Tyson ordered a carafe of still water.

'It's spring, not tap?'

'Of course, sir.'

Ava asked for her usual house white.

'It's important to stay hydrated,' Tyson informed her once they were alone again, before explaining why in detail.

When Ava's wine was placed in front of her, her eyes were glazing over, and she took a hefty swig because it was important to stay hydrated. Should she text Grace? Undecided, she opened the menu.

Her mouth watered as she read the description for the chicken Milanesa. She resolved to get through this, the date from hell, because there was nothing to eat in the cupboard back at hers and Grace's gaff except a can of baked beans, and she'd had beans on toast last night.

'I'm in the bulk-up phase, which means high calories and a protein-rich diet.'

'I think I'm permanently in the bulk-up phase,' Ava responded, laughing a little too loudly as the wine hit her empty stomach.

Tyson didn't crack a smile, and once again, Snakehips saved the day by choosing that moment to return and ask them if they were ready to order their mains.

'Chicken Milanesa for me, please.'

'And I'll have the five-hundred-gram sirloin, medium rare, with no salad or chips.'

'Just the steak, sir?'

'I'm protein only. Will I get a discount on my meal?'

Ava slunk down in her seat.

There was to be no discount, and Tyson handed his menu back like a champion defeated before checking himself out in the gleaming knife this time. Ava watched him perk back up and was surprised by what he said next.

'So, Ava, tell me about you.'

It was like being interviewed for a job as Tyson clasped his hands on the table before him. They were little, out of proportion to the rest of him. Or at least what she'd seen from the waist up, and she had no plans to see what lay below.

'Er, well, there's not much to tell. I'm from a small village on Ireland's West Coast, where my parents run the local pub, the Shamrock Inn, and I've been living in London with my twin sister, Grace, for the last year.'

That brought a flicker of interest. 'Are you identical?'

'Yes and no. We've both got the red hair and blue eyes, but I've a little birthmark, just here.' Ava pointed to her jaw. 'And Grace keeps her hair much shorter. Our style's different, too.'

At first glance, their faces were the same, but if you took the time for a slower second appraisal, you might spot the subtle nuances like the birthmark. Ava's features were watercolour to Grace's acrylic. Her jawline was softer than her sister's, too, which, more often than not, was set determinedly.

'It's not hard to tell who's who. And I've three other sisters. Shannon, the oldest, is a nurse; Imogen's an interior designer; and Hannah's our eco-warrior. And yourself?'

'I've got an older brother, Mike. He's a pro wrestler. Get it? Mike and Tyson – Mike Tyson?'

No. She didn't, because wasn't he a boxer? 'And are you from London?'

'Leyton. Mike and I still live with our mum because she supports our dietary needs and busy lifestyles.'

In other words, she ran about after them, Ava thought.

'And what do you do?' Tyson asked.

'For work, you mean?'

'Yeah.'

'I'm a freelance copywriter.'

It was met with a blank stare.

'Basically, I design and create print, digital, social media, video, television and radio advertisements. I'm working at an ad agency at the moment on a six-month contract. But what I'd really like to do is write a novel.' Ava had no idea why she'd shared that – perhaps because when she said the words out loud, it made her dream seem tangible.

'Then why don't you?' Tyson asked perfectly reasonably, smoothing a stray lock of hair back into place before chugging back his water and waiting for her response.

Why didn't she?

'Fear.' She realised it as she said it. 'Fear of failure. And I need more life experience behind me. I want to travel and see a bit. That was the point of coming to London.' She shrugged. 'Otherwise, I've nothing to draw on except Emerald Bay and my time at college.'

Mind, there were plenty of characters in the village, she mused. Poor old Paddy sprang to mind. He spent his days pickled and was in love with a life-size cardboard cut-out of a model from Heneghan's Pharmacy's Christmas perfume campaign. He'd called her Bridget. Other faces from home flitted forth – Mam, Dad and Nan. Just thinking of them made homesickness tug like an invisible umbilical cord. But when an image of Shane replaced her parents and grandmother so in focus she felt like she could reach out and touch him, she dragged herself back, realising Tyson's mouth was moving.

'"The road to nowhere is paved with excuses." Mark Bell, powerlifter, said that.'

The quote hit a nerve, but Ava didn't have time to dwell on it because her pounded and crumbed chicken dish, a wedge of lemon on the side, was placed in front of her with a flourish. It was swiftly followed by an enormous piece of meat which saw Tyson get busy with his phone.

'What do you think of "a man and his meat" for the caption?'

'Grand,' Ava mumbled through a mouthful of chicken. Christ on a bike!

But she was the sort of girl who'd always look for a silver lining in situations, so she concentrated on her meal. The tenderised chicken was delicious. Besides, she thought, risking a glance at Tyson, who was arranging his plate for a second take, the evening couldn't get any worse.

But Ava was wrong.

3

'Good night, was it?' The Uber driver, whose name had flashed up on Ava's screen as Erin, glanced back over her shoulder. Her black eyebrows were at odds with her shock of pink hair, and her nose stud glittered in the dim interior.

'Yes, thanks.' Ava clambered in the back, not wanting to confide it had been anything but. That would instigate a conversation.

The mist had settled into a pervasive drizzle now. As Erin concentrated on her side mirror, Ava stared out the window. It took forever for a break to appear in the traffic, the indicator tick-tick-ticking loud above the low radio volume. She was almost mesmerised by the shards of water illuminated by the streetlights when the car pulled out and began to move toward her flat. There were still plenty of people out and about. Although it was only nine o'clock, so she shouldn't be surprised.

She watched a group of girls still clad in office gear, arms linked, tottering toward the welcoming glow of a pub. One had a Santa hat on, another a blinking gimmicky red Rudolph nose, and was that a pair of antlers on the blonde's head? It was very early for a Christmas do given Hallowe'en had not long been.

Whatever they were up to they were having great craic, and for some reason, they made her think of her sisters. She'd a sudden longing to be sat round the fire at the Shamrock Inn with them. Those girls' night was only starting up, and she was ready for bed! Then again, it wasn't them who'd spent the last hour and a half in the company of @TysonThebody. They wouldn't be laughing like that if they had.

Ava had begged off dessert, saying she was too full, adding she'd better make tracks given her early start in the morning. It was a lie that could be forgiven under the circumstances, she'd told herself. It had also suited Tyson to pull the pin on the evening because he'd raised his eyes from the menu and announced he wouldn't be doing dessert either. Apparently, there were no pure protein puddings on offer. God loves a trier, she thought a few minutes later as they waited to pay, and he pumped for a discount on his meal once more. Snakehips had stood firm, however, and finally, Tyson had begrudgingly swiped his card and paid for his steak.

'Can I get a receipt, please, mate? It's a business expense, like.' Then, stuffing his card back in his wallet, he looked at Ava. 'I'd offer to split the bill with you, but it wouldn't be straight down the middle as you had two wines with your meal, and I'm a firm believer in equal rights.'

The only response to this Ava could formulate was, 'You're an arse.' Rather than say this, though, she hastily paid for her meal, two wines included. The sooner she was in a taxi, putting distance between herself and Tyson Hiscock, the better.

Unfortunately, in her haste to exit the restaurant, she became momentarily wedged in the entrance with Tyson. She blamed his enormous thighs. Her eyes had saucered when he'd stood up from the table at their meal's end. They were like a set of hormone-plumped turkey drumsticks wrapped in denim, and thinking she had no wish to know about his giblets, she'd wriggled herself free from Carlito's doorway and toppled out onto the pavement. A spot of fancy Irish-dancing footwork had followed as she'd tried to stay upright, but Tyson had grabbed her, steadying her just as faceplanting had seemed inevitable.

'Whoa there, girl,' he'd said as though she were a filly breaking free for a canter.

'Thanks,' Ava had mumbled, flustered by her near tumble. She'd tucked her hair – which had fallen down despite Grace's earlier bobby-pin assault – behind her ears, all set for an awkward but quick goodbye before calling an Uber. 'Right, well, lovely meeting you but early starts and all that.' Her tone had been brusque, but she'd been too late, because Tyson's eyes had been half closed, his lips wet and parted as he'd honed in for a goodnight kiss. Quick as a flash, Ava had turned her head so that he wound up licking her cheek.

He'd actually licked it. The memory, still raw, saw her rubbing at her cheek, pulling what Grace called her broccoli face (she wasn't a fan of the brassica) before letting her hand fall back to her lap. The purple-haired Trolls doll dangling from the rear-view mirror caught her attention. It should have had pink hair like Erin's, she thought, as her mind started to wander.

Shane.

His name echoed in her head like she'd stood at the mouth of a cave and called it out.

Ava used to believe in soul mates. That there was this one person with whom you would feel a connection that words couldn't adequately explain because it ran too deep. She'd fancied herself luckier than most because she had two – Shane and Grace. The idea had made her smile smugly because, in Shane, she'd had her romantic mate and best friend and, in her twin, her sister and other best friend. Ever the yin to her yang, Grace had said she read too many romance novels when Ava spouted this. Either way, she couldn't let herself believe Shane had been 'the one'. Not anymore, because the thought of being eternally single was depressing.

Ava's breath left a foggy patch on the window as she turned away from it – and her thoughts – to see Erin's jaw working as she chewed gum. Music was playing softly, and her fingers tapped along to the beat on the steering wheel.

The car smelled of cheap air freshener, and, curling her nose, underneath the chemical summer-breeze aroma, there was the scent of an ashtray in need of emptying. It was hardly a limo, but still and all, it was a tenner that could have been better served elsewhere. She'd been eager to put tonight's disastrous date behind her by cosying into her fleece PJs and losing herself in the book she was reading. Books were an escape from her thoughts; the sooner she was back at the flat, the better.

Suddenly a Miley Cyrus hit came on and Erin turned the volume up sharply, making Ava jolt. Erin's eyes locked on hers in the rear-view mirror. 'It's a good song.' A challenge flashed in them, as if she was expecting Ava to disagree.

'Mm.' Ava smiled back even though she was heartily sick of the song, and by the time the Uber nipped into a space a few doors down from the two-up two-down she shared with Grace, she knew she'd have 'Flowers' stuck in her head for the rest of the night.

'Thanks a million. Have a good night,' Ava said, letting herself out, but Erin didn't reply, presumably checking her phone for her next job.

She closed the car door, and as she approached the front door with its blistered paint, she dug her key out of her coat pocket, nearly dropping it when Binky pounced from the shadows into her path.

'Jaysus, Binky! You gave me a fright.' Her heart banged against her chest as she glared at the cat, whose unblinking yellow-eyed stare back at her said she couldn't care less. The plump tabby then followed her to the front step and flopped down on her back legs, tail flicking as she waited to be let in.

Binky lived three doors down from the overpriced, poky

terrace with its peeling wallpaper and antiquated plumbing she currently resided in. London rents and the cost of living, in general, had been a shock, especially given she'd come here intent on saving and going travelling. So far, she'd only managed to travel back home to Emerald Bay for Christmas and St Paddy's.

The cuddly cat liked to spread the love by calling in on her neighbours, and Ava worried the cat treats she'd plied her with might be responsible for her expanding girth. As such, she'd vowed not to buy any more, knowing she wasn't doing her any favours by spoiling her. Ava was desperate for a little cat or dog, but their landlord had a strict no-pets policy. Binky was a house-guest, not a permanent resident, which, when you thought about it, was ideal, because when she'd finally saved enough to allow her to go tripping around Europe or wherever, she wouldn't have to worry about her.

Ava's phone began vibrating in her coat pocket as she turned the key in the lock and shoved the door with her foot. She nearly tripped over the missile intent on getting inside.

'Sodding cat,' she muttered, not meaning a word of it, patting her coat pocket as she shut the night out with her back-side. Her phone could wait a moment.

'Grace?' she hollered up the stairs, not expecting an answer but waiting for a beat. There was no sound except the usual protesting pipes as someone ran the hot water tap next door, and Binky scratched the front-room sofa.

'Cut that out, you,' Ava admonished, reaching around the door and patting about on the wall until she located the light switch.

Binky dropped back down on all four paws and padded around the sofa, before nimbly jumping up to begin kneading the blanket she and Grace would pull over themselves when watching the tele.

Ava moved toward the sofa, stepping over Grace's discarded

trainers before sinking down alongside the cat. Binky gave a contented sigh as Ava tickled behind her ears for a moment. She admired her boots briefly then unzipped them. They were glorious tan ankle boots that went with everything. Still, they did pinch, and she revelled in freeing her feet and wriggling her toes for a few seconds before straightening. 'Well, Binky, I suppose the kettle won't turn itself on.'

Binky mewled in protest as Ava got up, keeping her in her line of sight as she shrugged out of her coat and tossed it over the back of the sofa. There was a thud behind her as she left the room, and the cat trotted toward the kitchen at the end of the hall.

'I've no treats for you, Binky, if that's what you're thinking,' she said, going through the motions of making a milky brew to take upstairs with her. 'And don't be making me feel guilty. It's for your own good, like.'

Binky tracked her every movement, hope shining on her whiskery little tabby face, and Ava sighed. 'All right, but just one, mind.'

She stretched up for the packet of kitty treats on the fridge and slipped her feline friend three biccies. Then, carrying her mug carefully, she headed upstairs.

She'd her pink fleecy jim-jams on, her face washed and teeth brushed by the time she remembered her phone was still in her coat pocket. She left Binky curled up at the foot of the bed and slipped back downstairs to get it.

The muffled sound of the neighbours' television through the wall and the churning wheels of a bus passing outside greeted her as she lifted her coat and dug out her mobile. She'd not even got her foot on the bottom stair when it leaped to life, reminding her of the missed call from earlier. Then, seeing her mam's name flash up, Ava's throat constricted. It was late for her to be ringing. What had happened?

'Mam?'

'Ava, I've been trying to get hold of you.'

Ava could hear the worry in her mam's tone. 'Sorry, I—

'Never mind. Is your sister with you?'

'No. Grace is at the cinema. What's going on?' Ava gripped the banister tightly and pressed the phone so hard against her ear it hurt. Please don't let her mam be ringing about Nan, she thought, her mind turning instantly to the oldest member of their family.

'Would you sit yourself down, Ava.'

'I am,' she fibbed, but she knew whatever was coming, it would be bad.

'Ava, love, it's Shane. He's missing.'

The stair she'd one foot planted on seemed to shift like sand, and she let go of the rail and collapsed down on it in a crouch.

'Ava?'

Shane was missing? It didn't make sense. 'I don't understand.'

'There was a storm at sea this morning, love. It wasn't fore-cast. Poor Rory.' Nora Kelly's voice snagged. 'He's beside himself, as are Conor and Michael. He said the weather blew up out of nowhere. He'd not seen waves like it in a long time, and Shane was swept overboard before they knew anything about it.'

Ava shook her head, feeling like she'd water in her ears. Her mam's voice seemed far away.

'Are you still there, love?'

'I'm here, Mam.'

'Did you hear what I just said?'

'There was a storm.' Ava's words trembled, and she was cold, but she couldn't succumb to the panic threatening to over-ride practicality. 'When, Mam? When did it happen?'

'Early this morning, but Rory only brought the *Mona Kate* back to the harbour at dark. He got a signal to call the Coast-guard once the worst of the storm passed and refused to bring the boat into shore until the Irish Coastguard sent a helicopter up and the lifeboat was dispatched.'

Shane! Ava inwardly screamed, refusing to let the thought of the Atlantic's swirling black waters swallow her. Hysteria wouldn't help. She tried to stay calm. 'Where are you now, Mam?'

'I've just arrived back at the Shamrock. Nothing more can be done tonight except pray, and that's what the whole village is doing. The search and rescue operation's wound down until first light.'

Ava needed to be there, too.

'Mam, I've got to go. I need to book a flight.'

'You're coming home?' There was no surprise in Nora Kelly's voice, nor any protest.

'Shane needs me, Mam. Of course I'm coming home.'

4

'Ava, what the feck are you doing? It's after midnight.' Grace leaned against the door frame, and the way her words lacked form around the edges and the lateness of the hour suggested she'd had a bigger night out than the cinema. Her wet hair was plastered to her face, her coat reeked of damp wool, and a piece of silver tinsel was now draped around her neck like a scarf.

'The film wasn't a patch on *Love Actually*,' she slurred. 'So Christy, Ella and I called in at the Bird in the Cage afterwards. The craic was mighty. They'd Christmas karaoke – already, can you believe? – and you know yourself how much better everybody sounds after a few drinks. So that made up for the film, especially when Christy sang "Santa Baby". You should have seen her posing and pouting about the place. She put Kylie to shame, so she did.' Then, blinking slowly, she came back to her original question. 'What are you doing?'

'Packing.' Ava hadn't heard the front door go; nor did she look up now as she focused on repacking her carry-on case for the umpteenth time.

Once she'd ended her call with her mam, she'd allowed

herself a few seconds to sit on the stairs repeating, prayerlike, 'He's not dead, Ava. He's missing, and missing means there's hope.' Then she did pray because hope had to cement itself foremost in her thoughts. She wouldn't allow doubts to creep in, and her pleading chat with God had steadied her hands enough to google flights.

Texts had bounced in one after the other from her sisters as she scrolled the Ryanair site, but she focused on her task, and only when she'd booked the airline's first flight out of Gatwick to Shannon Airport in the morning did she read them. Her older sisters were holding faith that Shane would be found alive, which was comforting. It wasn't that long ago Shane had been a part of the Kelly family, and when things had soured between them as a couple, Mam had remarked she missed him buzzing in and out of their home like it was his own. Ava wasn't the only one the break-up had affected, Nora Kelly had added. Invisible battle lines had been drawn when she'd left for London, but they'd been erased at the news of his accident.

This time when her twin spoke, Ava paused long enough to look over.

'Where are we going?' Grace giggled, stepping into the room and collapsing at the end of her sister's bed. She clapped. 'Did you snag a last-minute, all-inclusive to Ibiza?'

'No, and get that coat you're after wearing off if you're going to sit there. It's soaking, and it stinks.' Ava wrinkled her nose at the wet wool smell.

'Did Mam not ring you?' she asked tersely, not in any mood for a tiddly Grace as she folded her jeans and then unfolded them, staring at them for a split second and deciding to wear them tomorrow. A glance at the slim, antique gold wristwatch her mam and dad had bought her for her twenty-first birthday informed her it was already tomorrow. She'd wear as many layers as she could manage, she decided, fetching another sweater. Her ticket allowed for one piece of cabin luggage, and she had no clue how long she'd be staying in Emerald Bay.

Grace ignored her sister's request to remove her coat as she pulled her phone from her cross-body bag and stabbed at it before squinting at the screen. 'I've two missed calls from Mam. What's she after then?' she said more to herself than Ava. She waved the phone at her sister. 'Is it too late to call her back, do you think?'

It wasn't, because Ava knew their mam wouldn't be sleeping. None of the Kelly clan was sleeping. There was no point in Grace ringing their mam now, though, because there'd be nothing new to report until morning, so she cut to the chase. 'Mam was ringing to tell you Shane's missing at sea.'

'Shane Egan, the fishy-arsed eejit?'

Ava could see her words hadn't properly penetrated Grace's fug, but anger flared nonetheless. 'Don't call him that!' There'd never been any love lost between her twin and Shane.

This time, the sharpness of Ava's tone pierced Grace's alcohol-woozy brain, and she rubbed at her temples. 'Shit, sorry. That wasn't nice, but you don't usually mind.'

'I do mind, Grace. I just don't let on that I do.'

'But I don't understand. Missing?' She raked her sister's face for clarification.

'He's missing, Grace! M-I-S-S-I-N-G.' Ava fought hard to keep control as her voice rose several notches. Her nostrils flared as she inhaled, exhaling slowly to calm herself enough to relay the basic facts as she knew them. 'There was a storm. It wasn't forecast, and Shane went overboard. The Egans stayed at sea until the search began, but now it's been called off until dawn.'

Grace digested this information for a second or two, then, like the twist of a child's kaleidoscope, her eyes became focused, the news sobering her up faster than a bucket of cold water being tossed at her. 'Feck.' Then her forehead crumpled. 'But why are you going home? He's your ex, remember? Mam and everyone will keep you up to date with what's happening.'

Ava stared at her sister incredulously. 'I'm on a Ryanair flight at 9.20 a.m., and I'm going because I need to be there when he's found.' Her voice was steely as she added, 'Alive.'

Grace nodded slowly then held her hand up as though warding her sister off. 'Don't take this the wrong way, but you don't think you'll give him mixed signals? You know, by being there.'

'Oh, for feck's sake, Grace! No, I don't. It's called human decency, is all. I was with the man for five years. I owe it to him and his family to be there.'

'But they've been awful to you, to us, since you split with Shane.'

Grace wasn't letting it drop, and Ava choked back all the things that her sister's insensitive remarks had made boil up inside her. Things like how coming to London was a mistake, because she hadn't known how sepia her life would feel without Shane in it. Or how you could live in a city with over nine million people bursting at its seams and still feel lonely. And yes, the Egan brothers had behaved like surly eejits on her return visits home, but they were looking out for Shane was all. So, rather than letting her anger boil over, she told Grace that instead. 'It's no different from how you, Shan, Imo and Hannah look out for me. You've been just as offhand with him and his brothers.'

Seeing she was getting nowhere, Grace heaved a sigh and stood up, throwing her arms open. 'C'mere, Ava. I get it. I do.'

'Take that coat and the sparkly stuff off before you strangle yourself with it,' Ava demanded.

This time, Grace dislodged her bag and slipped out of her coat, letting it puddle on the floor before flinging the bedraggled tinsel like a lasso. It landed on the bedpost. Ava stepped into her sister's arms, grateful for the human warmth, and returned her sister's hug just as fiercely. She tilted her head, resting it on her twin's shoulder as a wave of exhaustion crashed over her.

You're not going to cry, she told herself, even as the sob forced its way up her throat and burst the dam with a hiccupping cry. Her body juddered as she uncorked her tears and let them pour forth.

Grace's words were razor sharp, her breath warm on Ava's hair when next she spoke. 'What you said earlier, Ava – you're right. They'll find him. Sure, Shane's been around the ocean all his life.'

Then why didn't she say they'd find him alive? Ava thought, pushing back from her sister and wiping her nose with the back of her hand. Her hair fell across her face, and she tucked it angrily behind her ears because they both knew how cold and unforgiving the Atlantic was this time of year. Neither sister would acknowledge aloud how hypothermia would swiftly take hold if, by some miracle, Shane had managed to stay afloat.

'I should never have left,' Ava sniffed, at a loss as to what to do between now and when she could leave for the airport.

'Ava, cop yourself on. Shane's a fisherman. He'd have been out on that boat today regardless of whether you were there. That sort of stupid talk's no help to anyone, especially not Shane.'

Her sister was right.

Grace softened. 'OK then, let's see what you've got in your case. You know you're a hopeless packer.'

Ava stepped aside, watching with eyes that felt wrung out as Grace tipped the contents of her case on the bed and picked a maxi dress out of the mix.

'I don't think this will be much use to you.' She tossed it to one side, then began rolling the necessities tightly so they wouldn't crease and packing them in tightly.

'You can put your toiletries in once you shower,' Grace said, zipping the case shut and hefting it onto the floor. 'What time's your flight again?'

'Nine twenty.'

Grace checked her watch, a clunky modern version of Ava's. 'Sure, you've hours yet. You need to try and get some sleep. And don't be looking at me like that. At the very least, you should get some rest.'

The last of the adrenaline fuelling Ava seeped out of her, and her shoulders slumped. She was tired. Her arms were goosy with cold thanks to the temperamental central heating, and it was a relief to clamber between the fleece sheets. She let her sister pull the duvet over her then flicked her bedside light on as Grace switched the main light out. Ava reached for her phone, set the alarm for six and was about to rest her head on the pillow when a tired, panicked thought occurred. What if her alarm let her down?

'Grace, will you set your alarm as a backup?'

There was no reply, and twisting to look back over her shoulder, she saw the room was empty. It'd be grand. There was no reason for her alarm not to go off.

She turned the light off and squeezed her eyes shut but less than a minute later gave a weighted sigh. There'd be no chance of resting, let alone sleeping if she was lying here worrying about oversleeping.

Before she could fling back the covers, though, Grace had appeared, slipping in next to her and draping an arm across her protectively. 'Alarm's set,' she murmured, her breath a mix of mint and alcohol.

It was what Grace had always done since they were small, Ava thought, her eyes boring into the dark as she stared at the linear shape of her desk. Whenever she couldn't sleep, be it from a bad dream or worry over a late school project, Grace would jump in alongside her, and Ava would find comfort in her sister's strength. Everything would be all right because she had Grace, and Grace was fearless. Her sister was the sort of girl who'd run pell-mell into the sea, whereas Ava was more inclined to hang back and dip a toe in first.

It wasn't surprising then, she thought, her mind refusing to switch off as Grace began snoring softly, that Grace had been the first to announce her plans to leave Ireland after college. Ava remembered how just the thought of Grace being in London and her being in Emerald Bay had made her feel like she'd be losing a part of herself. It hadn't helped her and Shane, being at odds because Ava wanted to explore new horizons, too. He refused to entertain the thought of leaving Emerald Bay, saying it was because of Jody, his beloved dog, but there was more to it than that. She was sure of it.

For her part, Grace had soon begun a campaign to get her twin to come with her to London, urging her to cut her ties with Shane and join her for the excitement of being young and free in what was an extension of the very cool and happening suburb of Hackney, where she'd found a flat to rent. 'We'll have a blast,' she'd cajoled. 'And you know yourself you're far too young to settle down with Shane or anyone. Don't let life pass you by, Ava.'

The latter remark had hit a nerve because Ava didn't want to moulder away in Emerald Bay, never having seen anything. She wanted to travel. There were so many places she wanted to see and things she wanted to do, and the English capital seemed as good a place as any to start. Of course, that wasn't to say she didn't love Shane, but she knew her future didn't lie in becoming a glorified housekeeper for the Egan males. Sure as eggs, that would happen if she did what Shane wanted and moved into the family's dilapidated cottage with its tacked-on extensions.

Grace's arm was dead on her, and she tried to dislodge it, feeling like she was being suffocated. Tonight, her sister's presence wasn't comforting, because her mind kept twisting its way back to the fact that Grace was behind the biggest mistake she'd ever made – burning her bridges with Shane. They'd tried to make things work, but his attitude, combined with distance and the feeling they were pulling in different directions, had seen her call things off between them.

Shane had told her there was no going back if they broke up. And still she'd walked away.

5

Morning finally dawned as it always does, with Ava's alarm signalling it was time for her to get up and Grace's shrilling simultaneously. She'd managed two, maybe three fractious hours of sleep, and the first thing she did after rubbing her scratchy eyes was check her phone.

There was no news.

Grace had dragged herself up too and, playing Mam, tried to tempt her with toast, telling her she was no good to anyone hungry. But food was the last thing on her mind, and Ava had refused, deciding to leave a few minutes early for the station because Grace's fussing was making her even more antsy.

They'd hugged each other hard in the doorway, Grace perhaps a little harder, and then Ava had set off down the road, her case trundling behind her. She'd felt her sister's eyes hot on her back and, turning, saw her still standing on the front step. Ava had flapped her hand at her, herding her inside – not least of all because she'd freeze in just her pyjamas.

Before she knew it, Ava was buckled into her aeroplane window seat, staring at the blanket of grey outside. Inside the terminal building, an enormous bauble-laden Christmas tree had already been erected. Now she was trying to ignore the tinny Christmas compilation music filtering through the speakers. The world felt out of kilter, because although she'd planned to spend Christmas with her family, she hadn't been due to go home for weeks yet.

The music gave way to the cabin crew demonstrating the aircraft's safety features, and she knew she should be paying attention as they climbed upward, but nothing would have registered anyway. It would be no good to ask her for help putting on the oxygen mask in an emergency. She wasn't the only one she saw turning her head from the window and side-eyeing the suited man beside her. He was tip-tapping importantly on his phone, but on the bright side, the woman in the aisle seat who'd reminded Ava a little of Rita Quigley from Quigley's Quill bookshop in Emerald Bay was all but taking notes on what yer man there was after doing with the lifejacket.

She leaned her head back against the seat. Despite the coffee she'd knocked back after checking in, her lids were heavy. But trying to nap was pointless. The brown liquid was swishing around her empty stomach. There'd be time for food and sleep when Shane was found. And she wouldn't think of him chilled to the bone, lost, she resolved.

So, instead, Ava cast her mind back to another time, thinking how strange it was that you could know someone your whole life and one day see them differently.

2016

The Kellys had been surprised and relieved waking up that morning to find all that angry grey hovering over their little corner of the world had been washed away. Even better, the sun had, at last, deigned to appear. Given it was the summer holidays, July had been rubbish so far, but today had all the makings of a long overdue scorcher. The only person happy with the rainfall they'd had was Lorcan McGrath. As a sheep farmer, he was fond of the wet stuff, so he'd spouted in the pub last night.

Ava and Grace were scratchy with being cooped up inside the Shamrock with nothing much to do except the chores their mam and nan set for them. There were just the two of them home these days, with Hannah having recently moved to Cork while Shannon and Imo, given the eleven- and nine-year age gap between them and the twins, had long since flown the nest.

Nora joked that once Grace and Ava were packed off to college, she and their dad would have a grand old time of it. Grace had quickly pulled her equivalent of the broccoli face before telling their mam not to get any ideas of running about the place starkers or the like because they weren't teenagers anymore, and Nan would still be there keeping an eye on them. She'd earned herself a flick with the tea towel for her troubles.

The sisters had agreed there was only so much clearing and wiping down of tables in the pub listening to the likes of old Enda Dunne going on about what a good woman their nan, Kitty Kelly, was a girl could do. It wasn't how a pair of soon-to-be seventeen-year-olds should spend their last hurrah before beginning their final year at school.

Hence Grace's desperation to hit the beach this afternoon, having been texting frantically from the moment she'd got up, making plans to meet up with their crowd down at Emerald Bay later. The sandy inlet would be thronging, and Ava wasn't in the mood to join in because she wanted to work on a poem. It had been forming over the last few days, but the words kept teasing her, refusing to reveal themselves, and if they were to become clear in her head, then she needed to be by herself, somewhere quiet like the park.

This was why she was lying on her bed with a hot-water bottle pressed down on her belly, feigning cramps because it was the only way she'd get out of going to the beach with Grace.

Downstairs, she could hear the familiar clattering of lunch

being cleared away, and she turned to stare out the window. The sky was a cloudless blue, the sun was high and there wasn't so much as a whisper of wind. It wasn't a day to be lying on your bed in an airless room, Ava thought, wishing they'd hurry up downstairs so she could sneak off.

As twins, Grace and Ava knew one another inside out and understood most things about each other. Grace, as the more outgoing of the two, however, was a people person who blossomed in the company of others. Ava said she was a social butterfly who suffered from FOMO – fear of missing out. Whereas Ava, while not anti-social by any means, was happy to be left to her own devices occasionally, too. She needed to be.

Grace couldn't comprehend this and would nag at her to join in with whatever she was up to, so when Ava heard an elephant thundering up the stairs, forewarning her Grace was heading her way, she arranged her face to look suitably miserable.

Half a second later, the door burst open, and Hurricane Grace swept into the room.

'How's the tummy?' she asked, appraising Ava before she moved to the wardrobe and flung it open. Her short sundress, worn over the top of her green bikini, revealed legs bronzed not by the sun – both sisters were apt to ripen to an angry pink under its rays – but by self-tanning lotion.

Fake tan worked a treat and was a godsend for those blessed with milky skin like theirs in the summer months – unless it came into contact with a hot tub. Grace had learned this the hard way when she'd got pally with Daisy Doncaster last summer, because her family owned a hot tub. She'd made Ava and the rest of the Kellys laugh, arriving home from her first visit to the Doncasters with wet togs rolled up in a towel, saying, 'Sure, the hot tub's not all it's cracked up to be.'

She'd said she felt like she'd been dip-dyed, having gone in the water one colour and come out another. Served her right for having her head turned by a hot tub in the first place. They were Irish, not Swedish; Nan had tutted she'd be sniffing out saunas next.

'Not great,' Ava fibbed, replying to her sister's question. Grace was making her dizzy, darting here and there, fetching and stuffing items into her beach bag before finally sliding into her flip-flops, pulling her sun hat down low and slinging the bag over her shoulder before rummaging around inside it. 'Sunscreen, check.'

Satisfied, she raised her gaze to Ava. 'Last chance. Are you sure you don't want to come? It'll be great craic. The lads are bringing the portable barbeque down to the beach. Mam's given me a packet of sausages, Brid's bringing the bread and sauce and Martina's got a six-pack of RTDs. Sure, you don't have to swim. You can hang out, like.'

'No.' Ava shook her head. 'I don't want to spoil the party with my miserable face.' She pulled an extra wretched expression for good measure.

'Poor you, but fair play.' Grace gave her a pitying glance before gathering herself up. 'Ah well, things to do, people to see. I'll catch you later, then. Hope you feel better by the time I get back.'

The implication was that she was no fun when laid up.

With that, she swept from the room. The only evidence she'd ever been there in the first place was the clothes spilling out of the dresser drawers.

'Shut the door,' Ava shouted after her sister, but Grace was halfway down the stairs and either didn't hear her or chose not to.

Ava couldn't be bothered to get up and close it herself; instead, she picked up her book. Half an hour and then she'd head off, she decided, because Mam and Dad would be back behind the bar by then, and Nan would be heading out to her crafting group.

'How are you feeling now, love?' Nora Kelly appeared in the doorway a short while later.

'Mam! You gave me a fright. I never heard you coming up.' Ava dropped her book, losing her place. She could be very stealthy when she wanted to be, their mam. Nora Kelly firmly believed in the element of surprise when it came to suspicious goings-on in her household, like her youngest daughter lying on top of her bed on a hot summer's day.

'Sorry, I should have knocked.' Nora gave Ava the once-over. 'Grace said it's the period pain.'

'Mm.'

Nora raised an eyebrow. Ava regularly suffered from cramps, and she clearly remembered picking her up a packet of pills from Heneghan's that usually did the trick a fortnight ago. 'You know you'll feel better if you get up and about. Go and enjoy the fresh air.'

'Ah, don't, Mam – you sound like Ms Roche.' The PE teacher always flapped away efforts to get out of any sporting activity because of period pain with a no-nonsense, 'Physical activity is the best way to take your mind off it.'

Nora wasn't contrite. 'All I'm saying is it's not too late. Your sister's still downstairs trying to cadge the chops your nan's got thawing for tonight's stew to take to the bay. Are you sure you don't want to go with her?'

How many times would she have to say she was sure? She was one hundred per cent sure, Ava griped silently, seeing an expression she couldn't read flit over her mam's face as she said, 'I'm too heavy for swimming.'

It was the second fib she'd told in half an hour, but if her mam and Grace would accept her as she was, then there'd have been no need. That was the problem with being one of five. You were expected to enjoy all the rambunctiousness a big family brought all of the time. She thought Dad was the only one who understood, not meeting her mam's keen eye as she plucked at her quilt cover. It was why he loved his unusual pastime – for a publican at any rate – of botany. It was an escape to wander the countryside on his own, at one with nature as he sought out the wildflowers of Connemara. A time to reset himself.

'All right then,' Nora said finally. 'Rest up. I'd best get down and give your father a hand. We've had word a coachload of Americans is on their way.'

Ava gave her mam a wan smile as she left her to it, the door clicking shut behind her.

Twenty minutes later, after pausing to snaffle an apple from the fruit bowl in the middle of the farm-style dining table large enough for the whole family to sit around, she closed the kitchen door behind her.

The car park was busy as passengers stepped down from the coach her mam had mentioned was due. Ava watched for a moment as they stretched and paused to admire the diorama of lush green fields stretching beyond the hedgerow across the road before making their way toward the rear entrance of the Shamrock. Mam and Dad would be run off their feet, she thought, hesitating. If it wasn't for her supposed sore stomach, she'd have been called downstairs to help. Still and all, Grace was off enjoying herself. Why shouldn't she?

Guilt tugged, but her smile was polite as a man with a camera slung around his neck passed her. He was wearing a yellow cap with the letter 'B' embroidered on the front. A Boston Red Sox fan, she mused, familiar with the emblem thanks to a lovely Bostonian couple who'd stayed at the Shamrock for a few days last summer.

It was only a short walk down the lane to the park, which was just as well because the sun was fierce. She was pleased to see that the expanse of grass was indeed deserted, with the swings hanging lonely and the roundabout still. The mams and babbies who'd usually be clustered about with their takeaway coffee from the Silver Spoon must have opted for the cool waters of the bay. Shading her eyes, she glanced over to where the holly bush grew. The spot was popular with Emerald Bay's youth, but no cloud of illicit vaping steam or cigarette smoke was giving the game away today.

Walking past, she headed to her favourite spot. The ancient sycamore tree would offer shade, and the grass, a touch too long after all the rain, tickled her bare ankles as she cut across it. Ava couldn't wait to kick her sandals off! The ground would be damp, but she didn't care.

When she reached the thick trunk, she flopped down with a happy sigh, unbuckling her shoes and tossing them to one side. Her back rested against the bark. Overhead, rays of light danced through the thick canopy. Then, fetching her pen and notebook from her tote bag, she settled herself down to write. It was a relief when the words she'd been waiting for came.

Ava wasn't sure how long she'd been in the park polishing her verse to within an inch of its life – she always lost track of time when writing. Not that it mattered. Remembering the apple, she munched on that before tossing the core toward the sparrows. Then she rolled on her tummy, rested her head on her hands and closed her eyes. The heat and all that concentrating had made her drowsy. Sometimes when the wind was blowing a certain way, you could hear the roar of the Atlantic from here, but not today. All she could hear was a bee or wasp far enough away not to be a worry. Her body was heavy with relaxation, sinking into the earth. *Bliss*, she thought as her mind began to drift.

Someone was shouting, and she blinked back from her stupor, aware a dog was barking.

'Oof!' The air squished out of her like a punctured tyre as a dead weight landed on her back, gone as quickly as it had arrived. *What was going on?* Her eyes flew open as she rolled over, her skirt bunched up around the tops of her legs, in time to see a black dog gambolling off. Well, it was more of a pup, she thought, annoyed at the interruption.

'Sorry about that! She got away on me.' A figure came running toward her.

Ava put her hand up, using it as a visor, and saw it was Shane Egan.

Present

The crackling intercom brought Ava back to the here and now, and she stared out the window as the pilot announced they'd begun their descent. She was surprised to see the fugue-like cloud cover had dissipated, to be replaced by cobbled-together patches of green fringed by a body of water. The roiling waves that had taken Shane appeared calm from up here, and she prayed that wherever he was, he was staying strong.

6

Ireland

Hannah smelled like honey, Ava thought, relieved to sink into her sister's embrace. She'd offered to pick her up, having been working on the front line of the Feed the World with Bees project she was embroiled in by distributing wildflower seeds and offering advice on hives in nearby Bunratty. The sight of her sister, with her mound of hair and baggy dungarees worn with an Aran knit underneath, waiting for her in the arrivals hall had been comforting.

'Thanks for coming to get me, Han,' she said, pulling free from the hug, eager to get on the road.

'Don't be silly, and give me that,' Hannah bossed, taking the handle of her wheelie case from her. 'C'mon.'

Ava's step faltered as she saw the front page of the local newspaper someone had left lying on a seat. *Local Fisherman Missing*, screamed out at her. The photograph of Shane, inordinately proud of his catch as he held up the enormous bass, made her chest tighten. It was black and white, but in her mind, it was colour. She could picture the way his blue eyes were sparkling, see the stubble that appeared the moment he'd finished shaving, the yellow and navy of his oilskin bib and braces, and the muscular silver body of the fish, remembering when it had been taken.

Hannah, tracking her gaze, stopped. 'They'll find him, Ava. Mam said they're doing everything they can.'

If they hadn't found him, they weren't doing enough, Ava thought but didn't say as her sister tugged her along behind her.

They exited the airport to a murky, calm day, and Ava crossed the tarmac to the waiting rust bucket covered in bee propaganda stickers.

'Still waiting for Elon to sponsor you with that Tesla, then,' Ava remarked dryly, sounding more like Imogen than herself, because it was the sort of thing she'd say, as her sister unlocked the car and tossed her case into the back seat. She didn't wait for Hannah's reply as she slid into the passenger seat. Hannah climbed behind the wheel and gripped it tightly for a moment, squeezing her eyes shut.

'Are you OK?' Ava's brow creased. Shane missing would be affecting her too, she realised, as it would all the residents of Emerald Bay. It wasn't just about how she was feeling, and she needed to remember that.

'Yeah, I'm just doing my thing.'

'What thing?' *Was she praying?*

'I'm sending up a silent prayer Doris here will start. She's been temperamental lately, and working for non-profit means until Elon comes to the party, I'm stuck with her. But don't be worrying, Ava – I'm not going to ask you for petrol money given the circumstances.'

'Oh. Thanks.' This wasn't good, Ava thought, closing her eyes and doing the same, because she was desperate to get home. There'd be time to query why Hannah had decided to call her car Doris later.

'OK, here we go.'

Ava opened her eyes and fixated on Hannah's hand as she slotted her key in the ignition, mouthing, 'Come on.'

There was a click and nothing more as her sister turned the key. She thought Dad could come and get them, and reached for her phone.

Hannah read her mind. 'Oi, ye of little faith – hang on a sec.' As she wiggled the key about in the ignition this time, the car spluttered to life.

'Thanking you.' Hannah raised her eyes heavenward before shooting her sister an 'I told you so' look and reversing out of her space. 'Do me a favour, would you? Text Dad to tell him we're leaving the airport. I promised to keep him updated. You know what he's like.'

Ava nodded, checking her phone to see if there were any updates first, but there was nothing new other than a text from Grace asking if she'd landed. She didn't have the energy or inclination to respond to that so just did as Hannah asked, banging out a quick message to their dad before letting the phone drop in her lap. Her head was woolly, and resting it against the seat she stared listlessly at the road ahead.

Hannah had begun prattling on about a new incentive the Cork City branch of Feed the World with Bees was rolling out, and now and again, Ava made an 'mm-hmm' noise to show she was listening. She wasn't, though. She was back in the park with Shane in that wrinkle in time.

2016

'You need to keep that dog of yours on a lead,' Ava snapped, glaring up at Shane. They knew of each other, in that way of growing up in a small village. He'd been a year ahead of her at the playgroup in the church hall Mam used to take her and Grace to. And in the infants and high school, too, but she didn't *know* him. Shane had held himself aloof from the crowd she and Grace knocked about with since his mam had died. All she knew was he'd opted not to do his final year and then go to college, even though he was bright enough to. He'd joined the family fishing business straight from school instead.

Grace thought he was cute but way too moody. Ava wasn't so sure, though – not about the cute, because he definitely was, and her eyes grazed over his dark hair, clipper cut short. Would it be bristly or satiny if her hand was to run over it? She hoped her face hadn't coloured, giving away her thoughts. But she wasn't finished yet, because he also had nice eyes, and eyes were windows to the soul. They were blue, but not in a boring way. Indigo sprang to mind. She liked that description, and her fingers itched to jot it down.

'Feck! Sorry, like. I didn't see you there.' Shane looked uncomfortable and shoved his hands in his short pockets.

His plain black T-shirt was crumpled, as if he'd picked it up off the floor of his bedroom and put it on. Perhaps he had, Ava thought. It wasn't like his mam was there saying to him no child of hers would be leaving the house looking like that, as Nora Kelly was apt to do.

'I only let her off the lead because I thought no one was about.' Shane's eyes moved past her to the dog leaping about after a white butterfly. 'Jody, c'mere to me now!' His voice was sharp; the dog's ears twitched this time, and she angled her attention toward him. He repeated the call, and she skulked back over.

'You won't hit her or anything, will you?' Ava asked, alarmed.

'Course not.' Shane shot her a surprised glance. 'Why would you think that? She's young, is all. She'll learn.'

'Sorry.' Ava felt bad for assuming the worse. 'It was just you sounded so angry.' That's what Grace meant by moody, she realised. He gave off this undercurrent of anger. It crackled from him like electricity, but given the cancer had taken his poor mam, he'd every right to be mad at the world, because it was unfair.

'I'm trying to train her. She's only five months old,' Shane supplied, shrugging her apology off, seeming unaware of her appraisal.

Ava reached a tentative hand out, feeling Jody's wet nose as she snuffled it. 'She looks a little like Enda Dunne's Shep,' she said, referring to the retired sheepdog as she petted Jody's silky black coat.

'She's a Labrador–Border collie cross.'

'Well, whatever she is, she's gorgeous.' Ava smiled as the dog collapsed down next to her, tongue lolling, lapping up the attention she was giving her.

'She'll let you do that all day,' Shane said, his worn trainers scuffing the ground.

'Why aren't you on the boat with your dad and brothers today?' Ava craned her neck, looking up at him.

'Dad gave me the day off. I didn't feel too good when I got up this morning.'

'But you're better now?'

'I am.'

Ava studied him for a second, wondering if he needed to be alone, too. There was something about the oddity of their meeting here in the park like this that saw her confide how she'd pretended to have a sore stomach, leaving out the finer points.

'Grace doesn't mean anything by it, but if I don't want to join in on the craic, like, she thinks there's something wrong and harps on and on at me until I give in. I didn't feel like it today, and I couldn't be arsed arguing with her,' she finished.

Jody rolled on her back, and taking the hint, Ava rubbed her belly.

Shane squatted down and picked up a stick, tracing it through the loose soil around the sycamore's base. He pointed to her notebook with the pen lying on top of it. 'What's in your book there?'

Ava snatched it up and shoved it back into her bag.

'Sorry, I didn't mean to pry.'

She'd overreacted. 'No, it's OK. I write a little, is all.'

'A diary, like?'

'No, poems, words and ideas. I want to write a book one day, so I jot things down when they come to me. The poetry helps me get stuff out, my feelings and things.' She waited to see whether he'd smirk or make some smart-arse remark, but he did neither.

'What I said about telling my dad I didn't feel good – I wasn't sick, not physically.' He didn't look up from the patch of soil he was digging into with the stick. 'Since Mam died, I have these days where I don't want to be part of' – he dug harder – 'well, anything, I suppose. It passes, but I feel like I have this great weight crushing me, and all I want is to be left alone.'

'But you're not alone. You're talking to me.'

'I am.' Shane's indigo eyes settled on hers, and Ava felt something shift between them as he stopped digging and sat down next to her.

Present

The horn blaring dragged Ava rudely back to the present. 'Jaysus, Hannah!' She jumped, seeing her sister's hand sitting heavily on it.

'What? He was driving up my arse like an eejit.' Hannah stopped honking and gestured at the shiny SUV that had overtaken them, slapping her hand down on the steering wheel. 'If a poor sheep happened to be out on the road, it wouldn't stand a chance; not to mention yer man up there would kill himself or someone else to boot.'

They both knew wandering livestock was a possibility in this part of the world.

'Fair play,' Ava conceded, rubbing her eyes, which smarted with tiredness, then glanced about, trying to get her bearings. She hadn't fallen asleep but had been a million miles away.

On her left, craggy green and brown hills sloped high, and on her right, a low stone wall traced the road. Windswept grasses clung to the rocks, the Atlantic surging on the other side. The ever-changing Irish sky was an undecided obsidian with an opening in the clouds through which shards of light streamed. It was an almost biblical scene, Ava thought, her gaze returning to the ribboning road ahead. They'd be home soon.

Checking her watch, she saw the news was about to come on the radio. 'Does that work?' She pointed to the car stereo.

'Yeah, but reception's not good out here.'

Ava fiddled with the knobs, but all she got was static and crackling.

'Told you. And Mam would ring you if there was anything to report,' Hannah said softly.

She was right, but it didn't offer any comfort, and Ava crossed her arms over her chest, hunching down in her seat.

7

The ruins of Kilticaneel Castle were imposingly situated overlooking the cove of Emerald Bay. Usually, the sight of it still standing proudly all these centuries later filled Ava with excitement because she was nearly home. Not today, though. She was too focused on getting to the harbour around the next bend.

Fairy lights were draped over the jumble of wharf buildings and would twinkle welcomingly once the light faded. That would be down to Isla Mullins wielding clout on the tidy town committee, Hannah muttered, adding that given she was a shop owner, Isla had a vested interest in ensuring Christmas came to Emerald Bay as soon as the first fairy light was switched on in Galway. Ava didn't comment.

As for the small port, with its red and blue fishing boats jostling in the green waters that gave the village its name, it usually offered a picturesque photo opportunity for those tootling along the Wild Atlantic Way. Today, however, it was eerie, given it was depleted of boats. There were no tourists in sight either, although there was a cluster of people milling about by the harbour wall as Hannah pulled the car over at Ava's urging. She'd wanted to carry on to the village, telling Ava there was nothing they could do here besides freeze, but Ava had been insistent.

'I need to hear what's happening first-hand,' she told her sister. Her leg was out the door before Hannah had come to a complete stop.

'I don't want to risk turning the engine off in case Doris decides not to start again,' Hannah said, pulling the handbrake up but keeping the car idling. 'I'll wait here for you, but don't be long, because I'll be burning petrol.'

About to climb out of the car, Ava twisted back in her seat to look at her sister. 'Don't wait, then. There's no need. You go on to the Shamrock. I can ring Dad later, or I'm sure someone in that lot over there will give me a lift back to the village.' She pointed across the road, making out a few familiar faces.

Hannah frowned. 'Don't worry about the petrol-burning thing – just go and find out if there's any update, and I'll wait for you. I don't like the idea of you hanging about there alone.'

'Hannah! Don't be daft. I won't be on my own, will I?'

'I don't mean that. I mean without me or one of the family.'

'You don't need to hold my hand. I'm not a child,' Ava barked – then told herself Hannah was only doing what any big sister would do by looking out for her and wound her neck back in. 'Sorry. That wasn't fair, and listen, I appreciate you picking me up and all, but I promise I'll be all right. You g'won home. Besides, you know what Dad's like. If you don't show your face in the next fifteen minutes, he'll start with the pacing.'

Liam Kelly insisted on keeping abreast of his daughters' movements while they were driving the open roads. If he'd had his way, they'd all be getting about in matching bright-yellow cars, because he insisted yellow was the most visible vehicle colour in adverse weather conditions.

Shannon, whose nursing work included home visits, which saw her driving all over the countryside, had succumbed, nick-naming her car BB, short for Big Bird. Hannah had said if Elon got in touch, she'd pump for the yellow Tesla, if there even was one, while Imo wouldn't relinquish her red sports car for all the tea in China, and as for Ava and Grace, well, they'd no need of a car in London. If they mentioned they were in the market, though, he'd be in their ears doing the hard sell on a banana mobile.

Hannah checked out the milling group over the road, weighing up her options. Then, with a sigh, she stilled the engine. 'I'm not going anywhere. You're right about Dad, though. You head over while I call him and tell him where we are.'

'Thanks, Hannah.' Ava gave her sister a conciliatory smile and swung her other leg out of the car, closing the door behind her.

The salty wind whipped strands of hair across her face, blinding her momentarily. She grabbed a handful of hair, impatiently holding it back from her face as she crossed the road, glad of her coat but wishing she'd had the foresight to put a hat on. The waves slapped hard against the harbour wall, and seagulls circled overhead as she set her sights on the small huddle of people and made her way toward them.

A little apart from them, a burly man about the same age as her dad by the looks of him, wearing a high-visibility vest, was speaking earnestly into a walkie-talkie. Carmel Brady from the Silver Spoon cafe was bustling about filling paper cups from a large thermos with a liquid Ava realised was mulled wine as the scent of citrus, cinnamon and spice caught on the air. And there was Shane's aunt, Yvonne, white-faced beneath her bobble hat, shaking her head as Carmel offered her a cup of the comforting wine. Seeing her, Ava's step faltered. If anyone knew what was happening, it would be Yvonne – or Vonnie, as she was known – but she wasn't sure of the reception she'd get, given how the other Egans had behaved toward her since she'd split from Shane.

It was too late to worry about that now because Vonnie had seen her, and Ava raised her hand, acknowledging the woman before letting it fall to her side as she approached.

'Ava?' Vonnie, who had the Egan dark colouring and a weather-beaten face, fixed her with dull eyes weighted down by the bags beneath them, a surprised note inflecting her weary tone as Ava reached her. 'I thought you were in London.'

Shane's aunt was a capable woman, but it was clear the stuffing had been knocked out of her. She ran the fishmonger and takeaway side of the family business with her husband and sons, working alongside Rory and his lads on the boats. She was popular among locals because, despite features that could loan themselves toward looking hard, she kept up a cheery banter as she plunged the wire baskets into the bubbling hot oil of an evening. That and her generous scoops of chips.

'I was, but Mam phoned me and told me what had happened. I had to come.' Her eyes pleaded with Vonnie for understanding, and she automatically reached for the older woman's gloved hand. They'd always got on well when she was with Shane.

To her relief, after a moment's hesitation, her hand was grasped gratefully, and she felt the pressure of Vonnie's fingers pressing into hers. 'Is there any news?' Her eyes swung away from Vonnie, squinting out to the sea beyond the harbour, but there was nothing to see – only the undulating body of water, the shadowed mounds of distant islands and the hard, flat line of the horizon.

Vonnie shook her head. She appeared almost shrunken inside her blue puffer jacket as she took a deep breath. 'There's no point me soft-soaping it for you, Ava. It's been over twenty-four hours. Things aren't looking good. I'm sorry, love. I know you and Shane were close once upon a time.' Her voice was hoarse with exhaustion and caught on the last sentence.

Ava wanted to wrench her hand away and cover her ears as

her gaze swung wildly about, searching for the man in the high-vis vest, who'd disappeared. He must be part of the search and rescue effort. She'd find him and demand he tell her exactly what they were doing out there to locate Shane, but Vonnie, sensing what she wanted to do, held on to her hand tightly, and if she was surprised by the strength of Ava's reaction, she didn't let on.

'No. Let the man do his job, Ava. Rory did everything right. He made the man-overboard call to the Galway Coastguard the moment he could get a signal, and the R115 was sent up from Shannon Airport as soon as the conditions were considered safe.'

'R115?'

'Rescue 115, the helicopter.' Vonnie was matter-of-fact as she spieled off the rescue coordination efforts as though memorised by rote. 'A Mayday relay was put out on the VHF to all vessels in the area to proceed to the MOB. Sorry,' she said, catching Ava's bewildered expression, 'the man-overboard position and the Costello Bay Coastguard Unit were straight on it. The big ALB lifeboat's been launched from the Aran Islands base, too. Rory and the lads went out again at first light, even though I begged them not to.' The bobble atop her hat wobbled as she shook her head. 'They're running on empty and in no fit state to be out on a boat. It'll be a blessing if it's not four people they're searching for before the day's done. My Eric and the boys are out there, too.'

'He might have made it to one of the islands,' Ava shot back. She wouldn't give up hope. The waters around here were littered with stony outcrops and sandwiched between the Aran Islands off Galway and Achill Island, a little to the north off Mayo. It wasn't a stretch for him to have made it to land. Shane was a strong swimmer, and he'd been around the water all his life. His odds were better than most. He'd know how to deal with big seas.

The lines surrounding Vonnie's eyes softened, and seeing the sympathy there, Ava bit down on her bottom lip, feeling powerless. She didn't want pity. She wanted hope. Her inability to do anything made her want to rail at someone to let it out.

Vonnie's phone began ringing. Letting go of Ava's hand at last, she pulled it out of her pocket, shading the screen from glare. 'It's our mam ringing from the retirement home.' She glanced up briefly. 'I'll have to take it. Sorry, Ava.'

'Of course,' Ava said, waiting until Vonnie had answered before disregarding her request that she let the Coastguard do their job as she scanned the parked cars to see if she could find the man in the orange vest. She spied him sitting in a four-wheel drive and hurried toward it. She'd only taken a few steps when a fella she didn't recognise stepped in her way, bringing her up short.

'Excuse me,' she muttered, trying to step past him, but his rangy frame blocked her.

'Do you know him, then? Shane. It's tragic, all right – what's happened.'

He took a step forward, holding the device up. 'So, are you related to Shane or a family friend?' His teeth had a purplish stain that suggested he'd been enjoying the warming effects of Carmel's mulled wine a little too much. She must be on the tidy town's committee, too, doling that stuff out in November.

'Clear off, Jeremy Jones.' Hannah muscled in alongside her sister, squaring up to him. 'You're a vulture, so you are.'

The man stared at Hannah briefly through narrowed eyes, and then they glimmered with recognition. 'I don't believe it. Not you again. Sure, what are you doing here? I can't see any protected trees, or is the Green Peace boat secretly mooring up here in Emerald Bay?' He pretended to scan the harbour. 'No. I can't see that either. It must be Shane Egan who brought you down here.'

'It's none of your business.' Hannah stood her ground, her arms crossed, feet planted wide.

He shook his head, looking toward Ava. 'A word of advice. Her sort will only get you into trouble.' Then he swivelled about and walked off toward the parked cars.

'Who on earth was that?' Ava stared at her sister, who uncrossed her arms and relaxed now he was a safe distance away.

'Jeremy Jones, eejit reporter. He works for the newspaper in Galway. I've had a few run-ins with him. He knows which side his bread's buttered on that one. He ran that front-page picture of me and some fellow greenies chained to an oak tree in Galway shortly before the Garda carted us off for trespass. He'd had his palm greased by the developer, and his story made us out to be unhinged do-gooders with more time on our hands than sense. Mam and Dad went mad going on and on about the shame of having a law-breaking tree hugger in the family. Still, it was worth it, because you can't go around chopping trees down willy-nilly for so-called progress. And,' she finished smugly, 'we saved the old oak despite Jeremy Jones and his one-eyed reporting. Thanks to our collected signatures, the developer had to build around it.' She barely paused to draw breath. 'Oh, there's Vonnie. Have you spoken to her?'

Hannah's words were washing over the top of Ava's head, and she never heard the question.

'Ava?'

'What?'

'I asked you if Vonnie had anything to tell you?'

'No, nothing new.' Ava shook her head and glanced toward the man in the vehicle, but her sister's diversion had put the lid back on her simmering anger, and she realised Vonnie was right. She'd not be doing Shane any good by pestering those trying to help him. Instead, the magnetic tug of the sea drew her gaze once more.

'I'm going to get a cup of that mulled wine Carmel's after passing around before she runs out and heads back to the Silver Spoon. Do you want one?' Hannah asked.

'No thanks, and you know it won't be just a mulled wine you'll be after getting – it'll be an interrogation as to my being back, too,' Ava said, well aware those in Emerald Bay's goods and services business were thick as thieves when it came to goings-on in the village.

Her hightailing it back to hold vigil for Shane Egan even though they'd broken up a year ago would indeed be classed as goings-on worth a mention.

'If it's free, I can take it.' Hannah winked and strode toward the cafe owner.

Ava watched her go for a moment, wrapping her arms around herself, then looked back at the sea, whispering into the wind, 'I'm here now, Shane. Come home to me. Do y'hear me? Come home.'

8

Hannah flapped her hands at the persistent seagull swooping over her head as she sipped her warming wine. 'Go away,' she mumbled after swallowing the last mouthful. 'You wouldn't like it anyway.'

The seagull squawked and glided downward, resting on the harbour wall and watching the sisters with a beady eye.

'Did Carmel give you the third degree?' Ava asked. She'd been studiously avoiding eye contact with the cafe owner, having felt her curious gaze on her more than once.

'Of course.'

If Mam was here, she'd have told Hannah to wipe her mouth, Ava thought, ignoring her sister's moustache stain as she mimicked Carmel's conspiratorial whisper.

'Tell me now, Hannah, were Ava and Shane back together, because they kept that quiet?'

Ava rolled her eyes. Emerald Bay and its village drums would drive you mad.

'You'd have been proud of me,' Hannah continued, 'because I was all very vague and mysterious about why you're back even after she offered me a top-up of the mulled wine.'

Ava's mouth betrayed her with a twitch, because there was nothing vague or mysterious about her sister, who wore her heart on her sleeve.

'Carmel was after saying how Mam's stepped up organising folks, though. She's put together a cooking roster for Rory and co, and Vonnie's side of the family. And she sent Dad up to the Egans' to collect Shane's dog.'

'Jody,' Ava supplied, stricken that it had taken her until now to think of her, but her mind had been so full of Shane.

Jody was his best friend, and the feeling was mutual. He'd told her once his father had allowed him to get the pup, hoping it would help fill the hole losing his mam had left. Her death had hit the whole family hard, obviously, but Shane had a sensitive side to him and, being the youngest, he'd struggled to cope. It broke her heart to think of the poor dog pining, not understanding what was going on. Her eyes burned as she swallowed the lump that had formed in her throat. Shane would know the village would rally around, which gave her a modicum of comfort.

'Jody.' Hannah repeated. 'Anyway, Carmel said there's been no end of volunteer dog walkers and that she's claimed a spot in front of the fire in the pub.'

Ava realised her teeth were beginning to chatter at the mention of fire; it felt cold enough to snow and she lifted her gaze warily to the leaden sky praying it would hold off until Shane was found. She thrust her hands deep into her coat pockets, silently cursing its wool-blend label. Despite its hefty price tag, she began to suspect it was more blend than wool. That wind blowing in off the sea was cutting right through her. Her eyes flicked to her sister, who didn't even have a coat on. But apart from her blue lips, you'd never know she was frozen as she kept up a steady stream of chatter. She interrupted her. 'Thanks, Hannah,' then linking her arm through hers drew her sister close.

'What for?' Hannah huddled in.

'For being here.'

'Sure, where else would I be.'

They lapsed into silence, both aware that darkness would begin to encroach in another forty minutes and the search would be called off for the day. Ava's lips were working in silent prayer when Hannah nudged her.

'Oi, Mam's here. At least, I think it's Mam. There's a possibility we're after sighting the Irish Yeti.'

Ava turned in the direction Hannah was gesticulating to see Nora Kelly, rugged up in a hat, scarf, coat, gloves and boots, and snickered despite the current situation. Their mam appeared lopsided thanks to the canvas tote bag used for picnics and the like weighing her down. As she bustled nearer, she called, 'They're forecasting snow, you know. You two must be frozen. For the love of God, have you no sense? Where are your hats? And, Hannah, you'll catch your death. I can't believe you're out in this without a hat or a coat.'

Neither sister replied because their mam had a point, although, for Hannah's part, she'd be hard-pressed to fit a beanie overtop of her locs. Nora was still tutting when she reached them a second and a half later, depositing the bag on the ground and flexing her arm. 'That's better.'

Then, before they knew what was happening, both sisters were pulled into an embrace which ended with a kiss on their foreheads, leaving behind a lipstick imprint.

'Now then,' Nora said, her tone leaving them in no doubt she was in charge. 'You head off home, Hannah. There's no point in you being here, too. I put the immersion heater on before I left so you can have a hot shower when you get in, and your nan's been cooking to feed the five thousand. Neither of you will be going hungry.' She shot her youngest daughter a concerned look. 'And if I know you, Ava, you won't have eaten since I rang and told you what happened. I've a slab of buttered brack for you to have in the meantime.'

She was right. Ava had been surviving on caffeine, and even though her stomach protested at the thought of food, she'd be no good to Shane fainting from hunger. It was a relief to have her mam's no-nonsense presence here, taking charge of the situation. A comfort to feel like she was that little girl again who, having grazed her knee, would have it kissed better by her mammy. There would always be a part of her who believed her mam held the power to make everything better with a simple maternal kiss.

Hannah didn't need to be told twice, and after giving Ava's arm a final squeeze, she hurried back to her car. Ava crossed her fingers that Doris would start while Nora fussed with the contents of the bag she'd brought with her. There was a spluttering across the street and a toot as the car juddered forth, just as her mam flapped out the old tartan blanket they used as a picnic rug.

'Here – let's put this around you,' Nora said, draping it around Ava's shoulders before pulling her hat off to reveal chestnut hair needing a roots retouch, flattened by the pom-pom beret Liam had bought her for her birthday. 'We'll put this on you, too.'

'Ah, no, Mam – you'll be needing that,' Ava protested.

'No, I won't. The internal furnace is beginning to flare.' Nora fanned her face with her free hand to prove her point.

There was a reason her mammy was president of the Menopausal and Hot Monday night group, Ava thought, watching her cheeks begin to pinken as though she were curled up in front of the fire that would be roaring in the Shamrock. Accordingly, she let her pull the hat down low over her ears, grateful for the reprieve from the wind.

Nora studied her daughter for a moment, concern etched into the fine lines spanning her eyes, and then she busied herself, pouring a mug of steaming tea from the thermos. 'I know you don't normally take sugar, but I added a teaspoon or two because it's good for times like this.' She passed the brew to Ava, who took it gratefully, then retrieved the food parcel she'd also brought and unwrapped it.

Ava blew on the hot liquid before taking a tentative sip. A teaspoon or three, she thought, wincing at the sweetness, but the second sip was better, and warmth had begun to flood her veins. She even managed to nibble on the fruity loaf, which, combined with the tea, had a rallying effect on her. Nan's brack had magical properties. 'Thanks, Mam,' she mumbled through her mouthful, getting a chuck under the chin instead of a telling-off.

'Shannon's been in a terrible quandary over staying or going,' Nora said, a frown embedding itself in eyebrows over-plucked back in the early noughties.

'What do you mean, Mam?' Ava wasn't aware Shannon had been planning a trip back to the States to see James in Boston— assuming that was what Mam was referring to. She'd have thought her sister would have mentioned it on one of their regular FaceTime catch-ups.

Nora steepled her hands to her mouth. 'You don't know. Of course you don't. Not with everything that's been happening.'

Dear God, what now?

'I left it to Shannon to tell you, but she obviously didn't want to in a text. James's mam, Hazel, died last night. Hannah doesn't know yet either. They were all there with her – James, Maeve, the boys.'

'Oh.' Ava's eyes filled, blurring her vision. She'd never met the woman in person but had chatted to Hazel Cabot online. She knew how close James and his brothers were to their mam, and Shannon thought the world of her. Maeve Doolin, who resided in one of the thatched cottages before you reached the village of Emerald Bay, was loved by locals. Her and Hazel's story was simultaneously heart-breaking and heart-warming, and had been the talk of the village for a while there. Thanks to James, Maeve's grandson having travelled over from Boston determined to reunite the pair, and Shannon, Maeve and Hazel had a semblance of a happy ending.

'I know it was on the cards, but it doesn't make it easy. 'Tis terrible sad is what it is,' Nora lamented, her shoulders sagging.

Hazel Cabot had had uterine cancer, and Ava's mind flitted to Shane's mam. Different cancers but equally devasting. Then, remembering what her mam had said about Shannon being in turmoil, said, 'She should be with James, Mam. He needs her. Maeve will need them both. Haven't I got you, Dad, Nan, Hannah and Imo here with me? I'll talk to her later. Tell her to get on a plane.'

Nora nodded. 'They're all back at the pub, desperate to see you.'

Ava could picture the scene, and she longed for the cosy warmth of the Shamrock Inn, her dad's burly, solid presence and her sisters' easy banter, the pub filled with the faces of people she'd known all her life gathered to support one another. But she longed for Shane more. 'I can't leave, Mam, not yet. Not while there's any light left.'

'No, of course you can't. I understand.'

'Do you, Mam? Because I'm not sure anyone else gets it. I don't see how they can when I've only just admitted it myself. I still love him, and I know I might be too—' A hiccupped sob cut her off.

Nora put an arm around her daughter, holding her tight. 'Oh, Ava, love, don't go down that road. Not yet. And I know you've still got feelings for him. Sure, I'm your mammy, aren't I? And I don't mind telling you, you've worried your dad and me. You've not been yourself in a good long while, no matter that you keep telling us all you're fine and dandy living the life with your sister over there in London.'

Ava leaned her head on her mam's shoulder, not arguing with what she was saying as she breathed in the familiar scent of her. Then, straightening, she finished her tea while her mammy peered past her.

'Is that Vonnie over there?'

Ava nodded.

'Will you be all right here for a minute while I go and let her know we're all holding the family in our prayers? There's more tea in the flask if you want it.'

'Course I will. Thanks, Mammy.'

Ava helped herself to the tea, and she'd nearly drained her second mug by the time Nora returned.

'The poor woman. She's bearing up but only just.'

The light was growing greyish now, almost pixelated. Both women lapsed into silence as they watched black specks moving steadily toward the harbour. If they'd found him, it would have been radioed to shore, and an ambulance would be on standby, Ava knew, and the thought of Shane spending another night braving the elements made the tea and brack want to come back up.

'Ah, sweet and merciful Jesus,' Nora said quietly.

Ava dragged her eyes away from the approaching boats, surprised to see her mam's face ghostly pale in the gloaming as she rocked on her heels. 'It's bringing it all back.'

What her mammy told her next was completely unexpected.

9

'What do you mean this is bringing it all back, Mam?' Ava was perplexed. So far as she knew, nothing like this had happened before in Emerald Bay.

'This waiting for news.' Nora flapped her hand like she was swatting a fly. Her agitation was plain to see. 'It's as though Father Time's fiddled with all the clocks, making them tick to a different beat. The daylight hours speed by, night falls fast and then the hours until dawn crawl.'

She was right, Ava realised, thinking back over how slowly last night had passed and what a blur today had been. Tonight was sure to be an interminable wait, but at least she was here in Emerald Bay, close to Shane and her family. She still had no clue what her mam was on about, and curiosity was a welcome diversion from her panic that the search had been called off for the day. 'When were you ever waiting for news like this?'

This time she got a straight answer. 'When your great-grandda disappeared at sea.'

Ava's eyebrows disappeared into her hairline, and her mouth hung open. This was the first she'd heard of her great-grandfather's demise at sea. To be fair, she'd never actually asked how he died. Still, it wasn't the sort of thing you brought up in general conversation or even thought about, for that matter. Besides, Mam wasn't inclined to instigate conversations about her childhood. She supposed she'd simply assumed he'd died of old age. But why had she never heard mention of him or this before?

Nora studied her daughter's face, reading the question there correctly. 'Close your mouth, Ava. I don't like talking about that time, and you girls never asked. That's why.'

'Do Dad and Nan know?'

Nora nodded. 'It's not a family secret. It's ancient history, is all. Or at least it was. With all this happening now, it feels like it was only yesterday, not forty-odd years ago.'

'I didn't even know he was a fisherman.' Ava was perturbed by her murky knowledge of her maternal great-granddad; her maternal grandparents, too, for that matter.

She and her sisters had grown up at the Shamrock Inn, living with their granddad and nan Kelly, who'd passed the business on to their dad, Liam. It should have gone to his older brother, their uncle John, but aside from their dad's odd anecdote about when he was young, John was never mentioned other than to say he hadn't been seen or heard from in years and, sure, every family had a bad apple lurking in the crop.

Finbar Kelly, their paternal granddad, had died when she and Grace were young, but they had firm, fond memories of him. As for Nan, she'd always been there, a part of their home, cooking up a storm for them all, and if her erstwhile firstborn son's name was ever brought up, her face would pucker and her lips would tighten, but it was her eyes that would hint at the hurt lurking beneath the surface.

Her mam's side of the family, the Nolans, was different. They were like vaguely sketched characters in a story you'd never got to the end of, aside from her mam's awful, all-too-vivid cousins that was – Frankie, Brendan, Tom and Colm Nolan.

The four brothers lived in nearby Ballyclegg and frequented the Shamrock regularly on account of the family discount Nora gave them on their pints of ale. It was only a minor discount, mind, but given the amounts of ale the Nolan brothers consumed, they considered the trip to the Shamrock to be worth their while. They had a sister, too, Maureen, who used to run a guesthouse in Dublin, but Ava couldn't recall having met her. Then there was Mam's older brother, Uncle Tiernan who'd emigrated to America when he was barely in his twenties. He was hit and miss at keeping in touch, but Mam wrote to him regularly with family news, and his wife, Sydney, never missed Christmas and birthday cards.

These days, her mam and uncle sporadically video-called one another on WhatsApp. Mam would drag you into the conversation if you were lurking in the background. Always awkward when you've never met the person looming out of the screen at you. Zoom meetings and the like were different because you weren't talking to family. It was work. As for their parents, there'd been some sort of falling-out, which Mam never discussed.

So far as Ava knew, it had never been resolved, and then it was too late, because neither of her maternal grandparents had made old bones. The closed expression settling on her mam's face now told her she wouldn't glean any more from her on the subject today either.

Ava sighed. Families were a complicated business, and trying to work out the ins and outs of hers was giving her even more of a headache, so she shelved the mystery of what had happened to her great-grandda for another day and concentrated on the boats returning to the harbour. She could make their colours out now, and their engines were audible.

Her mind leaped ahead, theorising that Shane had been found alive and well, but for reasons she'd find out shortly, the news hadn't been radioed in. You never knew, she thought with a shot of optimism as she craned her neck, trying to see who was on what boat.

The whiff of diesel, oil and fish grew stronger as her hope slowly evaporated. There was no sign of Shane as the fishing boats moored, just the fishermen who'd joined in the search for him. One by one, they clambered from their vessels, weary and defeated.

None of the searchers were saying it out loud, but it was an unspoken truth written on their bone-tired faces that, given the sea's temperature, Shane would have been lucky to have survived much longer than an hour in it, and cold-water shock was an all-too-real risk, setting the odds against him.

She overheard someone saying the lifeboat had returned to its station but would be out again at first light. They weren't giving up! Ava grasped hold of this with all her might, her stomach turning over at the sight of Rory, Michael and Conor, their tread heavy as they made their way up the jetty. Ava met Rory's gaze, and his blue eyes, so like Shane's, flickered momentarily with surprise, but then the light dimmed, and he gave a small shake of his head.

It told her what she already knew.

Shane wouldn't be coming home tonight.

10

Ava stared out the window of her mam's new car to where Benmore House was lit up like a lighthouse on its lonely perch. The grand home Imo had recently had a hand in renovating had been built up there in the days of the landed gentry as a visual reminder of the hierarchy between the Leslie family and the villagers. The lights twinkled in the myriad windows, signalling the family was in residence. It was apparent nobody traipsed after members of the Leslie clan switching lights off after them while going on about money not growing on trees. Unlike Liam Kelly, who had a sixth sense when it came to lights being on in unoccupied rooms. Even if you had only left it a moment ago.

Nora Kelly was attempting to lighten the heavy atmosphere by spouting off about the features of her yellow (of course) Volkswagen Golf, named Vera. It sounded suspiciously like she'd memorised the salesman's patter. Ava wasn't listening, though, as she wondered whether Shane could see Benmore House from wherever he was.

Then she became aware of something odd happening around her nether regions. A spreading warmth reminded her of the one-time-only wee she'd taken in the swimming baths in

Kilticaneel. 'Mam, I think there's something wrong with your car. My seat's after getting hot.' Her eyes widened toward her mam's profile, waiting to see if she'd suggest they open their doors, drop and roll before the car exploded.

'Ah, not at all. That will be the heated seats, Ava. The steering wheel's heated, too. Have a feel of it if you like.' She took one hand off the wheel.

'No. You're grand, thanks. I'd prefer it if you kept both hands on the wheel.'

'It's all part of life's little luxuries,' Nora tittered, obviously pleased with her new vehicle. Then, keeping her eyes on the road, she began fiddling with the various bells and whistles on the dashboard. Suddenly, the windshield wipers swished into life, and the car stereo began belting out Harry Styles.

'Sorry about that.'

She stabbed at various buttons, and the next thing Ava knew, she was reclining, staring at the padded ceiling.

'Mam!'

She was flung upright again so quickly she was in danger of whiplash, just in time to see the row of quaint thatched cottages that heralded their arrival at the outskirts of the village. They'd soon be driving down the village of Emerald Bay's main road.

'Sorry,' Nora muttered again. 'I'm still figuring out what knob does what.'

Ava didn't deign to comment, staring out at the cottages. They were all in darkness, which wasn't surprising given Maeve Doolin, the only permanent resident in them these days, was in Boston with her family. The other two were holiday lets, and it was low season. And then they were passing the homes of the villagers whom Ava knew – had known all her life. Had Isla Mullins, in her tidy town committee capacity, been in the locals' ears regarding getting into the Christmas spirit as well? She wondered, seeing holly wreaths were already adorning doors, and she'd hazard a guess that tucked away in kitchen pantries, the plum puddings would be pickling in whiskey. Under normal circumstances, the blow-up Santa the Brady family displayed in their window each year would have raised a smile, but this evening, the jolly sight just made her feel sad.

They passed under the red Christmassy bow strewn across the street, signalling they were now on Emerald Bay's main shopping street. Without the welcoming glow from inside the shops, the fairy lights, bunting, angels and snowflake decorations seemed forlorn. Ava half expected to see tumbleweed blowing toward them as she eyed the curve of pastel pink, yellow and green buildings. The pavements, too, were empty.

Shannon's best friend, Freya, the owner of Mermaids, had shut her vibrant blue art gallery and jewellery shop for the day. All the signs were turned to closed in the windows of Isla's Irish shop; Eileen Carroll's woollens shop, The Knitters Nook; and Rita Quigley's bookshop, Quigley's Quill. Nobody was putting the world to rights in the Silver Spoon cafe. Still, Dermot Molloy's Quality Meats made Ava blink, because the butcher never closed early in case someone needed last-minute sausages or the like for dinner. In fact, the only shop still open was Heneghan's Pharmacy, and Ava could see Nuala on the telephone while Niall Heneghan was beavering away in the dispensary. People needed their medication no matter what drama was unfolding, she supposed.

'It's been hit and miss as to who opened today, and those that did shut their doors early. Apart from Heneghan's, and I think the Bus Stop is still open,' Nora said before Ava could ask where everyone was.

Ava wasn't surprised the Gallaghers were reluctant to toss away the chance of a sale of a loaf of bread or pint of milk. Their plans for a world cruise when they retired were common knowledge.

'At times like this, people want to gather together, Ava.

There's strength to be found in solidarity, and it was standing room only in the Shamrock when I left earlier.'

Ava wasn't sure what she wanted. To be left alone or be surrounded by people she knew and loved? But she did know there was a slim-to-none chance of the former.

The Shamrock Inn glowed with a warm welcome as they slowed for the turning. Ava noticed the profusion of petunias that had tumbled from the window boxes in spring on her last visit home had been replaced with hardier seasonal pansies, their explosion of yellow and purple offering cheer on a winter's day.

Nora pulled in around the back of the pub and, stilling the engine, said, 'You'll be pleased to know the bees are hibernating.'

'It wasn't me that made a fuss about them. It was Imo,' Ava replied, angling her head toward the conspicuous hives down the bottom of the beer garden. Still, she was pleased she wouldn't have to add getting stung to her list of worries. The hives were courtesy of Hannah and her quest to feed the world with bees.

'Imogen's given up her campaign to get rid of them since she tasted the honey your father was after harvesting from them. You want to see him decked out in his beekeeper's garb. He thinks he's the bee's knees, so he does.'

Nora thought herself hilarious, but Ava winced at the cheesy joke as she waited for her mam to get her giggles under control. The hysteria was probably down to stress, she decided.

'He's been selling jars of fresh honey in the pub and thought he had a nice little sideline going until Hannah caught wind. She's making him donate his earnings to Feed the World with Bees.'

That drew a laugh from Ava. Hannah never missed a beat, she thought, getting out of the Golf, and you had to admire her tenacity.

The two women hurried over to the kitchen door, eager to escape the chill, and Ava stepped inside after her mam.

The sight of Shannon, Imogen and Hannah sitting around the table nursing mugs of tea was welcome. So, too, was seeing Nan at her usual station, stirring an enormous pot on the stove. The savoury aroma of what she had simmering away there promised a hearty, rib-sticking meal. There was a collective putting down of mugs. Shannon and Imogen scraped back their chairs in a manner that, under normal circumstances, would have had their mam telling them off. Still, these were anything but normal circumstances, and even though she grimaced at the sound, Nora stayed silent.

Meanwhile, Kitty had let go of the spoon in her hand, uncaring as it slid down the pot into its bubbling contents in her haste to be the first to get to her granddaughter. She hugged Ava fiercely while Shannon and Imogen waited their turn. Nan smelled of onions, but Ava didn't care as her breath was squeezed from her. Kitty didn't offer platitudes, seeming to understand all her granddaughter wanted from her was phys-ical comfort.

'Nan, give the rest of us a look-in.' Imogen was fidgeting behind her.

Kitty released Ava and, seeing Nora had taken over at the stove and was trying to retrieve the spoon with a pair of tongs, elbowed her daughter-in-law out of the way.

The normalcy of her mam and nan vying good-naturedly for the position of top dog in the kitchen was as comforting as the aroma from the pot, Ava thought, turning to her sister. She used the half second before Imogen embraced her to appraise her.

Imo smelled the same – expensive – but there was some-thing different about her. Ava took a step backwards as she was released, and it came to her then as her sister tucked her hair behind her ears, revealing a grave expression. Her hair was shorter. It bounced on her shoulders instead of hanging down her back, but it wasn't just that. The polished veneer Imogen wore like a hard shellac nail varnish had been wiped away, leaving a softer, more natural version underneath, and her glow wasn't down to something luminous from a bottle either. Ryan O'Malley would be responsible for that.

'Listen, Ava, I know we haven't always been complimentary where Shane's concerned since you two broke up, but that was just us—'

'Being protective big sisters,' Ava supplied. 'I get it, Imo. You don't need to say it.'

'But I do,' Imogen insisted. 'I want you to know I'd— well, we' – she glanced to a hollow-eyed Shannon hovering behind her and Hannah still sitting at the table, who both nodded – 'we wouldn't wish this on Shane and his family. Not in a million years.'

Ava managed a nod, determined not to crumple, as Imogen stepped aside to let Shannon greet her properly. She was shocked by the dark circles under her sister's eyes, although she shouldn't be, she thought as Shannon flung her arms around her.

'Shan,' she said, pulling away from her and holding her at arm's-length, 'I'm OK. You need to go and be with James and Maeve.'

Shannon studied Ava's face and then nodded. 'I'll go upstairs and book my ticket in a minute. Hazel's death was expected, but they weren't ready to say goodbye. None of them were, me included. She was a lovely woman, and I wish I'd had longer to get to know her.' She sniffed, her eyes shining brightly as she took hold of Ava's hands and pumped them gently. 'They will find him.'

Ava nodded. Her determination not to dissolve into a blubbery mess weakened as she saw the tear trickling down Shannon's cheek.

'I shouldn't have broken things off with Shane and gone to London,' she spluttered, her voice thick.

'Oh, Ava,' someone said – she wasn't sure who. A chair scraped, and the spoon clattered back in the pot as she was surrounded by a Kelly family cuddle which, to the uninitiated, would look like a rugby scrum with Ava the ball in the middle.

'Nora.' Liam Kelly burst through the door connecting the family quarters to the pub, coming up short at the spectacle that greeted him.

'Is this hug exclusive to the female members of the family, or can I join too?'

'Hi, Dad,' Ava croaked, craning her neck through the middle as she came up for air.

'Hello there, Marigold,' Liam said, calling her by the nickname he'd bestowed her with when she was little, after the Connemara wildflower. Deep railway-track worry lines ran between sandy eyebrows that seemed to have taken on a life of their own since he'd stepped over to the dark side of his fifties. He moved toward the women in his life and put two beefy arms around them.

'It's strange, Grace not being here.' Hannah's voice was muffled.

'You two are never apart,' Imogen added as they pulled away.

'We're not joined at the hip,' Ava snapped. Then seeing the hurt flit across Imogen's face, she immediately apologised. 'Sorry, I didn't mean it to come out like that.'

The tension was diffused as Napoleon, Shannon's Persian cat, padded into the kitchen and mewled in that funny way that signalled he'd something in his mouth.

'What's that he's got?' Hannah asked, and they broke apart to see him drop his present on the floor in front of his paws before looking up at them with yellow-green eyes.

'That's his smug face,' Shannon said.

Imo squinted, and she let an enormous sneeze go. 'Mam, can you get me an antihistamine before my eyes start swelling?'

Nora opened the top cupboard and fetched the container where she kept all the pills and potions.

'How can you tell if he's a smug face?' Hannah asked.

'I'm with Hannah. It's a squished-in face he's after having, smug or not,' Liam stated. 'Ah, no, not another sock.' He bent down to retrieve the striped ankle sock, pocketing it as he straightened. 'I wouldn't mind if he stole them in pairs, but he lies in wait by the laundry basket and steals them one by one, more often than not hiding them. I've more odd socks than I know what to do with.'

'You could use them for puppets, Dad.' Imogen's eyes twinkled in Shannon's direction.

'I'd forgotten Dad used to do that.' Shannon's mouth curved. 'Mr Sleepy Sock.'

Imogen snorted.

'Who's Mr Sleepy Sock?' Hannah frowned, looking from one sister to the other.

'He was before your time. You, Grace and Ava are the tea-cosy generation,' Imogen said, referring to their father's penchant for donning the tea cosy as a hat when he was in a silly mood. 'Show them, Dad.'

'Yeah, show us, Dad,' Hannah urged while Nora shook her head, watching her husband pull the soggy sock over his hand and take himself into the hall.

'He used to do this when it was time to put our lights out,' Shannon explained, scooping Napoleon up and holding him close.

'We refused to turn them off until we'd had a visit from Mr Sleepy Sock,' Imogen said, looking at the door their dad was now hiding behind in anticipation.

Suddenly, Liam Kelly's sock-covered hand appeared around it, his thumb and fingers moving in time with the high-pitched voice he'd adopted. 'It's Mr Sleepy Sock here paying you a visit from the land of nod. Did you know all the little children in Ireland have their lights out now and are sound asleep apart from youse two?'

'You were such an eejit, Dad, but we loved it.' Imogen laughed, as did the others, and Ava smiled along.

She wished she was here under different circumstances, but all the same, she was glad to be home.

11

'Thanks, Nan, that was grand,' Ava said, her belly full of the Dublin coddle and soda bread that had been placed in front of her. She'd had no choice but to eat it as Kitty Kelly had kept a firm eye on her until she'd mopped up the last of the broth, and she felt better. Her sisters and mam had gone through to the pub as their dad needed a hand, making her promise to join them once she'd eaten.

Ava was desperate to see Jody, but Imogen had told her the dog had been taken out for a walk by Kyle Hogan. The teenage criminal mastermind behind Emerald Bay's great perfume heist had turned over a new leaf. Kyle had pinched a display bottle of perfume from Heneghan's Pharmacy for his girlfriend's Christmas present, only for her to return it to the pharmacy, complaining it had no scent. He'd spent every Sunday since engaged in community service, mowing the local park's lawn.

Their dad had already carted hers and Hannah's bags upstairs, and she'd unpack the little she'd brought later. Right now, though, she needed to fetch something from their room.

Kitty made to clear her bowl and plate away, but Ava waved her away, getting up from the table. 'You're not to be running after me now, Nan. I'm not an invalid,' she said mock sternly, carrying her dishes over to the sink. 'Besides, I need to keep busy.'

Kitty nodded her understanding, watching with wily blue eyes as her granddaughter immersed her dishes in the sudsy water, scrubbing them clean before leaving them to drain on the rack. 'There's a mountain of coddle left in the pot. I'll go through and see who needs a bowl, though I daresay no one will be hungry, given the plates of food that have been arriving all day. You want to see the bar top in there. It's like one of those all-you-can-eat buffets. It's what people do in times of crisis – cook.'

Ava raised a smile. Nan included, she thought. Growing up, there had been times she'd found living in a village the size of Emerald Bay claustrophobic. However, more times than not, she was aware that the sense of community amongst the locals was something special. Look at how they were rallying around Imogen's fella Ryan's family since his dad's stroke.

'I wonder if the Egans will be in.' They'd be better off here in a warm pub with people who cared about them than sitting at home waiting the night out.'

'I don't know, Ava.'

Ava turned to make her way upstairs but hesitated, spinning on her heel to see Kitty untying her favourite '*I don't need a recipe, I'm Irish*' apron. 'Nan?'

'Mm?'

'Mam's after telling me about her grandda going missing at sea, like.'

'I wondered if Nora would tell you about that. With young Shane missing, this was bound to bring it back for her. A terrible thing.' She shook her head.

'She didn't get into the nitty-gritty of it all though.'

Kitty eyed her granddaughter and said, 'It's not my story to tell, Ava.'

Ava was disappointed but didn't pursue it, because she had something she needed to do. 'I'm just nipping upstairs. Will you tell the others I'll be through shortly?'

Just as the Egans would be better off surrounded by people who knew them and Shane, so would she. Even though the temptation to hole up in her bedroom was strong.

Kitty hung her pinny on the back of the door. 'I will do.'

Ava had her bottom foot on the first step, her hand resting on the banister, when she heard her nan's voice again. Thinking she was speaking to her, she paused to listen, catching, 'And if Enda Dunne thinks he's after getting seconds of my coddle, he's another think coming.'

Poor old Enda, she thought, realising that Nan was muttering on to herself. Her worn-out eyes crinkled at the corners, thinking of the retired farmer with his permanent seat at the bar. Enda had an unrequited soft spot for her nan, although the jury was out on whether it was her nan or her cooking he was smitten with!

All thoughts of Enda Dunne were banished upon reaching the landing. Napoleon pounced playfully out of the shadows, and she nearly went flying.

'Don't be doing that,' she admonished, picking up the unrepentant little furball and tucking him under her arm as she flicked the hall light on. 'Sure, my poor heart is in a fragile-enough state as it is.'

Napoleon wriggled until she set him back down, and she heard him scamper down the stairs as she opened her bedroom door.

Ava switched the light on in the room she'd grown up sharing with Grace and Hannah, realising her mam must have been up and drawn the curtains earlier. It was still strange even now to be met with the blue-and-white Cape Cod aesthetics instead of the purple and pink of their childhood. That was down to Mam redecorating as soon as they'd all moved out, so she could let the freed-up bedrooms when they weren't home during the busy summer months. This time of year, the accommodation side of the pub was quiet, but come June, July and August, it paid to check with Mam before rocking home to make sure their room was free, or you might find yourself kipping on the sofa in the TV lounge!

One thing that had yet to change, though, was the three beds. They were still in a row like the three bears' beds from 'Goldilocks', and Ava's eyes were immediately drawn to her own. Her case was set at the foot of her bed, waiting for her to unpack it.

It was tempting to kick her shoes off, rip back the covers and crawl beneath the sheets. She'd pull them over her head to block everything out until morning, but tempting as it was, she knew she'd only lie there brooding.

Hannah obviously hadn't been upstairs yet, because of all the sisters, she was the messiest, and her bag, like Ava's, was standing to attention at the foot of her bed. By tomorrow morning, the contents of that carryall would be strewn everywhere, and the bedcovers crumpled. She and Grace used to run a piece of string along the floor as a demarcation line when they were younger, and there'd be ructions if Hannah's mess strayed over it.

She turned her gaze to Grace's bed in the middle. It was going to be strange sleeping in here without her sister. Grace had been calling, but Ava hadn't picked up, so she'd rung Shannon instead, who'd given her an update on how she and everyone else was doing. There was nothing more to be said.

Ava ignored her case. Its scant contents could wait to be hung up. Instead, she moved over to the wardrobe, yanked the doors – still prone to sticking – open and removed the neatly folded woollen blankets from the top shelf, placing them by her feet. Then, stretching up on the balls of her feet, she began patting about in the far corner of the shelf until her fingers connected with what she was looking for.

Molten relief surged as she returned to her usual height with the small lilac box, bow on top, in her hand. It was a stupid place to have left something precious, but she hadn't wanted to take it to London. What was in this box signified her past; London was the future, or so she'd thought at the time. Accordingly, as Grace had been downstairs hollering it was time to leave for the airport, she'd shoved it up there, hoping no nosy guest would find it.

The box fit in the palm of her hand, and she carried it over to her bed, sitting on the crisp blue-and-white-striped spread before opening it. Inside was a smaller, red velvet jeweller's box, which she snapped open.

There it was. Her gold sweetheart locket nestled on the cushion. Ava held it up by the chain and watched the heart-shaped locket spin briefly before dropping it into her open palm and feeling the solid weight of it settle there.

This was her connection to Shane, and she fought to breathe as she unclasped it, sadness pressing against her chest as she gazed at the photographs nestled inside.

Snapshots of happiness frozen in time stared back at her. Ava closed her eyes, recalling the grittiness of the sand beneath her bare feet as she'd shouted Shane's name over the wind, her finger pressing the camera button as he turned, sooty hair tousled, eyes creased with mirth. He'd been watching Jody dancing at the sea's edge, chasing waves, her excitable barking muted by the sea's song. Goose bumps flared down her arms like she was at the bay, locked into that scene, bracing against the salty breeze.

She smiled through her tears, remembering how she'd put her phone away and gone to shiver alongside him; then the scratchiness of his wool sweater and the faint smell of lanolin as he pulled her to him and rubbed her warm.

Grace had taken the other picture of them sitting next to one another in the beer garden, her head resting on Shane's broad shoulder. The Shamrock loomed in the background, and Ava pressed her eyes shut to conjure the warmth of that sunny afternoon, fancying she could still taste the green onion flavouring from the crisps they were sharing mingling with the sweet taste of her shandy.

She remembered what had come before. How she and Grace had arrived home earlier than expected from college that Friday afternoon, and, wanting to surprise Shane, she'd gone down to the harbour to meet him off the boat. The seagulls had squawked overhead as she'd pressed her index fingers and thumbs into a heart shape and held it up for him to see as Rory nudged the boat into its mooring. Shane had been first off the boat, ignoring his brothers' jibes as he'd strode toward her. He'd smelled fishy, but she hadn't pushed him away, laughing about it instead as his lips had landed softly on hers. She did the same now to the locket, holding it up to her lips and squeezing her eyes shut.

Shane had given it to her on her twenty-first birthday, and the lump forming in her throat began to hurt. The memory of how he'd surprised her with it shone as bright in her mind as the pictures in her locket were...

12

_____

The shindig celebrating their twenty-first birthdays had been Grace's idea. Ava would have preferred a slap-up meal somewhere with Shane, Mam, Dad, Nan, her sisters and their various boyfriends. But Grace had been insistent they mark the occasion with a hooley. 'You're only twenty-one once, Ava, and, sure, you can go out for dinner any old time,' she'd said before turning her attention to their parents, informing them that given they were poor college students home for the holidays, it was their parental duty to host it at the Shamrock.

The promise of a free bar until 10 p.m. had been all the encouragement their fellow student friends needed to come and sample the delights of Emerald Bay. As such, the pub was jammers when the big day rolled around. The hired jukebox was pumping out classic old danceable sounds and, being a balmy night, the partygoers had spilled into the beer garden. Mam was frantic, trying to get bite-sized nibbles into their imbibing guests. At the same time, Dad was in danger of RSI, so often was he pulling pints.

Ava, who'd lost sight of Shane in the throng, collared Grace to ask her if she'd seen him.

'No. And don't worry about him. This is our party, Ava. He's likely outside talking to someone.'

'I'll just go and have a look.'

'Aves! C'mon. It's my birthday, too, and I've hardly seen you.' Grace pulled a petulant face. Then 'Brown Eyed Girl' came on the jukebox, and she began jigging about, turning several admiring heads her way. 'Ah, I love this song! Look, Imo's already breaking out her moves.'

Before Ava knew what was happening, she was pulled into the mix of bodies dancing in the space that had been cleared of tables specifically for that purpose. There was nothing for it but to enjoy the song and dance, she decided, throwing herself into it alongside her sisters. Besides, who wasn't partial to a bit of Van Morrison?

By the time it ended, she was out of breath and giddy.

Grace left her to weave her way through the melee until she finally saw Shane. He looked incongruous with a plate of sausage rolls in his hand. She thought that Mam must have given him them to pass around, pushing past a girl with a sheet of black hair hanging to her waist to grin at him before swiping one. She popped it straight in her mouth. 'Yum – Nan's sausage rolls are the best.' Then, seeing Shannon passing by empty-handed, she took the plate off him before she missed her chance.

'Oi, Shannon, can you please pass these around?' Ava called to her sister.

Shannon eyed her and Shane for a second then sighed. 'I was going to get a well-earned drink, but g'won, give them here. It is your birthday, I suppose.'

'Aves, I know your mam and dad have a speech planned for later, but do you think we could slip away for an hour? I still need to give you your present?'

'Oh yes?' Ava waggled her eyebrows suggestively, pleased when he laughed. Then she took hold of his hand. 'I like the sound of that.'

They moved outside.

'Do I have to wait until we get to wherever we're going, or can I have it now?' Ava asked, following Shane to his car.

He dug his keys from his good jeans and waved them under her nose. 'Patience, Ava, patience. All will be revealed shortly.' Then he unlocked the car, and she clambered in.

Ava relaxed back on the headrest as they drove up Main Street. The shops were in darkness, and the road ahead was empty. It wasn't long before the lights from the homes dotted about Emerald Bay twinkled behind them, and she shifted in her seat to study Shane's profile. 'C'mon then. Tell me. Where are we going?'

Shane didn't take his eyes off the road. 'Down to the bay.'

'But it's nearly dark.' Ava stated the obvious.

'There's a full moon tonight. You'll see it in a minute when we clear the bend.'

He was right, Ava saw as they passed the last of the houses leading to the village and rounded the corner to cruise along the coast road. There, shimmering in the space between land and sky, was a giant pearl.

'It's gorgeous,' she breathed as the car bounced over the gravel, pulling up near the spectral ruins of Kilticaneel Castle.

The sound of their doors banging shut was loud in the still night. She glanced around to see if any teenagers who sometimes parked up here after dark were about, but there were no other cars in the area reserved for visitors to the castle and the bay it overlooked. She tilted her head heavenward to see the sky – now inky and dancing with celestial energy – thinking how beautiful it was as she let Shane take her hand and lead her toward the coastal path.

The shushing waves of an ebbing high tide were louder

now, the grasses on either side of the path rustling – a hedgehog maybe? Ava hoped it was a hedgehog at any rate. The shrill cry of a kestrel that had forgotten to roost made her jump, and Shane gave her hand a quick reassuring squeeze. There was no need to use his phone torch to light the way, because the moon had created a snaking silver path for them to follow, and they reached the shore without incident.

'You know Jody will be jealous if she finds out we've been to the bay without her,' Ava said, slipping her heels off and holding them in her free hand. The wet sand was coarse between her toes, and she scrunched them up, waiting while Shane crouched down and untied his laces.

'I won't tell her if you don't.' He glanced up at her and gave her a wink.

Seeing him trying to balance on one leg as he pulled his sock off made her smile. Ava gulped in greedy lungfuls of the briny air and then held her arms out wide as though she was Kate Winslet in *Titanic*. Only she was embracing being twenty-one and in love. Anyway, Shane was much more handsome than Leonardo, in her opinion.

The tight knee-length dress she'd had to shimmy to get into was more green than teal in the silvern light. She spun around as fast as her restricted movements would allow, her head thrown back until she was dizzy, like she used to as a child. Shane caught her before she toppled over onto the sand.

'Steady on,' he bubbled as he held her in his arms like she was a swooning maiden on the cover of a romance novel.

Ava joined in with his laughter. She was tipsier than she'd thought and dizzy to boot.

'You looked like a mad mermaid just then with your green skirt and hair flying out.'

'This was exactly what I needed, Shane. Thank you.' Ava reached up and stroked his cheek. He was clean-shaven for a change. What with the crisp cotton shirt, his good going-out jeans and shaving, he'd made an effort for tonight's party, and she loved him all the more for it.

Shane reached down and picked the lock of hair that had floated across her cheek while she spun, holding it between his thumb and forefinger. 'When we were in infants, I used to think your hair was made of gold.'

'Mam used to tell us it was. Grace and I believed her for the longest time. And how come you never told me that before?'

'I was five at the time.' Shane's expression softened. 'I think I thought you were beautiful even back then.'

Ava's heart contracted. Shane wasn't one for spouting sonnets and the like. He wasn't one for romantic gestures either, but could you be anywhere more romantic than where they were now? And it had been his idea to come here.

'I love you, Shane Egan,' she said softly.

'And I love you, Ava Kelly.'

He lifted her toward him, and she could feel the imprints of his fingers on her back and the strength of his arm supporting her. The sound of the waves faded to white noise as the warmth of his breath at the moment before his lips reached hers tickled her face. Her body tingled, feeling the softness of his mouth as it pressed down against hers, and her arms reached up so she could rest her hands on his shoulder.

'Ava.' Shane pulled away from her slightly.

'Mm?' She was still in the dreamy moment, her eyes half shut.

'I don't think I can hold you much longer.'

'Oh.' Her eyes opened in time to see his apologetic grin, and she laughed as he righted her so she was standing on her own two feet once more. 'Thanks for not dropping me.'

'You're welcome.'

He was digging around in the pocket of his jeans, but Ava ignored that, because she'd decided she wanted to mark this moment, right now, by doing something she'd never done before, something neither of them would forget. She unzipped her dress.

'Er, Ava, what are you doing? Not that I'm complaining or anything.'

'We, Shane Egan, are going skinny-dipping,' she stated, slipping out of her dress.

'You what? You do know we live in Ireland, not the Bahamas?' His eyebrows were arched incredulously as she stood in her underwear, her hands already around her back, busily unhooking her bra.

'I'm aware of that, and you heard me,' Ava bossed in her best schoolmarmish voice. 'So come on. Off with your kit!'

'You're a mad mermaid, all right.' Shane shook his head before giving in and stripping off.

Standing starkers under a full moon, they took one another's hand, leaving their clothes in a pile on the sand, and charged down to the water whooping. As they plunged into the icy Atlantic, the whoops turned to laughing shrieks. Ava, the water up to her waist, her upper body one big goose bump, her lower body burning with shock, began to drag Shane back toward shore.

'Oh no you don't! This was your big idea. You're not getting out until you've gone under.'

'Ah, no, Shane!'

'Count of three. We'll do it together.'

Ava knew there was no getting out of it, and turning to face the oncoming waves, she joined in the countdown. 'One, two, three!'

She threw herself under the next tunnel of water, feeling bubbling seawater rushing past her ears before bobbing up like a seal. Shane was still dry from the torso up, and she spluttered her indignance, scooping water with her hands and splashing him. He futilely tried to shield himself as she shouted, 'You cheated!'

He was laughing as he began wading back to the beach, but Ava was having none of it, and her legs pummelled through the frothy surf in determination to stealth bomb him. She leaped on his back, and they both went under, struggling to right themselves as the sand dragged beneath their feet.

'That wasn't fair,' Shane coughed, water clinging to his lashes as his eyes shone with laughter.

'You deserved it,' Ava declared with a satisfied smirk as he shook himself, much like Jody would when she'd been playing in the surf, sending water droplets flying.

They exited the sea as quickly as they'd charged down to it, their teeth chattering when they reached the mound of clothes. Shane chivalrously handed Ava his shirt to use to dry herself off.

'I've got a spare T-shirt in the car and a couple of towels in the boot. I'd have brought them down with us if I'd known we would need them,' he said, catching the scrunched-up, damp shirt as she tossed it back to him. He did his best to pat himself dry, but as he tried to get his jeans back on, Ava told him to hurry up, and he began grunting about there being nothing worse than trying to put jeans on over wet skin. At last, he zipped them up and, decent once more, shoes in hand, they hurried back up the path, relieved to find the parking area was still empty.

Shane fetched the towels from the boot and wrapped one around Ava's shoulders, opening the car so she could get in while he dug around in the back for his spare T-shirt. Once his chest was covered, he got behind the wheel, turning the engine on and blasting the heater. They sat there in silence, waiting for the shivering to subside.

'I don't know how I'm going to explain this.' Ava patted her matted locks, then flicked on the interior light and inspected her face by pulling the sun visor down. As she'd suspected, she had panda eyes. She was doing her best to remove the black streaks from underneath her bottom lashes when Shane spoke up.

'Tell them you were caught in a rain shower. It's Ireland after all. Ava?' A note of uncertainty crept into his voice. 'I was going to give you this down on the beach, but then you started stripping off.'

Ava forgot about her smudged mascara as she saw the lilac box he was holding out to her. 'What is it?'

'Open it and see.'

She took the box nervously and lifted the lid to see a smaller, red velvet case inside. Ava eagerly pulled it out of the box and snapped the case open. Her mouth formed an 'O' upon seeing the locket nestling inside, and she picked it up, holding it up to the light. 'Shane, it's gorgeous,' she breathed. 'I love it. Thank you.'

'You haven't seen what's inside it,' Shane pressed, looking pleased with himself.

Ava opened the locket, and a swell of emotion surged, seeing the photos tucked inside. The right words wouldn't come, so she held the necklace out to him instead. 'Would you put it on for me?' Angling herself so she faced away from him, she lifted her salty hair up, waiting for Shane to drape the necklace around her neck and fasten the clasp.

'Done,' he said a second later.

She let her hair fall and straightened again before dipping her head to admire the locket nestling against her décolletage. 'It's the most beautiful thing I've ever been given. Thank you.' She stroked the smooth gold heart, vowing never to take it off.

But she had.

13

Present

Nora Kelly's voice calling up the stairs pulled Ava back to her current reality.

'Ava, love, are you coming down?'

This time there was no swallowing the lump in her throat, and it hurt too much to reply. Instead, Ava dropped her head into her hands and began to sob. She was unaware of the footsteps up the stairs or the creak of the bedroom door opening as her body juddered. Ugly crying. The mattress dipped beside her as Nora sat down and pulled her to her.

'Where is he, Mam?' Ava hiccupped.

'I don't know, Ava, love. I don't know.'

Nora let her sob it all out, and eventually, the well ran dry. 'That's been building all day that has. It's good to get it out,' she said, holding Ava tightly.

Ava pulled away from the embrace. 'I need to blow my nose.' Her voice was nasally, and her eyes were hot and felt puffy.

'Wait here – I'll fetch some tissues from the bathroom.' The bedsprings creaked as Nora got up, and Ava swiped under her eyes, trying to compose herself. Her mam returned, pressing a wad of tissues into her hand, and Ava trumpeted into them.

'I've a cold flannel here. Lie down, and we'll put it over your poor eyes.'

It was nice to have Mam take charge, Ava thought for the second time that day, doing as she was told.

Nora had folded the flannel and draped it across her daughter's eyes like a sleeping mask. 'How's that?'

'Grand, thanks, Mam.' Ava's throat ached, and she couldn't do anything about that, but the coolness of the flannel was already soothing the tension drilling behind her eyeballs. Nothing would make her feel better other than Shane being found, but the bawling had helped release the overflow of emotion.

'I'm going downstairs to make you a cuppa. I'll be back in two shakes.'

True to her word, Nora reappeared with a mug of sweet milky tea in next to no time. Ava removed the flannel and put it on the bedside table before sitting herself up.

'Thanks, Mam – just pop it down there.' She indicated the space next to the flannel, and Nora set the mug down.

'What's that you've got in your hand there?'

Ava was unaware she was still gripping her locket and unfurled her fist.

'Your locket. I remember Shane giving you that on your twenty-first. Although, we never did get to the bottom of why you looked like a bedraggled mermaid when your father and I gave our speech.'

'And you never will.' Ava rustled up a smile. 'It was on the shelf down the back of the wardrobe, where I left it when I moved to London.'

Poor Mam's eyes were weary Ava noticed as she let the locket fall into her lap. She reached for her tea and took a sip.

The heaped teaspoon of sugar dolloped in there had a galvanising effect. She knew crumpling into a heap wouldn't help Shane, so it was time to pull herself together and be strong. She'd had her wobble, but there were to be no more.

'Is Jody back from being walked, Mam?'

'She is, and she's claimed her spot by the fire again, lapping up all the attention she's after getting. Dermot Molloy said he'll walk her back to the Egans later. His youngest two won't give her a minute's peace. Apparently, they've been mithering their daddy for a dog.'

An image of the black Lab cross stretching languidly by the fireside as she was petted floated forth. Shane always said she was a floozy. Give her a pat, and she was anyone's. Ava was suddenly desperate to be the one patting her.

Nora perched on the side of the bed then, and Ava gulped her tea.

'Slow down. We don't want you choking on that.'

Ava didn't slow down.

'Would you like me to do your locket up for you?'

Lowering the mug, Ava said, 'I would – thanks, Mam.'

'Sure, it's better around your neck than lying about in your lap like so.'

Ava passed her mam the locket and downed the rest of the brew before shuffling over to sit on the side of the bed beside her.

'Turn around and hold your hair up,' Nora directed, then: 'Whoever designs these things must be from Lilliput. They're so tiny,' she muttered, fiddling about with the clasp while Ava turned her back to her mam and scooped her hair up.

'You should wear your glasses more.'

'There's nothing wrong with my eyesight.'

Ava held her free hand before her and mimicked her mam, trying to read her grocery list. 'Is that lemon creams or bourbon creams I'm after writing down?'

'Cheeky madam! There – got it.'

The clasp clipped into place, and Ava let her hair fall, putting her hand on the heart to press it against her chest. It felt like a talisman, and if she promised never to take this off again, Shane would come home to her. She didn't realise her lips were moving until her mam spoke up.

'You could try doing that with the rosary beads.'

'You're as bad as Father Seamus, Mam. I've been praying.'

'Speaking of whom, he's downstairs in the pub. He'll pray with you if you like?'

'You mean tell me God still loves me even though I haven't shown my face in church since Easter?' Ava replied, tongue-in-cheek.

'That's highly likely.'

Ava didn't need to look at her mam to know she was trying not to smile.

'That hair of yours could do with a brush,' Nora stated.

'I don't want to look in the mirror, because I know I look a fright.'

'Nothing washing your face and running a brush through your hair won't fix. Why don't you go and sort yourself out in the bathroom and fetch the hairbrush for me? I'll sort you out.'

'OK.' Ava dutifully trotted into the bathroom, turning on the hot tap and wincing as she caught sight of her swollen features.

Once the water was warm, she splashed her face several times, then patted blindly about for the towel she knew would hang over the rail and rubbed her skin dry. There was a hairbrush in the top drawer, and Ava took it back to the bedroom, handing it to her mam before sitting on the floor in front of her with her back resting against her legs.

Nora gently teased out the windblown knots and began rhythmic strokes, as she had every night when Ava was a child. It had always been a bone of contention with her older sisters that Ava and Grace hadn't been subjected to the Nessie Doyle bowl cut anywhere near as much as they had. Ava and Grace would always reply that it was because their hair was made from gold.

'Shall I count, Mam?' It was how she'd learned to count to one hundred, sitting here like this of a night.

'If you like.'

The monotonous counting and gentle brushstrokes were as good as any yoga session. By the time she'd reached one hundred, she was still exhausted but calmer. Nora put the brush down, flexing her wrist as Ava stood up.

'Shall we go downstairs now, Mam?'

'That sounds like a good plan.'

14

Liam Kelly was pouring a pint of Guinness with the same level of single-minded focus da Vinci must have applied to the painting of the *Mona Lisa* when Ava trailed into the pub behind her mam. She nearly tripped over the box of Christmas decorations from which tinsel spilled. The box had been left forgotten on the ground beside the flip-up counter at the end of the bar.

'That's a health and safety risk, Mam,' Ava muttered, but Nora had already been pulled into a conversation with Clare Sheedy.

She bent to pick the box up and nudged the plates of food cluttering the bar top aside to make room for it. Then, as her dad let the pint he'd been pouring stand, Ava surveyed the cosy space.

The Shamrock Inn was heaving, but it wasn't humming with its usual good cheer. At first glance, it seemed the entire village had gathered here to hold vigil for Shane, and a sombre atmosphere prevailed. Flickering candles burned to stubs in the windows to symbolise hope and the community's prayer for Shane's safe return.

The low hum of conversation died off as punters noticed Ava, and heat reddened her cheeks at the unaccustomed attention. Her dad's wink reassured her as she hovered awkwardly, and Shannon waved for her to join them. Her sister was perched around a table with Imogen, Ryan, Hannah and Freya. She'd pull up a chair next to them in a minute, she decided as her eyes raked the other tables to see if the Egans were here.

There was no sign of them. Over by the fire, Jody's black coat gleamed as she languished in front of the leaping flames beside the hearth. Two little Molloy children kneeled on the floor, stroking her. Mam had mentioned they were desperate for a dog.

She itched to pat Shane's beloved dog, who'd been as good hers, too, but as she made her way over to Jody, she found herself being waylaid by Isla Mullins. The Irish souvenirs shopkeeper was hard to miss in a green sweatshirt with a rainbow and a pot of gold emblazoned on the front.

'We're all praying he comes home safe, Ava.'

Isla's mouth was set in a grim line as she laid a hand on her forearm, and Ava rustled up a tremulous smile, biting at her bottom lip because she'd done enough crying.

One by one, the familiar faces of Eileen Carroll, Rita Quigley and Nessie Doyle swam before her, echoing Isla's sentiment. Even Mrs Tattersall, who was notoriously annoyed with anyone who dared to breathe the same air as her, had a kind word this evening. Of course it was tempered with a gripe about how mobility scooters had no place being in a pub as Mr Kenny nearly ran over her foot in his haste to get to the gents. They all startled as he made use of the horn to clear the way.

Ava extradited herself and made it to the fireplace, where she greeted the Molloy littlies. She was never entirely sure which child was Siobhan and which was Sinead as she crouched down in front of the black dog.

'Hello, Jody. How're you holding up?'

Her hand ran down the Lab cross's silky coat, and Jody's tail began thumping when she heard Ava's voice. She raised her head, pinning Ava with her soulful gaze, as though checking it really was her, before scrabbling to her feet. Her wet nose nuzzled at Ava's hand.

'I've missed you, Jody, girl.' She kissed the top of the dog's head and wrapped her arms around her, wondering if the animal she'd adored and had found so hard to leave had felt abandoned when she'd moved to London. The thought of Jody pining cracked her heart a little more, and she marvelled over her forgiving nature as she made her affection for Ava clear.

Dermot Molloy was holding up bags of crisps, which sent the younger of his offspring hurtling back to join the rest of their family, and Ava got to her feet.

'Come on, Jody. We'll go and join the others.'

This time it was Father Seamus who stepped in front of her, the expression on his round face grave. She could smell the whiskey he was partial to when he called in at the Shamrock on his breath. He held the empty Waterford crystal tumbler reserved especially for him in his hand as he said, 'Ava, I know this is a worrying time, but I want you to know there's power in prayer, and every single person in this village is praying for Shane.'

Herself included, Ava thought, and her voice when she spoke had a rawness to it. 'Thanks, Father. Have you been to see Rory, Conor and Michael?'

'I've not long got back from their house.'

It was a silly question, but she had to ask. 'How are they holding up?'

'As well as can be expected.'

Ava hesitated, then blurted, 'I should call round myself, but I'm unsure of the reception I'd get.'

There was little that went on in Emerald Bay that Father

Seamus wasn't privy to, messy break-ups included, and Shane's brothers had made it more than clear they backed their brother.

'There are bigger things on their mind, Ava, but you should be with your family now. When I left, Rory and the lads were ready to turn in for the night. They want to be back out on the water at the crack of dawn to carry on with the search. Besides, you know yourself, Rory's not one for sitting about talking things over, and the apple doesn't fall far from the tree with his lads.'

Ava nodded her agreement, understanding Father Seamus's tactful way of telling her to leave the Egans be just now because gruff described Rory and his sons at the best of times. Shane's sensitive side must have come from his mam.

'And so, as you know, I'm here for you too if you'd like a word with Him.' He raised his eyes heavenward in case she was in doubt as to whom he was referring to. 'You know where to find me, even if it's been a while since we last saw you there. I'll let you bring your friend with you, too, if you decide to pay us a call.'

Ava detected the light briefly dancing in button-bright eyes that didn't miss a beat as Father Seamus ruffled the top of Jody's head.

'I do, and I'll bear that in mind. Thanks, Father.'

'Then I hope to see you there, Ava, and remember it's times like this we need to surround ourselves with those that love and care for us.' He eyed his tumbler as though surprised to find it empty. 'Now then, I'm off to see if your dad can spare me a second tot – given the circumstances, like.'

The corners of Ava's mouth twitched because, circumstances or no circumstances, the good Father would have been heading up to the bar for a second tot regardless, given that it would be on the house. Mam insisted on it, much to their dad's chagrin. Nora Kelly was determined to make up for her girls' lax ways where Mass was concerned. And many a word had

been exchanged when tallying up the takings as to how plying
Father Seamus with whiskey wouldn't give the family a free
pass through the pearly gates.

Imogen's beau, Ryan O'Malley, saw her approach over the
rim of his pint glass, and he stood up, coming around from the
table in his clumpy work boots. She was folded into a bear hug
before she knew what was happening, breathing in wood chips
and plaster dust. The genuine gesture surprised her but
warmed her, too, given she'd not had much chance to get to
know him. The little she'd gleaned from Imogen as to why he'd
returned to Emerald Bay, having made a good life in London,
was that he'd taken over the family's building company after his
father suffered a debilitating stroke. That said a lot about his
character, Ava thought as the rough flannel of his shirt
scratched her cheek.

Shane had a similar shirt, and fresh pain stabbed her, but
she wouldn't go down the rabbit hole of memories again.
Instead, she considered how good this burly builder was for her
sister. Being home in Emerald Bay suited Imo, and thanks to the
marvels of the online world, her interior design business hadn't
been impacted by her move from Dublin. Her work involved
more travel these days, but it seemed a small price to pay for
how happy she was.

Ryan released her, and she smiled her thanks. He didn't
offer platitudes, but he didn't need to, because the hug had said
it all, and he crouched down to say hello to Jody while Freya,
who'd hopped off her stool, squeezed her in greeting. Shannon's
best friend's blue hair tickled Ava's nose, as did her soft floral
scent. She stifled a sneeze as she looked over Freya's shoulder to
see there was no sign of Oisin. It wasn't surprising, though. Not
from what Shannon had told her. Freya described the man she
was head over heels about as 'free-spirited', whereas Shannon
thought 'selfish arse' was a better fit.

Another stool was found, and Ava shuffled between

Shannon and Imogen. At the same time, Jody settled at her feet under the table.

Hannah was leaning over the table, talking to Imogen, whose eyes had glazed over. 'Tiny homes reduce your individual environmental impact and energy consumption by forty-five per cent.'

'You just googled that.'

'What are you on about?' Ava butted in, looking over at Hannah, whose cheeks had that high colour, signalling she was on her soapbox.

'Imo and Ryan are thinking about building a house. There's a section with a view of the bay they're interested in, and I'm telling them this is their chance to step up and do their bit for the planet.'

Ava knew they were living in Ryan's parents' house while Mr O'Malley was undergoing a rehabilitation programme in Dublin. 'That's exciting, Imo!' It was the first she'd heard about herself and Ryan taking such a big step forward in their relationship. Her sister was a fast operator.

'Thank you, Ava. It is. Or it would be if the environmental crusader over there didn't keep harping on at us about the virtues of living in a kennel with windows.'

Ava couldn't help her grin. Imogen might have changed, but there was still plenty of the Imo she knew and loved in the mix, too.

'Your children will thank me one day,' Hannah replied sanctimoniously. 'Have you been in touch with Grace, Ava? She's been texting me continuously, wanting to know where you're at.'

'I'll flick her a message now.' Ava felt bad for ignoring her sister's voicemails but had nothing to tell her. Still and all, she should have been in touch, because if Grace was going through the hell she was right now, she'd want to be there for her, and it wasn't fair to freeze her out. They'd always been hyper-aware of what each other was feeling, something they accepted as part and parcel of being identical twins.

She dug her phone out and tapped out a quick message, apologising for not getting back to her sooner but saying there was nothing new to tell her. She stared at the text for a second and added she was doing OK under the circumstances and had plenty of shoulders to lean on.

'How did you get on with booking your flight?' Ava asked Shannon, leaving her other two sisters to it.

'I fly out at ten thirty tomorrow morning,' Shannon replied.

'Thanks a million, Ryan,' Ava said as a Baileys was placed before her. She hadn't wanted a drink, but taking a sip of the creamy sweet liqueur, she was glad he'd fetched her one. 'That's good, Shan. Have you told James?'

Shannon nodded and then shrugged. 'I wish things were different all around.'

'Me too.' They gave one another a half-smile of under-standing.

Ava saw their dad had left their mam manning the bar and was rallying up Dermot Molloy and Ollie Quigley, who had the giveaway black cases in their hands, signalling a session would soon be underway. 'I think your services are going to be required.'

Shannon swivelled on her seat to see what Ava meant, just in time to see Ollie set his fiddle and guitar cases down on the table closest to the fire. Dermot had brought his uillean pipes, and Liam was polishing his tin whistle as Shannon slid off her stool to join them.

All conversations trailed off as Liam Kelly put the tin whistle to his lips, and the sweet, pure sound filled the pub. Shannon was standing in front of the fire, and as she began to sing, her melodic voice both haunting and angelic, the fine hairs on Ava's arms stood up. She knew she wasn't the only one affected by the ballad.

Ollie began to pluck softly at the guitar strings, and as the quartet reached the gentle chorus, the villagers joined in, their voices united, arms about shoulders as bodies swayed along to the song 'A Fisherman's Life'.

By the time the song ended and Jody gave off a mournful howl, there wasn't a dry eye in the pub.

May God give you...
For every storm, a rainbow,
For every tear, a smile,
For every care, a promise,
And a blessing in each trial.
For every problem life sends,
A faithful friend to share,
For every sigh, a sweet song,
And an answer to each prayer.

— *IRISH BLESSING*

15

'He's alive, Ava. They've found him. They've found Shane!' Nora Kelly rushed to Ava's bedside, her voice rising an octave with each word.

The sheets were pulled up to her chin. She hadn't expected to sleep so heavily, but the last twenty-four hours had taken their toll, and after crawling under the covers sometime after midnight, she hadn't stirred since. Hannah's soft snores across the way reassured her she was home at the Shamrock, and even though her mam's words penetrated her subconscious, she didn't prise her eyes open, convinced she was dreaming. And if that was the case, she didn't want to wake up.

The rough shake convinced her otherwise.

'Ava!' The impatience in her mam's tone penetrated the sleep fog. 'Did you hear what I said? Shane's alive. It's a Christmas miracle is what it is! He's going to be all right. They're bringing him ashore now, and I'm guessing the ambulance will be on standby to take him to the hospital in Galway.'

'Mam?' Ava hauled herself upright, searching her mother's face for confirmation of what she was saying.

Nora's pink fluffy dressing gown was knotted about her

waist and her hair mussed, but her eyes were bright and her skin glowing as she repeated what she'd said. The excitement caused her voice to grow louder, so she was almost shouting.

Across the room, Hannah, too, jolted awake.

'He's alive, Mam?' She tossed back her bedcovers and sat up, rubbing her eyes.

The tears that burst forth as Ava realised it was true Shane had been found and would be OK took her by surprise.

'He's suffering from hypothermia, and he's dehydrated, but he's alive all right. It's a Christmas miracle, girls.' Nora repeated her earlier sentiment.

'It's fecking fantastic is what it is!' Hannah was jubilant.

For once, Nora didn't tell her daughter off for swearing as Ava giggled borderline hysterically at the remark. She'd woken up to find herself on an emotional see-saw, as elation bounced between disbelief and back again.

'Where was he found, Mam?' she managed to choke out, knowing she was wasting precious time asking but needing to know.

'I don't know all the ins and outs, love, but there's talk he was on one of the islands and that he'd found a cave to shelter in. Thank God he wasn't in the water long.'

'Will you take me down to the harbour?'

'Not in your pyjamas, I won't.' Nora had no control over the smile encompassing her face as she glanced down at her own attire. 'Now g'won with you and have a quick shower. I'll meet you downstairs in ten minutes. You too, Hannah. Your sister's after leaving for the airport shortly, and your nan is already cracking eggs into a bowl.'

Ava didn't need to be told twice. She leaped out of bed and narrowly avoided tripping over Napoleon for the second time since she'd arrived. Barging into the bathroom, she was grateful for small mercies like Imogen having moved into Ryan's; otherwise, she'd have been hammering on the door about now! One bathroom servicing five sisters had always been a flashpoint in the Kelly house.

Ava brushed her teeth while waiting for the hot water to kick in and sent up a thank-you prayer as she squirted body wash into the palm of her hand. Suppose her father had been outside the bathroom timing her shower, as he'd been known to do with five daughters under one roof. In that case, he'd have given her a round of applause when she emerged in record time! She dressed in a heavy knit and jeans, not bothering with any further titivations. Pulling her damp hair out from the neck of her jumper, she shouted, 'Bathroom's free,' to Hannah before haring down the stairs.

'Isn't it the best news?' Shannon, her case waiting by the back door ready for her flight to Boston, was an advertisement for comfortable air travel in a sweatshirt and leggings. She got up from the table and embraced her sister then gestured to the steaming mug on the table. 'I figured you wouldn't take long to get ready, so I made you a coffee.'

'Thanks, Shan.' Ava picked it up, her hand trembling with excitement at the thought of seeing Shane shortly.

'And I've scrambled eggs on the go.' Kitty didn't turn away from her task at the stove.

'Ah, Nan, thank you, but honestly, I won't be able to eat a thing, and as soon as Mam's down, I want to head off to the harbour.' Ava raised her eyes to the ceiling, hearing footsteps padding about, hoping she wasn't far off.

'The eggs are almost ready now, so sit yourself down, Ava, Shannon. Neither of you will be any good to your young men if you're a pair of skinny little waifs that get knocked down in a strong wind.'

Would Shane be her young man again? Ava wondered. She wanted it more than anything, but if he didn't feel the same way, she'd still be eternally grateful he'd survived. One way or another, she'd soon find out how he felt. The thought made her breath quicken.

Shannon was smirking. 'I'm a wee way off waif status, Nan. You know me – stress is my eating trigger. And these last few days have been stressful, to say the least.'

'Better eggs than chocolate and crisps at the airport, Shannon.' Kitty, playing mother hen, popped bread into the toaster. 'And as for you, Ava, a good breakfast will get you through whatever lies ahead today. Protein is what you both need to sustain youse.'

Ava wasn't going to waste her breath arguing, so she pulled out a chair next to Shannon. Then, remembering why her sister was leaving for Boston this morning, she said, 'Be sure to pass on my condolences to James and his family – and to Maeve of course – won't you, Shan? It's terrible sad.'

'Of course I will, and it is, but it's wonderful, too. That's what I'm holding on to.'

Ava couldn't see what was wonderful about dying of cancer, and her expression must have said the same.

'I mean that Hazel and Maeve connected. It wouldn't have happened without James. I've seen a lot of death in my job, and it's only right to be sad when someone passes, but it's OK to be happy about the life that was lived as well,' Shannon elaborated.

'I can see that,' Ava said after digesting her sister's words for a few seconds.

'It's such a relief, like, being able to leave knowing things at home are OK.' Shannon glanced toward Kitty and lowered her voice, leaning closer to her sister. 'I've been thinking about it since we first heard Shane was missing, and we were wrong. All of us. We shouldn't have pushed you toward moving to London like we did. It was because we were worried.'

Ava frowned. 'About what?'

'Grace was concerned about Shane's controlling streak and

the fact he could be jealous. We thought it would do you good to branch out. Dip your toe in the water, so to speak, and see what else – who else – was out there, because it's a big old world. We didn't want you to settle for the first fella who'd happened along.'

The words 'controlling' and 'jealous' were ugly, and Ava felt each of them like a slap. How dare Grace!

'Shane's not like that, Shan.' Her words were spoken softly, not wanting Kitty to be privy to the conversation, but her head shake was vehement. 'And I know my own mind.'

Grace's interference stemmed more from wanting her twin to come to London with her. It harked from a selfish place which, if you thought about it, raised the question of exactly who was controlling and jealous. As for her easily swayed sisters, they should have known better, given they'd known Shane since he was a youngster and how he'd been welcomed into their home. At the very least, they should have raised their concerns with her. But she wouldn't let any of that mar the euphoria she felt at his rescue. Not now, at any rate.

Shannon was oblivious to Ava's inner turmoil. 'Like I said, I'm sorry. We were wrong. I can see that now. I always thought Shane was a lovely fella, and I feel bad for all the fishy-arse jokes I've laughed along to.'

'I'm guilty of that, too,' Ava mumbled. Her laughter had been a defence mechanism against missing him. She'd been sick of standing up for him where her sisters were concerned, angry by his off-handedness toward her on her visits home. They'd both behaved badly because they were hurting.

'Anyway, I'm so happy he's been found.' Shannon paused, thinking over what she wanted to say next. 'You're your own person, Ava, and it's your life. Follow your heart from hereon in, do you hear me?'

Ava nodded, her grip on the handle of the mug loosening. She understood what Shannon was getting at and knew she was always considered the more fragile twin. But while she and

Grace might be identical, that didn't mean they weren't individuals, even if other people didn't always see it like that, and to be fair, sometimes they even got the line blurred as to where one of them began and the other ended.

'It's a second chance you're after being given. Grasp it with both hands, and don't let go this time.'

'I'm not going to.' Ava meant every word of it.

'Here we are.' Kitty placed two mounded plates of soft yellow eggs wobbling on top of thickly buttered toast in front of them. 'Eat up.'

'Thanks, Nan,' they chimed, picking up their knives and forks as Nora, Hannah and Liam clattered downstairs and through to the kitchen.

'That smells good. I hope there's plenty to go round, Mam,' Liam greeted his mother with a kiss on her cheek. 'Shannon, we'll hit the road in ten minutes once I've some sustenance. All right?'

'Grand, Dad. Thanks for taking me.'

'Ah, sure, it's not a bother.'

'Just a scraping of butter on Liam's toast, mind, Kitty,' Nora bossed.

Ava didn't need to see her nan's face to know she would be rolling her eyes and that she'd put an extra dollop of butter on her son's toast no matter what his wife said. To Kitty Kelly's mind, a little extra padding in winter didn't harm anyone, no matter what the doctor said.

'Sit yourselves down, all of you.' Kitty waved the wooden spoon like a baton, as if she was conducting her orchestra. On cue, chairs were scraped out from the table.

Ava had managed a forkful or two of the eggs but struggled to find room amongst the raw energy of anticipation.

Shannon nudged her conspiratorially, whispering, 'Tip the rest on my plate.'

She flashed her sister a grateful smile and did just that. Her reward as Kitty set breakfast in front of her son was a gratified smile at the sight of a clean plate. Meanwhile, ignoring Kitty's instructions to sit down, Nora served hers and Hannah's up, carrying the plates over to the table.

'You'll all look after Napoleon for me while I'm away, won't you?' Shannon asked, a forkful of food halfway to her mouth. 'It's not just food and water he needs. It's plenty of attention, too.'

'I'm not promising anything,' Liam replied. 'I had to chase your four-legged gremlin down the hall to retrieve my boxers this morning. Oh, and speak of the devil. There he is.'

Napoleon trotted nonchalantly into the kitchen and leaped gracefully onto Shannon's lap before licking his front paw and eyeing them all.

'Close your ears, Napoleon. Grandad loves you, really.' Shannon stroked the little cat, shovelling her food in with her spare hand.

'I have to say, though, I wasn't impressed being gifted Dad's underpants, Shan, especially because I wasn't sure if they were worn,' Hannah stated before asking her mam to pass the salt.

'Do you mind not talking about underwear at the breakfast table?' Kitty finally sat down to enjoy her breakfast.

'Sorry, Nan.' Hannah grinned, taking the salt pot and giving it a good shake over her eggs. 'Has anyone been in touch with Grace to tell her the good news?'

Ava hadn't. She hadn't thought of her twin once since Mam had given her the news, and now, after her conversation with Shannon, she wasn't in the right headspace to deal with her twin.

The back door burst open, silencing any further chit-chat of the underpants kind. Hannah's question remained unanswered as Imogen appeared.

'Oh good, you're still here, the pair of you.' Her eyes flitted from Ava to Shannon. 'I was worried I'd miss you. Ava, it's brilliant about Shane! Ryan and I danced a jig in the kitchen this morning. Literally. Poor Lulu didn't know what was going on.' Imogen referred to the little dachshund they'd inherited in Ryan's parents' absence as she stamped her feet on the mat. Then she tugged her mittens off, stuffing them in her coat pockets.

'It is,' Ava agreed, beaming at Imogen before downing the dregs of her coffee.

'Imogen Kelly, shut that door. You're letting all the cold air in,' Liam bellowed.

'You weren't born in a tent,' Imogen, Shannon, Hannah and Ava piped up in harmony, each receiving a glare from their dad as they giggled.

'Pull up a seat, Imogen. I'll not have it said anyone ever sat at my table and went hungry.'

'Your table?' Nora raised an eyebrow then flapped her hand at Kitty to stay seated. 'Imogen can see to herself, Kitty. Stop fussing.'

'I've had breakfast, Mam, Nan.' Imogen shrugged off her coat and draped it over the back of the empty chair.

Kitty made a humphing sound. 'Those seed things you're so fond of that get stuck in your teeth aren't what I'd call a proper breakfast.'

'Chia seeds, Nan, and they're highly nutritious.'

'Poppycock.'

Imogen's face danced with amusement, and she didn't answer back as she sat down. In the interim, Shannon and Ava had carried their dirty dishes over to the sink, leaving them on the side.

'Hannah, you're not to let your nan wash up, do you hear me?' Nora, too, got up from the table. 'Just let me fetch my coat, and we'll be off, Ava.'

'I hear you, Mam.' Hannah saluted. 'Nan, I'm not to let you wash up.'

She grinned cheekily at Kitty, who replied, 'She's a bossy wan, your mam.'

Ava donned her coat, winding her scarf around her neck while Imogen said her goodbyes to Shannon. Then everybody seemed to be on the move all at once, with Liam pushing his chair back, patting his belly and announcing he was ready to go. At the same time, Nora reappeared, rugged up to brave the elements.

'Ava, be sure and tell Rory and the lads we're made up for them, and once the young fella's back home, we'll have a celebration here at the pub.' Liam said, jamming her to him briefly before planting a kiss on her head while Shannon leaned down to kiss her nan's cheek.

'I feel like I'm always saying goodbye to one of you. Bíodh turas sábháilte.' Kitty wished her oldest granddaughter a safe trip in Irish, patting her hand. 'You look after that lovely lad of yours, James, and tell Maeve we're all thinking of her.'

'I will, Nan. Love you all,' Shannon called, and disappeared out the door, obviously not wanting them to see her tears at the goodbye.

'Don't worry, Nan – me and Imo will stay here and keep an eye on you,' Hannah reassured.

Imogen nodded while Kitty Kelly made a pooh-poohing noise. Ava smiled, overhearing her saying that if anybody needed keeping an eye on, it was the pair of them.

'Remember us to the Egans and tell Rory we've all been praying hard for this outcome.' Kitty's voice trailed after Ava, and she promised she would as she closed the door and traipsed after Shannon, Liam and her mam.

Liam and Shannon exited the car park first in a blaze of sunshine-yellow Hilux while Nora let her Golf warm up for a second or two.

The morning waiting for them was gloomy, with drizzle that would eventually soak you to your skin, but nothing could dampen Ava's mood. Nothing. She settled into the seat, this time prepared for the spreading heat beneath her bum.

As Nora was about to reverse, a car neither of them recognised pulled in alongside them.

'Who would that be at this time of the morning?' Nora, puzzled, rubbed at her window, which had already misted up from their breath. The pub wouldn't be open for a few hours yet. 'I don't believe it!' she exclaimed.

'Who is it?' Ava leaned past her mam to see for herself, her mouth falling open as she clocked who was behind the wheel.

16

'Ava, it's brilliant news! It's been all over the radio,' Grace gushed. 'You want to see the buzz of activity down at the harbour. I pulled over, thinking you might be down there, but obviously didn't see Mam's car. It's not hard to miss like Dad's, after all.' She giggled then shrugged. 'So here I am.'

'Here you are. But you didn't need to come, Grace.' Ava's statement was punctuated by puffs of white air. Her hand had automatically dipped inside her roll-neck, reaching for her locket as she stared at her sister unsmilingly.

Nora Kelly had stilled the engine and leaped out of the car as soon as she'd twigged who had just parked next to them. So Grace was recovering from being crushed into her mam's sweater-clad bosom as she stood alongside the grey sedan she must have hired at the airport. An uncertain smile was playing at the corner of her mouth at her sister's less-than-effusive greeting.

Ava supposed she shouldn't have been surprised to see her twin, because if the situation had been reversed, she would have been on the first flight home to be with Grace. Nonetheless, she *was* taken aback, because she could usually sense when her twin was near. Not today, though. Her mind was too full of Shane, and she didn't have time for her sister, because, here or not, Ava didn't want to hang about any longer.

Her heart sank as Grace stepped toward her, knowing there was no chance of getting away with a quick hello and catch you later. It wasn't in the Kelly DNA.

'What, no hug?' Grace's eyebrows, visible beneath the blunt fringe peeking from her green bobble hat, raised in puzzlement. She was wrapped in a matching coat with just the right shade of jewel toning in the green for their winter complexions. No twin liked being compared, but Ava would readily admit Grace was the fashionista of the pair. She was also overprotective, something Mam had once said stemmed from Ava having been poorly as a baby. In Ava's opinion, it was an overprotectiveness that sometimes erred toward bossiness. For the best part, she was happy to just go with the flow where her twin was concerned, but right now, Shane was her priority, and the sooner this meet and greet was done, the sooner they'd be on the road.

'It's only been twenty-four hours since I last saw you, but sorry.' Ava lunged awkwardly forward to greet her properly, knowing being stand-offish would result in questions which would only hold them up longer.

'That's better.' Grace grinned, her shoulders relaxing.

She smelled of a medley of duty-free perfume, and Ava imagined her perusing the array of fancy bottles on offer. For some reason, the mental image irked her.

'I'm glad you're here,' she fibbed, because even now, Ava was a pleaser. And to be fair, she was guilty of leaning heavily on Grace at times, perfectly happy to let her be the stronger of them. Was it any wonder Grace felt her twin needed her by her side? Right now, though, she wished her sister wasn't here and desperately hoped it didn't show on her face.

'And of course I had to come! I would have flown over with

you if the flight hadn't been fully booked. This morning's red-eye was the earliest one I could get a seat on.'

'Of course you did, love,' Nora butted in. 'Family needs to gather at times like this. Although you should have rung me or your dad and told us you were coming, because Dad could have brought you home from the airport. There was no need for you to be forking out for a hire car. And you'd have been able to see Shannon. That's where he's headed now, dropping her off for her flight to Boston.'

Ava was all but stamping her feet like a bull pawing at the ground, wanting to be off, but neither her mam nor Grace seemed to pick up on her impatience.

'I spoke to her last night, Mam, and asked her to give James, Maeve and the brothers my love. And I just passed them. I mean, that beast of a wagon Dad insists on driving is hard to miss. I flashed my lights, but either they didn't notice or thought I was a tourist, giving them a heads-up that Sergeant Badger was lurking in the bushes ahead.'

Nora smiled. 'He'd like to hear about his truck being hard to miss. That's the whole point of the yellow after all.'

Grace's grin was rueful. 'Don't you be starting on about yellow being the most visible colour on the road and all that. The next time I'm in the market for a car, I can tell you, Mam, he'll not be convincing me to buy a wee-coloured one.'

'Well, all I can say on the subject, Grace, is if that's the colour of your wee, then you need to up your water uptake.'

Ava wanted to scream with frustration over her mam and sister's light-hearted chit-chat when they should be on the road.

'Grace, Mam and I were about to head to the harbour. Come on, Mam,' Ava urged, returning to the passenger door.

'Grand – I timed that well. I'll jump in the back.' Grace also stepped toward the Golf, but Ava instinctively raised her hand.

'No!' Her voice was uncharacteristically sharp, and her sister and their mam blinked with shock at her tone.

Ava took a deep breath, dropping her hand. 'Sorry.' She couldn't be doing with this. Not now. 'I didn't mean it to come out like that. It's just—'

'It's OK, love. You've been under a lot of stress, and you want to see Shane,' Nora appeased, shooting Grace a look that suggested allowances should be made for her twin.

Grace approached the passenger side of the car where Ava was standing. She reached out, touching Ava's upper arm briefly. 'It's cool, Aves. I understand. I mean, you know Shane and I have never been the best of buddies, but I wouldn't have wished him harm, and honest to God, it's such a relief he's been found alive and well.'

Ava could see the hurt on her sister's face, but the words 'never been the best of buddies' reverberated. She didn't like the sick feeling building inside her and knew she'd been out of order snapping.

'No, it's not cool. I should have said there's no need for you to come with us, not when you must have been up in the middle of the night to catch your flight, and you've just driven from Shannon. I'm betting you've not had breakfast. If you're lucky, Nan will whip you something up.' They both knew there would be no luck involved. To be fed by Kitty Kelly was a foregone conclusion. 'So why don't you catch up with Nan and Hannah? Imo's there, too. And I'll catch you back here later.' She rustled up a smile, willing Grace to understand.

Her sister nodded a little too vigorously before saying, 'Grand. I am starved.'

'OK, that's sorted.' Nora clapped her hands, and Ava didn't hang about before clambering into the passenger seat.

Only when she'd closed the door, and her mam ducked back behind the wheel as Grace gave them a wave goodbye, did she allow herself a long, slow exhale.

. . .

The drizzle was settling on the windscreen as fast as the wipers could swish it away by the time they turned onto Main Street. Despite the inclement weather, though, a surprise awaited them.

'Mam, look! The tree's going up.' Ava pointed toward the square, where a boom truck with an enormous Douglas fir dangling from its crane was being guided into place by Dermot Molloy. Dermot Molloy's Quality Meats was the proud sponsor of Emerald Bay's Christmas tree, which seemed to grow bigger each year.

'I'd forgotten all about that, what with the good news this morning. I expect your dad will be out there soon with the ladder helping to decorate it.' Nora shook her head and said half to herself, 'So long as he doesn't fiddle about with the fairy lights until the rain's gone off.'

The year the lights had been switched on with great fanfare only to fizzle out, taking down the village's power supply with them, had become part of Emerald Bay Christmas folklore.

'He was talking about dusting off his Father Christmas suit to see if it still fits today,' she added.

The Christmas spirit had yet to fill Mrs Tattersall with goodwill Ava saw as they drove up Main Street. There she was with her headscarf knotted under her chin and a firm grasp of her trolley bag, gesturing furiously to a dropped chocolate bar wrapper a short distance from the Bus Stop mini supermarket. Out the front of which was a rubbish bin.

Ava watched young Ruby McGinn with the bronzed face, an anomaly given the time of year, stoop to pick it up, her head hanging as she righted herself and mooched toward the bin. Ava could imagine how that conversation was going. Mrs Tattersall would doubtless be threatening to telephone Ruby's mam and tell her she had a litterer for a daughter. *Did Mrs McGinn know littering was a fining offence that Sergeant Badger would be keen to hear about?*

Paddy McNamara, meanwhile, was in high spirits, swaying down the street, and from the movement of his arms, Ava guessed he was in full song.

In the pharmacy, Nuala was manhandling a blow-up snowman, tinsel strewn about her feet as she tackled the Christmas window. Ava waved out and received a cheery smile and wave in return. Meanwhile, across the road, the shopkeepers were out in force. Rita Quigley, Eileen Carroll – advertising the joys of wearing an Aran knit in winter – and Isla Mullins were attempting to drape fairy lights outside their shops, but it was a case of too many chiefs, by the looks of things.

The village was coming to life with the festive spirit as news of Shane's rescue spread, Ava surmised. This was more like it!

Nora didn't take her eyes off the road as they passed Mermaids, leaving the village shops behind, and fingers drumming the steering wheel, she asked, 'What's going on, Ava?'

'What do you mean?' Ava squirmed in her seat, and not because of the spreading warmth. She had an inkling as to what her mam was getting at.

'With you and Grace?'

The inkling was right, then. Ava stared out the side window as she toyed with how to word the effect the last few days had had on her. She had been off with her sister but couldn't help the simmering anger brewing where Grace was concerned. There was no sound in the car except for the rhythmic whoosh back and forth of the windscreen wipers as they drove past the row of thatched cottages. Today, a tour bus had pulled up, and a hardy group of travellers decked out in wet-weather gear aimed their cameras at the cottages.

Finally, she spoke up. 'I suppose I'm angry with her, Mam.'
'Why?'

'You heard her say she never got on well with Shane. And Grace kept telling me to move to London with her.' Ava's voice had a decided waver. 'And did you know she told Shannon, Imo and Hannah he could be controlling and jealous where I was concerned to get them on side with me moving? I mean, Shane? And what hurts, Mam, is that they believed her. Grace was the one being both those things.' Ava was on a roll now the dam had burst. 'I feel like they bullied me into making the wrong choice, because what if he'd died? What if I never got the chance to tell him I made a mistake and how sorry I am?' She didn't want to cry but was close to losing the battle.

'But he didn't die, Ava. He's very much alive, and that's what you need to focus on, not petty grievances.'

Ava bristled, not seeing what was petty about what she'd just confided to her mam.

'Don't hold on to grudges, Ava. It doesn't do you any good in the long run. They churn you up inside. I know.'

The grandparents they'd never met sprang to mind, but now wasn't the time to get into that.

'Your sister shouldn't have said that about Shane, but perhaps that's how she sees him.'

Ava started spluttering, but Nora lifted her hand from the steering wheel to silence her daughter.

'Ava, let me finish.'

With difficulty, Ava reined in what had been on the tip of her tongue. Her mam didn't have a clue. She wasn't a twin for starters. How could she understand the complexities of her relationship with Grace?

'I'm not a twin, but I am the mother of twins, and it's a complicated relationship between you. It always has been. It's a fine line to balance, needing each other and giving one another the space to live your own lives. Three can be a crowd, Ava. Grace will understand when she meets someone who makes her feel like you do about Shane.'

She might not be a twin, Ava thought, but sometimes their mam was a spooky mind reader. 'But I don't want to be piggy in the middle.'

Amusement flickered at Ava's turn of phrase.

'It's not funny, Mam.'

'No. You're right. Sorry.' Nora's eyes narrowed as they approached the harbour. In the distance, they could see the ambulance and a huddle of people clustered by the wharf. 'Things have a habit of working themselves out how they're supposed to, but I think you need to take some responsibility for your decisions as well. You were the one who broke things off with Shane, not your sisters. Why don't you try framing things differently and see your time in London tasting life without Shane as an experience? I know it won't seem like it right now, but his accident is an arse about face blessing in so much as it's crystallised how you really feel about him.'

Ava nodded, seeing her point, her hand already on the door handle.

'Would you hold your horses and wait until I've stopped the car, because I don't fancy your chances doing the drop and roll like they do on those American cop shows your father's fond of. Not with those potholes,' Nora warned.

Ava's hand stayed where it was, and when her mam pulled the handbrake up, she swung the door open. Nerves swelled like the rising tide about how she'd be received, but whatever happened between her and Shane would be his call.

Either way, she was glad she'd come home to Emerald Bay.

17

Ava pushed through the small crowd, all rugged up and watching the two black specks on the horizon making their way toward the shore.

She was dimly aware she recognised all the faces who'd gathered to see Shane brought home. His mate Ciaron was here, and there were his cousins and uncle, Vonnie's lads sipping the hot soup Carmel Brady was distributing. She figured they must have joined the search again this morning and returned their fishing boat when the good news was relayed, seeing they were decked out in their wet-weather gear.

The savoury, hearty-smelling soup was being gratefully received to warm those waiting at the harbour, and steam rose from paper cups clutched between mittened hands. Ava was careful not to knock anyone, not wanting scalding on her conscious as she edged her way toward Vonnie, who was standing near the jetty's edge. At least, she thought it was Vonnie – it was hard to tell under the coat and hat. Then she saw Jody beside her.

'Vonnie?'

Shane's aunt turned to see who'd spoken. Damp strands of

hair were plastered to her face despite the hat. The wet wool hug Ava received took her breath away but was welcome. Jody whimpered, and her wet nose nudged Ava's hand. Ava responded by crouching down to pet her and whisper that Shane was on his way home.

'You didn't give up hope, did you? You said he might make his way to one of the islands. And that's what he did,' Vonnie said.

Ava's gaze swung upward, and she shook her head. 'I couldn't let myself stop hoping.'

'You're a good girl, Ava Kelly. I always thought that, and I hope it works out between you and Shane. I really do.'

Ava's chin trembled as she opened her mouth to thank her, but the older woman had already moved on, firing out what had transpired.

'Rory radioed in to say Shane's conscious. His speech is slurred, and he's not making much sense. Classic signs of mild hypothermia.' She pointed to an ambulance positioned as close as possible to the jetty. 'He'll be taken straight to the hospital, and I suppose they'll want to keep him under observation for a few nights. But all things considered, he's doing well.'

Ava straightened and listened with her hands steepled to her mouth. Her mam appeared alongside them in time to hear the good news. Her voice shook as she conveyed how happy everyone in the village was to have had such a wonderful outcome.

'We're so grateful, all the family, like, for the support we've had. It means a lot,' Vonnie was saying as Ava allowed herself to think about her great-grandfather momentarily. How different the outcome had been for his wife, daughter and grandchildren.

The black shapes approaching the harbour were in sharper focus now as she mulled over her great-grandfather going missing at sea and the effect it must have had on her mam and their family to never have had answers. This was evident in her mam's glassy stare and compulsive nodding, even now so many years later, as she spoke with Vonnie.

At least this time there would be a happy ending, Ava thought, realising the black shape closest to shore was now orange. She rubbed her palms together like sticks trying to make a flame, willing the lifeboat to hurry up, feeling Jody press in close to her side.

Vonnie was still talking at a rate of knots. She tried to pay attention to what she was saying about how the lifeboat had spotted Shane on one of the smaller rocky island outcrops in the archipelago a little after eight that morning.

Thank God for his yellow overalls and bib. The colour would have been a beacon; otherwise, he could easily have been mistaken for a seal in the mist. She was unaware she was jigging up and down on the soles of her feet as voices quietened in anticipation of the lifeboat's arrival within the next few minutes.

Ava was hit by a visceral sense of having been here before. Waiting. She made a heart with her index fingers and thumbs and gazed down at it.

'People are saying it's a Christmas miracle.'

Ava swung around, and her eyes narrowed, recognising the man decked out like he was off to conquer Everest with a hungry expression as he waited for her to reply. Jeremy Jones, the reporter who'd had a run-in with Hannah. He must be hoping for an inside scoop on the rescue. There was no evidence of his recording device, but his hand was in his pocket, and she wondered if it was there. In his other hand was a hot cup of Carmel's soup. He had a faint ring above his top lip that hinted at the soup being tomato.

'It's that all right.' Nora's hands were clasped tightly. 'A Christmas miracle.'

'And how do you know Shane Egan?' Jeremy turned his attention to Nora.

'Sure, everybody knows everybody in Emerald Bay, and I've known Shane since he was a little fellow. My daughter here, Ava, and him were close.'

'Mam,' Ava hissed, tempted to put the elbow in. Nora Kelly's mouth was running away with itself.

'That's Mr Egan's aunt, am I right?'

'No comment,' Ava answered primly.

Just then, the hum of voices around them began buzzing like Hannah's honeybees around the hives in spring as the boat rose and thumped down over the waves to finally pull in alongside the jetty. The *Mona Kate*'s rumbling engine was audible as the fishing boat following close behind emerged from the sea fog. Ava forgot all about Jeremy Jones as she watched an ambulance officer swing into action, striding down the jetty to meet the lifeboat.

As she made to run after the woman, her mam grabbed hold of her arm. 'Not yet, Ava.'

Jody began to bark.

And then there he was.

A cheer rose as Shane was stretchered off the boat by the unit's crew members, who were all wearing white safety helmets. A thermal foil blanket covered him, and a strangled sob escaped Ava's lips. Her limbs felt light as she watched him be carried up the jetty toward the waiting ambulance.

Ava waved frantically, which was stupid given he was lying down, probably only half-conscious, but it was an instinctive reaction. So was breaking rank to move alongside the stretcher, ignoring her mam calling her back.

She was shocked by his milky pallor, but his eyes were open, and she wasn't wasting a second longer. Her thumb and index fingers made a heart, and she held it next to her heart, keeping pace with the two rescue workers either end of the stretcher. 'I love you, Shane,' she mouthed. Maybe it wasn't fair to accost him when he was most vulnerable, especially when she didn't know whether he still had feelings for her.

If we break up, Ava, that's it. There's no coming back from that.

She heard his voice clearly, as though he'd just opened his mouth and repeated the last words he'd said to her once more. Her teeth clenched so hard her jaw hurt. Ah, Jaysus, was she behaving like a fool? But Ava knew she had to try to make things right between them at the very least so they could be civil with one another. They'd known each other too long and shared too many secrets to act like they didn't know one another each time she returned to Emerald Bay. Those were conversations for another day, though. Right now, he needed to get to the hospital and under a doctor's care.

Then she saw it! A shadow of a smile as he registered her heart signal before she had to move away and the ambulance swallowed him up. It was enough for her, and she rocked on her feet, realising Jody's barking had ramped up at the sight of her master on a stretcher. Vonnie had a tight hold of the dog, and knowing Shane would want her to comfort her, Ava concentrated on soothing Jody while keeping one eye on what was unfolding.

The ambulance driver came around to the rear of the emergency vehicle and conferred briefly with his fellow medic. In the interim, Rory Egan rushed as fast as his wet-weather gear would allow him up the jetty. Ava hadn't been aware the *Mona Kate* had moored up, and she swung her gaze behind her to see a wiped-out Michael and Conor making their way over to their uncle and cousins. Vonnie checked if Ava was all right with Jody for a minute before hurrying over to join them.

Ava had managed to calm the Lab cross sufficiently, and she was sitting by her side. The frantic barking had settled to an occasional ruff. Rory caught her eye and acknowledged her with a weary nod before speaking to the two officers. His expression, as always, was unreadable, although the deep grooves either side of his mouth hinted at what he'd been through since Shane had gone overboard.

Ava watched as Rory climbed into the back of the ambulance. The second ambulance officer made to close the doors. Still, Rory reappeared a split second later, half stepping down as he sought out Ava, gesturing to her impatiently. Maybe things were worse than they'd been led to believe, and her legs liquified at the thought. Jody, sensing her panic, commenced barking again.

A hand on her back gently pushed her, and her mam's voice urged her forward. 'G'won, Ava. I'll look after Jody. Shane wants you with him. You can phone me from the hospital later.'

She felt like she was in a trance, hurrying over on wobbly legs. Someone – Rory or the ambulance officer; she couldn't be sure – helped her into the back of the vehicle. The doors closed behind her as she dipped her head and followed the female ambulance officer's instructions by sitting on the bench seat and pulling her safety belt on. Rory hadn't got back in behind her, she realised, her eyes seeking Shane while the officer wasted no time in attaching a drip.

He turned his head slightly, and their eyes locked. It was like the last piece of a puzzle slotting into place, and as the ambulance engine roared into life, there was no need for words.

18

Ava was pacing in the waiting area of the University Hospital Galway, unable to sit still, thanks to the pent-up nervous energy of the last forty-eight hours. The journey from that first phone call where her mam had relayed the awful news of Shane's accident to now might have been less than two days, but it had felt like a lifetime.

She shook her hands like she'd just washed them and wanted to air dry them, needing a physical release, a little like Nan did with her legs when she was plagued by restless leg syndrome. All well and good unless you were sat next to her on the sofa and she sprang into action! This must be what that felt like – a tingly, crawling sensation and an overwhelming urge to move.

Nobody seated nearby paid her peculiar behaviour any attention. Maybe they thought she was on drugs or having some sort of episode. Either way, their faces, tired and drawn as they waited for news about a loved one, spoke of far bigger things on their minds.

It was hard not to listen in on the conversations around her.

Like Ava, all of them were sitting or, in her case, pacing, waiting for information.

Ava didn't like hospitals. Well, who did? But she didn't like them like some people didn't like confined spaces or heights. She'd spent two weeks in hospital when she was three and a half – two weeks not understanding why she'd been separated from her twin and her family. There'd been a good reason of course. She had been battling bacterial meningitis. The infection was a killer, and fortunately, her mam had acted swiftly when Ava's temperature spiked, and she'd moaned her neck was sore and the lights were hurting her eyes.

Those two weeks had been traumatic for the whole family, and even though Ava's memories of being in the hospital were hazy, the smell of pine disinfectant and bleach mingling with an all-pervasive stewed-meat aroma was triggering. Still and all, she counted herself lucky to have emerged from the vicious illness unscathed.

Her phone ringing stopped her in her tracks, and she patted around for it before inspecting the screen.

'Hi, Mam.' Ava kept her voice low as she moved from the seating area to loiter alongside the vending machine. Unlike your red-haired, broken-arm woman sitting over there, she didn't want the waiting room to be privy to her conversation.

'How's Shane doing, Ava?'

Her mam's voice sounded far away, and Ava closed her other ear with her finger to hear her better. 'Have you got me on speakerphone?' She hated being on speakerphone. It was an annoying habit of her mam's where her daughters were concerned.

'Of course I have. We're all here wanting to know what's happening. Well, when I say all, it's your father, Grace, Kitty and myself. Hannah's after putting the Christmas decorations up in the pub before Isla begins mithering about them and keeping an eye on the bar. We decided it felt right to do so now. There'll be a hooley in here tonight to be sure.'

Ava heard her dad, sister and nan call out hello in the staticky background and responded in kind.

'Grace and your father are going to pick a tree from that farm near Kilticaneel in a short while. Preferably one we can get in the door this year, Liam,' Nora said pointedly. 'Oh, and Imogen's gone home. Would you believe your sister's on about cooking a fancy roast chicken for her and Ryan's dinner? I asked her, "What's wrong with an ordinary roast chook?" But that's Imogen for you. She always takes it one step further, and the last I heard as she walked out the door was she planned to stick a garlic-studded hot lemon up the poor chicken's backside. I'm telling you that can't be good now, can it?'

'It's down to that Jamie Oliver wan. He's a lot to answer for,' Kitty's voice echoed in the background.

'I asked Grace to go and look outside to see if an SOS smoke signal is coming from the O'Malleys' house, because I'm waiting to be summoned. You know yourself your sister thinks she should audition for *MasterChef* if she manages to boil an egg. So c'mon then, what's the doctor said?' Nora Kelly finally got off Imogen's lack of prowess in the kitchen and on to the pertinent matter.

'Not much. Shane was whisked off to the emergency department as soon as we arrived, and I haven't seen him or heard anything since. I'm hanging about in the waiting area.'

'Ah, well now, the good doctor will give him a thorough check, I expect,' Nora said. 'It's a shame our Shannon can't be there with you. She'd have given you a VIP pass to the emergency department.'

Ava doubted her sister's role as a public health nurse held much sway here in the ED.

'What's the tea like?' Kitty asked the million-dollar question.

'I don't know, Nan. I haven't tried it. Dad?'

'I'm here, Ava.'

He sounded like his mouth was full, and for a moment, Ava almost forgot where she was, hearing her mam admonishing him for taking advantage of the situation by sneaking a second sliver of apple cake.

She waited for her mam to finish, then asked him, 'Did Shannon get off all right?'

'She did. And I suppose you'll need picking up from the hospital at some point, too. I don't know, Ava. When I think of the years slashed from my life teaching you girls to drive just so I could hang up my chauffeur's cap once and for all, yet here I am still running after you all.' There was a bantering to his tone, and Ava knew he wouldn't hesitate to pick her up if she asked him to.

'Probably, Dad, but I'm only leaving once I've seen Shane settled on a ward for myself.'

'Fair play to you, girl.'

'I'm making your favourite corned beef and cabbage for dinner,' Nora's voice boomed, alarmingly loud.

'Mam, put the phone back down on the table. You nearly deafened me then.'

'Sorry, but your nan was after trying to take it off me.'

'Only to tell her that there's apple cake for afters.' Kitty got in on the act once more.

'There won't be if your son doesn't stop helping himself. He thinks I can't see him shaving little pieces of cake off the side like so.'

'I've no idea what you're talking about.'

'You look like a squirrel hoarding its nuts in its cheeks, Liam.'

'Give me the phone,' Grace demanded. A second later, she'd taken it off speakerphone as she said, 'They're mad, the lot of them. How are you holding up, Aves? I know you hate hospitals.'

'I'm grand.' Ava did her best to keep defensiveness from creeping in, especially after how short she'd been with her sister that morning. 'Or I will be when I've seen Shane.'

The lift doors down the corridor leading off from near where she was leaning against the vending machine pinged open just then, and an orderly carrying a bucket and mop stepped out.

'I could come to the hospital and sit with you? You might be there awhile. It can take forever to get through the emergency department.'

Ava was quick with her comeback, not wanting Grace to hold her hand. 'Ah no, you don't want to hang about here picking up germs unless you have to. But thanks for the offer.' She stood to attention, seeing a familiar figure walk through the main doors. 'Grace, I've got to go.'

She disconnected the call and chewed her bottom lip, watching as Rory, a craggier version of his sons, approached the information desk. He'd obviously been home and showered, because his hair was still wet, and instead of wet-weather gear and wellies, he was wearing a green cable-knit jumper and jeans.

She should have called over but stayed there, observing him as he spoke to the receptionist.

Rory Egan was a hard man to read. He wasn't one to give away much emotionally, something Shane had confided he'd struggled with when his mam died. There was no right way to grieve, though, she supposed. At least he hadn't stooped to Conor and Michael's silent, glowering treatment of her after her break-up with Shane. In all honesty, though, she'd have to admit to finding Rory Egan a little intimidating, which was why she was hesitating to alert him to her presence. What would he think if he looked over and saw her hanging about like so, though? She shuddered and croaked, 'Rory.' Then, after clearing her throat, tried a second time.

He turned away from where the receptionist was tapping busily into her computer, reacting to his name by holding a hand up.

Ava watched him say something further to the woman, who was run off her feet behind the front desk, leaving her to answer an incoming call as he strode toward her with his hands thrust in his pockets and an expectant expression on his face. The shadows under his eyes were as dark as the stubble prickling his jawline, she noticed as she told him what little she knew.

'They might be administering warm fluids to him intravenously for the hypothermia. It's called active core rewarming. He was given oxygen in the ambulance, and I think the drip the ambulance officer was after putting in was for dehydration, but I'm not sure.' Ava knew she was babbling but couldn't stop herself.

'I thought it was your Shannon who was the nurse,' Rory said when he managed to get a word in.

Ava gave a sheepish half-smile. 'Dr Google,' she said, holding her phone up. 'A nurse will come and tell us when we can go up to whatever ward he's put on.' She thought he smelled of Pears shampoo, and it reminded her of Shane.

A silence stretched between them, and Ava's gaze sought signs of a cafe as an escape. 'Er, shall I get us both a cup of tea? I know I could do with one.' Nan would be happy if she could give her a report later on the quality of the brew to be found at the Galway hospital.

'That sounds grand. White and one, please.'

Ava took a step away and then faltered. It was now or never. 'Rory, I, er, I wanted to tell you I'm sorry.'

'For what?' Thick eyebrows in need of a tidy hid what he was thinking.

'I hurt Shane.' Her fists were clenched, and her nails dug into her palms. 'I never wanted to do that.'

'I don't think that was just down to you, Ava, but what happened between you two isn't my business.' His reply was typically brusque.

Ava had managed to get this far, though. 'But I need you, Conor and Michael to understand, especially Conor and Michael, so would you tell them I'm sorry?'

Rory ran a hand through his damp hair and sighed, not meeting her eye. 'Don't think I condone those two lummoxes' behaviour toward you and your sisters, but they're grown men who don't listen to their father when he tells them they're behaving like arses.'

'They're only looking out for their brother. Sure, my sisters are the same. The thing is, I never wanted to break up with Shane, but I had itchy feet. I wanted to travel. Go and see a bit of the world, you know?'

Rory nodded his understanding even though, so far as Ava knew, he'd never gone further north than Donegal or south than Bantry. He was scratching at his chin now and still not meeting her gaze, obviously uncomfortable with his son's ex-girlfriend unburdening herself.

Ava carried blithely on. 'But Shane had no interest in leaving Emerald Bay, and it became this – this big *thing* between us. We weren't getting on well, because the more he refused to discuss the possibility of going somewhere new, the more I went on about it. Then Grace announced she wanted us to head to London, and I saw an opportunity. I could go, save some money and take off around Europe.' She gave a half laugh. 'And that worked out well – not. Jaysus, who knew it was so expensive to live in London? But at the time, I decided to get the travel bug out of my system and then come back and pick up where I left off with Shane. Have my cake and eat it.' Her lips curled ruefully, and she shrugged. 'Lots of people have to make long-distance relationships work. I thought we could, too.'

'Fair play.' Rory was gazing longingly at the sign for the Stem cafe.

'But we only fought more, and in the end, I said we should call it quits, and Shane made it clear there was no going back. I'm hoping I can change his mind, and if he does give us a second chance, I promise you I'll never do anything to hurt him again.'

'Christ on a bike, girl, is that all you wanted to say, because you took the long way around with that. And don't make promises you can't keep, because life has a habit of throwing you curveballs.'

'Sorry.' Ava was relieved to have got it all off her chest despite her long-winded explanation.

'Listen to me now, Ava. Shane's stubborn. All the Egan males are tarred with the same brush, or so Mona used to say.' His smile at the mention of his late wife's name was sad. 'We're too stubborn for our own good. He should have met you half-way, because he's not been the same lad since you and he parted ways.'

Ava thought this was likely the most she'd ever heard Rory say in one sitting, and he wasn't finished yet.

'Now, for the love of God, would you go and get those cuppas before I die of thirst.'

A small giggle escaped her lips, and she saw the faint indent of dimples she'd never noticed appear on Shane's father's cheek. His youngest son's were deeper but in the exact same spot.

'I will. White and one,' she repeated, walking away lighter of step.

19

Ava and Rory followed a family toting a helium Get Well Soon balloon and gift basket into the lift. The two small children clasping the hands of their parents didn't make a peep, probably having been told to be on their best behaviour, Ava guessed as the door juddered shut.

Shane was on the hospital's third floor in the high dependency unit, where he would spend the night. The wait before the doctor had sought Ava and Rory out to pass on the news that Shane was doing better than he should be given the circumstances had seen lunchtime come and go. Not that either of them could eat a bite. Then they'd sat together clock watching, and finally, as the afternoon edged toward early evening, word had filtered down. He'd been moved to HDU and they could go and see him. Ava had been glad of Rory's company to pass the time, and she suspected he felt the same. In the interim, Grace had called her twice, but she'd let her go through to voicemail.

The children's mother's perfume was cloying, and Ava held her breath as the lift travelled upward. Her lips felt dry, and she wished she'd brought lipstick with her but then told herself that even if Shane was awake, he wouldn't care whether she had dry or glossy pink lips.

It was a relief to leave the claustrophobic box, and it dawned on her she was growing immune to the disinfectant and unidentifiable food smells as she and Rory made their way over to the duty nurse.

'Hello there, we're here to see Shane Egan. He's not long been brought up.'

Ava checked out her name badge. Gemma. She hoped Nurse Gemma was good at her job, because she didn't look much older than herself. Her blonde hair was pulled back from her face in the sort of ponytail that would give a girl a headache, but her smile as she glanced up from the notes she was scribbling down was warm and invoked trust.

'Our very own Christmas miracle. Although you'll not be getting much out of him until tomorrow. He was sleeping when I last checked. It's the best thing for him.'

'We won't wake him, I promise. We'd just like to see him. I'm his, er...' What was she? She didn't want to be turned away, so she gestured to Rory instead. 'This is his father.'

Rory acknowledged Nurse Gemma in his usual gruff fashion, and with an understanding smile, she directed them to the unit Shane was in, telling them they'd find him in the second bed on the left.

Ava hung back in the entrance to the sterile, fluorescently lit space with its rows of beds on either side partitioned by blue curtains. Someone down the far end was snoring, and between rumbles, there was a steady click and whir of equipment.

'Would you like to go in alone, Rory?' she asked. This was a generous gesture on her part, given every possible body part was tensed in the hope she wouldn't have to wait long to see Shane for herself.

'No, sure, we'll go in together,' Rory replied, stepping onto the ward and taking the few short steps to the curtained-off cubicle where the nurse had said he'd find his son.

Ava relaxed her clenched muscles and hurried behind him, catching a glimpse of an older man connected to various tubes. His mouth was wide open as he slept in the bed closest to the doorway. Her bottom lip hurt as she nipped hard at it, stepping around the curtain to where Shane lay, eyes closed, an oxygen mask covering his mouth and nose. A white sheet and blue blanket had been folded at chest height, and his arms rested over the covers. On the back of his right hand, an IV catheter was taped in place, and clear tubing snaked from it to the bag of fluid dangling from the stand. A clip was attached to his finger, which was connected to the hospital monitor.

Seeing him hooked up to medical equipment, with a blipping machine keeping track of his vitals, was frightening, but his colour had improved. Or at least it appeared so. It was difficult to tell with the oxygen mask covering so much of his face. She mentioned this to Rory, being careful to keep her voice low, and he nodded. Ava wasn't sure if he was humouring her, though.

He gestured for her to take the only chair, positioned on the left-hand side of the bed, and she did so. She was grateful to sit down, because standing at the side of Shane's bed, staring down at him while he slept, didn't feel right. The temptation to take hold of the hand that wasn't punctured with needles and clips was strong, but that would be presumptuous. He'd been delirious when he'd been brought ashore earlier and was now asleep. She couldn't be sure he would even want her by his bedside once he was awake and aware of his surroundings. So, instead, she clasped her hands tightly, not sure what to do and self-conscious because of Rory's presence at the foot of the bed.

'It's good to see you, son,' Rory said, surveying his son for a minute or two, seeming to watch his chest's gentle rise and fall. Then, keeping his voice hushed, he said to Ava, 'I'm going to go and ring his brothers, let them know I've seen him and that he's doing well. I'll make tracks home after that. You'll need a lift back to Emerald Bay, too.'

Ava wrenched her eyes from Shane and sought out Rory. The frown between his eyebrows had softened now he'd seen his son again. It made sense to catch a ride with him rather than her dad coming to Galway only to turn around and head home again. But she was reluctant to leave Shane's side.

Rory read her indecision correctly. 'There's no point you being here tonight, Ava. You heard the nurse – sleep is the best thing for him. You can return when he's rested in the morning and up to a conversation.'

He was talking sense.

'You're right, and a ride home would be grand, thanks.'

'I'll meet you outside then,' Rory replied, digging his phone out, and with a last look at his son, he left Ava alone with Shane.

Ava studied Shane's face beneath the mask; her relief at being here with him now was all-consuming.

'Thank you for bringing him home,' she whispered into the antiseptic space around her. Then, unable to help herself, she unclasped her hands and pressed her fingers to her lips before lightly resting them on Shane's hand. 'I love you,' she whispered, hoping he could hear her in his dream.

Her phone ringing made her jump, and she cursed herself for not having thought to switch it off, fumbling to fetch it in her haste to turn it off. Annoyance flickered when she saw Grace's name lighting the screen again. She'd speak to her when she got back to the pub.

Shane didn't stir, and she half expected Nurse Gemma to stomp in and tell her off. At least the trumpeting snores from further down the beds had stopped due to the intrusive sound. That was something.

Her eyes flitted past the curtain in the direction of the entrance to the unit, not quite able to see it, and noticed the man in the bed opposite Shane was stirring. It wasn't visiting hours, and she wasn't being fair disturbing the other patients or keeping Rory waiting, not given all he'd been through and how long his day had been. So she stood up and gazed down at Shane. 'I'll be back tomorrow. Sleep tight.'

Ava crept from the unit and back toward the nurses' station. Gemma was still scribbling away behind her desk while Rory sat on one of three seats along the wall. A colourful print hung on the bland space behind him, and the other two seats beside him were empty. Seeing her, he stood and cricked his neck from side to side.

'Thank you,' Ava said to Gemma, hesitating because she wanted to add, 'You will take care of him, won't you?' but managed to refrain.

'He's in good hands,' Gemma replied, making Ava suspect she'd spoken her thoughts out loud after all. She gave her that smile again, and Ava relaxed a little.

'Ready?' Rory asked, draping an arm around her shoulder and giving it a quick and uncharacteristic squeeze before striding toward the lift.

Ava caught a peek of the flush that had crept up his neck and, knowing it hadn't come naturally, was warmed by his gesture of support as she joined him to wait for the doors to ping open.

As they walked toward the hospital's main entrance, Ava saw new faces had replaced those that had filled the waiting area's seats earlier. Night had fallen, too. Someone was walking toward them, and it took her shattered brain a second to register who it was.

Grace.

Their mam's catchphrase where her twin daughters were concerned ran through Ava's head for whatever reason. *There's no show without Punch.* She knew it stemmed from the old British Punch and Judy puppet shows and was usually voiced with exasperation about Grace popping up wherever Ava was or vice versa. Especially if one twin was in trouble for something or other.

Right then, though, she wished Grace would get back in her car, drive to the airport and fly back to London, because this show didn't need Punch.

20

'Hello there, Mr Egan. It's grand news about Shane.' Grace beamed her greeting, and a man in a leather jacket exiting the building turned to take a second glance at the redhead decked out in her emerald-green coat.

'It is, Grace, thanks,' Rory replied. 'I take it you've come to pick up Ava?'

Grace jingled the keys she was holding. 'I have.'

'I was going to get a ride with Rory, Grace.' Ava knew she sounded petulant but didn't care. 'Why didn't you ring before you left? I could have saved you the trip.' Ava recalled the calls she'd let go through to voicemail.

'I did. I tried more than once, but you didn't pick up.' Grace's tone wasn't accusatory; she was stating a fact. 'I thought I'd offer to come and get you to save Dad having to go out again after his round trip to Shannon.'

'I'll walk you over to where you parked,' Rory offered.

'Sure, there's no need, Mr Egan. There are two of us. We'll be fine,' Grace replied.

Rory was having none of it, though, making noises about not being answerable to Liam Kelly if anything were to happen to his girls. And so, bracing for the onslaught of frigid air, they passed through the exit and walked toward the parking area.

'Do you think you, Michael and Conor will be up to swinging by the Shamrock tonight?' Grace asked. 'There's been a celebration hooley underway in the pub all afternoon.' Plumes of white puffed from her mouth as though she were smoking.

'I suppose we will. We need to show our appreciation, like, for all the help we've had. We've enough food to feed us for a year piled up in the kitchen. I don't know what to do with it all,' Rory said as they were illuminated by an SUV's lights as it searched for the exit.

'I could swing by tomorrow and sort out what needs to be eaten and what can go in the freezer if you like?' Ava offered eagerly. She was keen to ingratiate herself into Conor's and Michael's good books. She could well recall their lack of proficiency in the kitchen. As for Rory, he was a basic cook but no housekeeper.

'I'd appreciate that right enough, Ava.' He nodded to them both as they reached the nondescript hire car. 'Drive safely now.'

'Will do. Same to you,' Grace said, unlocking the vehicle.

'Thanks, Rory. Hopefully, we'll catch you at the pub,' Ava called as he headed off, wishing she was going with him. She'd enjoyed getting to know him a little better. He'd always held himself aloof from her when she'd been with Shane, but there'd been a shift between them today. It gave her hope that things might work out with Shane, too.

'Ava, hurry up. You'll freeze standing out there like so,' Grace shouted out from behind the wheel before slamming the driver's door closed.

Ava climbed in alongside her sister, patting about for the seat belt. They sat silently while Grace flicked the car lights on, gunned the engine and reversed out of the space, obviously keen to get on the road. 'I've never heard Rory speak so much,' she said lightly a second later as she navigated out of the parking area.

'It's weird,' Ava confided, 'but I feel as though I got to know him more this afternoon than I did in all the years Shane and I were together.' She shrugged. 'I think coming close to losing someone changes a person. I mean, it has to, right?'

'I suppose it does.'

Ava rested her head back on the seat, yawning.

'It's been a big day, huh?' Grace indicated onto the road then joined the flow of traffic.

'Huge.' Ava remembered her sister had had an early start. 'You must be done in, too.'

Grace flapped her comment away. 'Nan sent me up for a nap this afternoon when she got sick of seeing my tonsils each time I yawned. So I'm grand now.'

Ava yawned again, thinking it was just as well Nan wasn't here with them now. Her eyelids fluttered shut, but her mind buzzed, and she knew she wouldn't drift off.

'And he's doing well? Shane, I mean, obviously,' Grace continued, ignoring her sister's closed eyes.

Ava picked up on the genuine concern behind the question, determined to put aside her irritation with her sister for muscling in. She was being irrational, because Grace only wanted to help. If anything, she should feel grateful for her presence. On the way to the hospital, Mam's home truths had hit their mark. She was angry with herself, and it was easier to put that anger onto Grace than to face it herself. 'Yeah, he is.'

'How long will he be in hospital?'

'I'm not sure. The nurses will monitor him in the high dependency unit for tonight. We were allowed to see him, but he was sleeping, and we didn't want to wake him. The doctor said how important rest would be to his recovery.'

She thought about how seeing him hooked up to the various drips and needing an oxygen mask had made her feel. 'It was scary, Grace. He was attached to all this stuff.' Her eyes were still closed, but she felt her sister's concerned glance alight on her.

'It would have been. But Shane will be OK, and that's what you need to focus on, because it's brilliant, Aves.' There was no guile in her tone as she reached over and patted her sister's thigh.

Ava opened her eyes and flashed a grin at her in the darkened interior. 'You're right, and it is brilliant. I think maybe it was a Christmas miracle he was found.'

'Ah, no. Not you and all? That word's been bandied about at the Shamrock all afternoon. I overheard Isla Mullins pushing the idea that Shane's island, as she's calling it, be declared a pilgrimage site. You know, like Croagh Patrick in Mayo?'

'You're not joking, are you?' Ava side-eyed her sister.

'No. And don't sound surprised. It's Emerald Bay we're talking about. Isla's gadding about the pub in a sweatshirt with 'God Bless Me, I'm Irish' emblazoned on it, and she's after having a Nessie Doyle bowl cut special done.'

A giggle escaped from Ava at the image Grace had conjured, and Grace grinned, pleased at having made her laugh.

'I think Isla's seeing euro signs at the thought of the tourism the village having its very own miracle site could bring, and I overheard her asking Father Seamus if he could have a word with the powers that be over there at the Vatican and get the process fast-tracked. The good Father was more interested in celebrating the "miracle"' – she made an air quote with her left hand, keeping the other on the steering wheel – 'with a few tots of Mam and Dad's free whiskey!'

Ava laughed properly this time, and it felt good. She knew it would make Shane laugh when he caught wind of it, and she hoped she would be the one to tell him, because she wanted to see his smile more than anything.

'What do you think of Imo and Ryan's news?'

'About wanting to build?'

'Uh-huh. Watch this space. We'll be bridesmaids before we know it.'

Ava groaned. 'It's exciting for them – the build, I mean – but can you imagine Imo as a bride? She'll be a nightmare.'

'A right bridezilla,' Grace agreed. 'Although she does seem different since she's moved back to Emerald Bay. More mellow. I think Ryan's good for her.'

'Mm, I think so, too.' Ava leaned forward and began to fiddle with the illuminated screen, searching for a radio station; she settled on one playing Lewis Capaldi.

Grace began drumming her fingers on the steering wheel, only it wasn't to the beat of the music, and Ava noticed the muscle in her cheek twitch. She knew that look and wondered what was coming.

'So, when we get back to the pub, I thought I could check out flights back to London now you know Shane's going to be fine. We could head back the day after tomorrow. How does that sound?' Grace didn't give her time to reply. 'It would give you a chance to go back to the hospital and see Shane before we go and, if you were serious about your offer, go round and sort the Egans' kitchen out. Rather you than me.' She shuddered for good measure.

Ava's insides twisted and tightened like a corkscrew while the muscle in her sister's cheek continued to twitch. A sure-fire indicator that, for all her nonchalance, Grace was unsure of Ava's response, because she knew her twin too well for her not to have picked up that things would be changing.

'Grace, I'm not coming back to London,' Ava blurted. 'Well, not permanently at any rate. I'll have to come back over and pack up my gear at some point in the next few weeks obviously,' she babbled, determined to get it all out. 'And don't be worrying about the rent. I'll pay my share until you can let my room.

Wasn't your friend, Sophie, talking about moving flats not so long ago? She might be interested.'

There, she'd laid it all out for Grace to digest, she thought, moistening her lips. She'd expected to feel better once it was off her chest, but anxiety about how her sister would take this news was making her skin prickle.

'But I don't get it?' Grace's eyes never strayed from the road ahead. They'd left Galway behind now for the quieter stretch of coast that would eventually wind them down into Emerald Bay.

'What's there to get?' Ava asked, a little bewildered, because it was self-explanatory. Nevertheless, she spelled it out. 'I've decided London's not for me.'

'But where's this all coming from? It's out of the blue, Ava. Is it to do with Shane?'

'Yes.' Ava raised her shoulders and let them fall. 'No.' She needed to make more sense. 'Things haven't worked out the way I planned in the UK, and Shane's accident has brought it to a head.'

'But we've had great craic. You know we have. I don't understand what you mean by things not working out?' Grace pinned her with her gaze.

Ava tensed. 'Keep your eyes on the road.' The last thing they needed was to have a car accident.

'Well, you pick your moments, Ava.'

'I didn't start the conversation. You did. And all I know is since we moved to London, I've been partying way too hard, trying to shake off Shane, but it hasn't worked. My feelings haven't changed, and I feel stuck there. The whole point of us going was to save, use the city as a base and explore a little of Europe between working, but I've less in the bank now than when we moved over, and the furthest we've been is Glastonbury.'

'OK, that's an easy fix. Let's rein it in a bit, then. I hear what you're saying, and it wouldn't kill us to stay home a little more.

We could pick a destination, like, I don't know, Budapest, that sounds cool, and save for one of those city breaks?'

Grace still wasn't getting it, Ava thought, slumping back into her seat frustrated. She didn't want to go to Budapest with her. She wanted to go with Shane. 'It's not that simple, Grace.'

'Yes it is.' Grace slapped the steering wheel.

'I want to see if Shane will give things another go.'

'What?'

'You heard me.'

'Don't be stupid, Ava. There's no going back. That's what you told me he said.'

'We all say stuff in the heat of the moment.'

'Like you are now. You're overwrought, which is under-standable, but you're not thinking clearly, because if you were, you'd see the reasons you broke up in the first place are still there. They won't have gone away because you left Emerald Bay for a while. Shane sees his future here, and you don't. See. It is that simple.'

Ava detected the impatience in Grace's tone, and her own voice raised a notch. 'For your information, I'm thinking clearly for the first time in months. I don't want to be in London, and I want to be with Shane.'

'I get it. You don't need to shout. But at what cost, Aves? You give up your dreams, move into the Egans' smelly, fishy house and wait on them hand and foot?' Grace snorted her derision.

'That's not going to happen, and I hate how you're always being smart about him and his family.'

'That's exactly what will happen, Ava, and you've changed your tune. It wasn't long ago you'd laugh when I said he and his brothers were fishy-arsed eejits.'

'Because it was easier to laugh than cry, and it's my life, Grace.'

Grace's breath huffed in and out, fogging a patch on the

windscreen as she calmed herself down. When she spoke up next, she'd changed tact, and her words were softer. 'OK, Ava. I've listened to what you've said.'

Ava wasn't ready to back down yet, though her heart was racing too much for that. 'Have you?'

'Yes, I have. I shouldn't have rushed things by talking about flights back to London. You don't have to make any big decisions tonight. Take a week or two to think about it. It will allow you to see how Shane feels about you before you make any drastic calls.'

There was sense in what Grace was saying, but a note of condescension riled Ava further. She was fed up with being pigeonholed as the younger, weaker sister. 'No, you're not hearing me, Grace. You never do. I don't want to stay in London anymore. Whatever happens or doesn't happen with Shane, I'm coming home to figure out what I want to do next. And would you slow down?'

Grace eased off the accelerator, her grip on the steering wheel cramp-inducing. 'But what about me? Where do I fit into all of this?'

'You love London. So stay.'

'Ava, we've never been apart for longer than a couple of weeks.'

'Oh, for Chrissakes! We're not kids anymore, Grace. We need to find our own way.'

'So you're choosing Shane over your twin, is that it?'

'Grace, can you hear yourself? You sound like a two-year-old. I wasn't aware it was a competition.'

'It's not; it's just...' Grace's voice trailed off.

'I should never have left him in the first place.' Ava forgot all about her mam's chat with her. 'You pushed me into breaking up with him and moving to London because it was what you wanted. It wasn't what I wanted, and it was a mistake. A great big fecking mistake.'

'That's not fair. You were feeling trapped in Emerald Bay. You wanted to go and have an adventure.'

Ava ignored that. 'You never liked me and Shane being together, did you?'

'Really? You're going to go there?'

'Why did you tell Shannon, Hannah and Imo that he was controlling? You know that's not true.' Ava had twisted in her seat, her eyes flashing as the blood began to rush into her ears. 'It was to get them onside, wasn't it? So they'd back you and convince me that London was a great idea because you were too scared to go alone.'

'No. I said it because if Shane loved you, he'd compromise. He won't, though, will he? He wants you under the thumb in Emerald Bay. I didn't want you withering away as a glorified skivvy to four eejit fisherman.'

'Oh, feck off, Grace. It's my life, not yours, and you had no right to interfere.' Ava turned to stare at the blackness, signalling she was done. Her breathing was still fast, but she didn't trust herself to say another word.

'You're a fool, Ava Kelly. When you wake up years from now and you've done nothing, been nowhere, I hope you remember what you just said to me.' Grace's shoulders slumped, and she stabbed at the radio as an annoyingly peppy song came on, turning it off.

The sisters drove the rest of the way to Emerald Bay in stony silence.

21

Ava was out of the car before Grace could pull the handbrake up.

She didn't bother to thank her sister for making the journey to Galway to collect her. She hadn't asked her to, she reasoned, closing the hire car's door with more force than necessary. Her feet crunched over the gravel as she strode past the other vehicles and into the beer garden, where the sensor light suddenly spotlighted her. She never saw the glowing tip of the cigarette or Lorcan McGrath, Emerald Bay's infamous farmer bachelor, until he stepped out of the shadows near the back entrance to the Shamrock.

'Hello there. How's life in the Big Smoke across the water?' Lorcan treated her to a smile that wouldn't find its way onto any toothpaste commercials in a hurry. His tweed cap was firmly in place, and his rolled cigarette gave off an acrid smell as the smoke spiralled past his weathered face.

Ava managed a tight smile in return, but she really couldn't be doing with this. Had he lost another tooth since St Paddy's Day? she wondered, aware he hadn't addressed her by name because he never knew which twin was which. 'I'm thinking of moving back to the bay as it happens, Lorcan.' She rubbed her hands together. 'It's freezing out here. I'm heading inside.'

'I'd like to know the stats in London,' Lorcan carried on, as if she wasn't standing there shivering.

Ava couldn't very well ignore him, and even though she knew Grace would be hanging back in the car park, waiting for her to head in, she asked, 'What stats?'

'The male-to-female-ratio stats. I've heard there are too many single women in Manhattan and not enough men to go around, so I've been contemplating taking a trip to the Big Apple. But, I thought to myself, if there's a shortage of men in London now, a trip across the water would be more cost-effective than flying all the way to America.' He adjusted the holey sweater he wore over his corduroy trousers. 'I have a lot to offer the right woman.'

Bad teeth, bad breath and body odour, for starters, Ava thought impatiently, rubbing her hands together. 'I'm sorry, Lorcan. I can't help you there. I haven't a clue about the male or unattached-female stats in London, but you could always ask Grace. She'll be on her way in any minute now.' Ava was in no mood to be kind. She excused herself and stepped inside the pub. Let Grace deal with lovelorn Lorcan.

The Shamrock Inn was heaving, filled with a decidedly festive air that had banished the sombre mood of the previous night. Shouts of laughter, clinking glasses and a general hubbub of chatter greeted her. In her absence, the bar had been draped with a holly garland bedecked with tiny red bells, and an expansive Christmas tree stood proudly in the usual spot by the window, decked out in festive trinkets. The star perched precariously atop it scraped the ceiling, and Ava was glad she'd missed the shenanigans trying to get that monster fir through the pub door. From where Ava stood, the tree sparkled with tinsel and shiny baubles, but she knew if she went over for a closer inspection, she'd find sentimental childhood ornaments and a selection of the origami decorations Kitty Kelly had had a hand in making last year dangling from its pine-scented branches. The fairy lights twinkling added the finishing touch.

A second sweep of the pub revealed no sign of Jody, and Ava guessed Conor or Michael must have collected her. Her back was slapped several times as the villagers she'd known all her life proclaimed Shane's safe return 'grand news'. She was nodding so hard that her neck hurt, and the smile plastered to her face made the corners of her mouth ache.

Ava managed to dodge her mam's awful cousin, Tom Nolan, as he readied himself to join in with the back whacking. She'd not have his hand anywhere near her, thanks very much – not given his fingers' up close and personal relationship with his nostrils.

Standing on tiptoes, Ava saw her parents doing a trade behind the bar, her dad having donned the over-the-top Elton John-style Christmas glasses he liked to dig out when he was feeling festive. She caught sight of Hannah clearing glasses from a table. There was no sign of Nan, but given the time, she'd likely be watching one of her television programmes.

She formed a hasty plan to skulk past her mam and dad, sneak out the back, through the kitchen and upstairs, avoiding any chance of the disharmony between herself and Grace being picked up on and explanations as to what had caused it being demanded. She'd sleep in Shannon and Imo's room tonight to avoid her twin. They both needed some space.

There was no such thing as making a quick escape at the Shamrock, though, and Hannah was already waving over. Ava held her hand up in return but moved in the opposite direction, darting around merry-making punters, thinking she might make it through to the sanctity of the kitchen undetected after all. Until her da's voice boomed out, calling her over to the bar.

Ava froze, a deer caught in the headlights, knowing she'd been spotted and that there was nothing else for it. So she sidled up to stand alongside Ollie Quigley. The fiddle player was waiting for Liam to finish pouring his pint, and she acknowledged him with a smile and a 'Yes, it is grand news.' Then, drumming her fingers on the wooden bar top, she said, 'Hi, Dad. Love the glasses.'

'Hello, yourself. Yours isn't the first compliment I'm after receiving, I have to say.' He pushed them back up his nose. 'Shane's doing well, I hear?'

'He is.' She gave him and Ollie, who was listening in, the low-down. 'The Egans will probably call in tonight. They want to show their gratitude for how everyone's rallied around them.'

'Sure, 'tis what folk do,' Liam grunted.

Ollie nodded his agreement.

Liam handed Ollie his pint, and he raised it at both Ava and Liam before moseying off. Liam strode to the till, and Ava watched her mam attempting to part Colm the Octopus from his cash. No easy task. He was another of her mam's charming Nolan cousins, but she'd pay for his pint if it meant hurrying things along, because the sooner she spoke to her mam, the sooner she could get out of here.

She felt something brush her left shoulder just then and stifled a shriek as she turned to see who or what it was. Two beady glass eyes were staring back at her. It took her a split second to register that the eyes belonged to Mrs Rae, Father Seamus's housekeeper. Or rather, the fox fur currently draped about her shoulders. Ava hated the thing, expecting it to suddenly spring into life and nip whoever was nearest with its sharp little teeth, but Mrs Rae thought it made her look like part of the landed gentry.

'How're you, Mrs Rae?' Ava enquired politely, once over her fright.

'Very well. It's Ava, isn't it? Grace is wearing her hair shorter these days.'

'That's right – very observant of you.'

'I don't miss much.'

I bet you don't, Ava thought, feeling Eileen Carroll's eyes boring into her. She was another one who didn't miss much. If that woman ever decided to sell her wool shop, a second career as a gossip columnist would be right up her alley. She ignored Eileen and concentrated on what Mrs Rae was saying.

'What good news we're after having about your young man being found safe and well. Although I thought you'd gone to London to live the footloose and fancy-free life?'

'I had, and he's not my young man.' *Not yet anyway*, she thought. 'And it's complicated, Mrs Rae. To be honest with you, I didn't find life very footloose or fancy-free in London.' Ava was saying more than she wanted to.

Mrs Rae shook her head, and a few wisps escaped the bun she always wore her hair in. 'I always say the grass is never greener. You know, Ava, in my day, things were simple. You were with a fella, or you weren't. On or off. Black and white.'

'I get the picture, Mrs Rae.'

'You young wans always seem to be in a terrible muddle as to where you're at. I blame the internet. You've too much choice is the problem as I see it.'

Ava wasn't sure what to reply, so she changed the subject, saying the first thing that came to mind. 'A few sherries tonight, is it?'

'I'm after having one celebratory tipple to toast the good news,' was the prim reply.

One my arse, Ava thought, being careful to keep a neutral expression on her face. It was a case of like priest, like housekeeper, because Mrs Rae's cheeks were exceptionally rosy, and there was an empty sherry glass in front of her waiting to be refilled, which suggested it was far from her first tot she was about to order.

Nora closed the till and stepped around Liam. 'How was

Shane?' she directed at Ava. 'I'll be with you in two ticks, Mrs Rae.'

Ava filled her in and, noticing her mam look past her, turned around and tracked her line of sight to see Grace conversing with Hannah. Great. Grace was probably telling her sister they needed to stage one of those interventions on her, like when a person needed to be sent to rehab. Her ears twitched as she swung back to her mam, who'd moved on to corned beef and cabbage.

'The plate's in the oven, but you might need to warm it in the microwave for a minute.'

'Thanks, Mam. I'm sure it will be delicious.' The last thing Ava felt like doing was eating, but she knew her mam had cooked her favourite especially, so she made a show of all but licking her lips in anticipation.

Nora's chest expanded, then, hearing Mrs Rae clearing her throat, she reached out to fetch the sherry bottle.

Ava thought she was probably frightened the little woman would set her fangy little fox on her if she didn't jump to as she inched away from its snappy jaw.

'Oh, and Shannon's arrived safe and sound in Boston,' Nora said, unscrewing the bottle and sloshing sherry into Mrs Rae's glass.

'That's good, Mam. She'll look after James, Maeve and the family. It's where she should be.'

'A little more now, Nora. 'Tis a celebration after all,' Mrs Rae urged.

Nora's lips pursed, but she did as she was told, glugging more amber liquid into the glass.

'I'm starving – thanks a million, Mam,' Ava fibbed, keen to disappear. 'I'll go on through now.'

She didn't hang about, calling out a 'Catch you later' to her dad. But she'd only taken half a dozen steps toward the adjoining door when someone caught her arm, tugging her back.

What now? Ava thought spinning around and finding herself face to face with a village idiot from days of old.

But no. It was, in fact, Isla Mullins. Ava tried not to stare at the Irish souvenir shop owner's new haircut, which, as Grace had warned, was a Nessie Doyle pudding bowl special. Instead, she focused on her sweatshirt logo. It was nearly as bad.

'Isla,' she greeted her, waiting for her arm to be released, but Isla had a firm hold of her coat sleeve and meant business.

'A little birdy's after telling me you've been to the hospital to see Emerald Bay's very own Christmas miracle man, young Ava.'

'If you mean Shane' – she knew full well she meant Shane – 'then yes, I've been to see him.'

'And how was he?' Isla scrutinised her intently.

'Asleep as it happens. But doing exceptionally well.' As soon as 'exceptionally' slipped out, Ava regretted her choice of wording and wished she could take it back. Isla didn't need any further encouragement on the miracle front.

Isla's expression was smug. 'Exceptionally, you say?'

'What I should have said was "well" – he's doing well, Isla.'

'It's nothing short of a miracle Shane Egan being found alive like so, Ava. Have you heard about my plans to push for the island he was rescued from to be made a holy site?'

'I did hear mention.'

'I'm telling you, the world will want to hear about this. I've been looking over my shoulder all afternoon, expecting the place to be stormed by your international news people any minute in search of a good story for their networks.'

'Oh, there's plenty to keep the international news people busy as it is, Isla.'

'But it's all doom and gloom. You know yourself if you tune into the six o'clock news on the television that it's all long faces and people dropping dead like flies, that sort of thing. No, what the world needs to hear is an uplifting story of miracles and survival against the odds. Especially with Christmas on its way. And if it brings a bit of foot traffic Emerald Bay's way, then all the better.'

'You've obviously thought about this, Isla.' The woman didn't miss a beat when drumming up business for Emerald Bay's retailers. Mind, if a second miracle occurred, and where Shane had sheltered was made a holy site, then the sight of Isla Mullins with her medieval monk haircut would scare the hardiest of pilgrims off.

'I have, and that's why I caught hold of you. Have you any insider information about what happened on that rock where Shane was found? It's for the miracle cause, like.'

'Well...'

Isla leaned closer, keen for the inside scoop, but speaking of scoops, Ava saw Evan Kennedy over her shoulder. He was sitting with Jeremy Jones, the reporter. What was he still sniffing about for? Evan was undoubtedly informing him he was distantly related to the American Kennedys. Evan was fond of namedropping, especially where the tourists were concerned, because when he got to the part about how he suffered the curse of the Kennedys, there was usually a free pint in it for him. She doubted Jeremy would stump up for an ale, though.

At least he wasn't talking to Isla. That was something. It would be all over the local papers about Shane being a living, breathing Christmas miracle if she caught on that he was a reporter. Shane was the sort of fella who didn't like a fuss on his birthday, let alone when he'd had a near-death experience, so she hoped the journalist would get fed up listening to Evan and go on back to where he'd come from.

'Don't be holding out on me now, Ava. It's for the good of the masses.'

'I'm not holding out. I told you Shane was asleep when I went in to see him.'

Isla's face sagged, but at least she let Ava's arm go, at which point Ava excused herself and made a run for it, escaping into the kitchen.

She closed the door and leaned against it, and thinking about Grace, she was suddenly unsure whether she wanted to be alone with her thoughts after all.

22

Kitty Kelly's voice carried from the family room as she admonished someone's silly behaviour on the television. Ava peeled off the kitchen side of the connecting door to the pub. Should she pop her head around the door and say hello to her nan? She'd want an update on how Shane was faring but didn't like being interrupted while watching her favourite soaps. No. She'd leave it for now. Still, she set her sights longingly toward the hall, because the temptation to head straight up the stairs was strong. Instead, she slipped her hand inside an oven glove and fetched the foil-covered plate from the oven. Her mam had gone to the trouble to cook her favourite dinner – the least she could do was try and eat it.

There was no point setting a place at the table or heating her dinner in the microwave as her mam had suggested. She opted to eat standing at the kitchen worktop, bracing for a struggle, but Nora Kelly always managed to make the corned beef melt in the mouth and, to her surprise, she made short work of the meal. She hadn't realised how hungry she'd been, although the food, as delicious as it was, did little to lift her mood. Her fight with Grace had quashed her good spirits about Shane. It made her resent her twin that little bit more, she realised, scrubbing the plate vigorously and leaving it to drain. At least Grace had stayed in the pub. She could have followed her to the kitchen to continue their argument, Ava thought, her tread heavy on the stairs.

There wasn't much to toss in her case as she gathered the scant things she'd brought to carry them down the hall to Shannon and Imogen's room. The curtains were still open, and after dumping her case on Imogen's bed, she pulled them to. Napoleon was a comforting sight, curled up loyally on Shannon's pillow, and he opened one eye at the intrusion but didn't stir.

'Hello, you.' Ava climbed on the bed to pet the Persian, the fuzz around the edges of her brain an indicator the day was beginning to catch up with her. She heaved a sigh. 'Napoleon, I've got to tell you, it has been the strangest day.'

As she stroked him, her fingers got trapped in a knot, and she recalled Shannon telling her he needed to be brushed daily. Her sister wouldn't have had time to see to him this morning, and with everything that had been going on, she'd probably forgotten to assign the task to whoever was willing.

Her eyes moved to the dressing table, where an antique silver hairbrush and comb set passed down to Shannon by their nan was displayed.

'No, Ava, not a good idea,' she told herself, knowing Shannon had a container in the top kitchen cupboard where Mam kept their first aid bits and bobs filled with Napoleon paraphernalia, including a self-cleaning cat hair brush. So, reluctantly, she clambered off the bed and made a quick trip back down the stairs, relieved the coast was still clear, to fetch the brush.

Her reward on her return as she set to work with the brush was Napoleon's deafening purr. He was stretched out with a complete lack of decorum, blissed out by the brushstrokes.

Although, as she gently tried to untangle the knot she'd discovered, he mewled indignantly, patting her with his paw.

'I'm sorry, Napoleon, but it's got to be done. We can't have your mammy coming home from America to find you looking like your aunty Hannah with the locs, now can we?'

There was no reply. Napoleon was a sulker, Ava decided as she continued speaking. 'Listen, how about I ask your mammy to pinch a little of Aunty Imogen's pricy salon conditioner next time she gives you a shampoo?'

There was a mewl which Ava took as a *yes, please.*

As she continued to run the brush over his coat, she opened up about what had transpired earlier. 'Grace and I had words on the way home from the hospital. We never have words. It's left me feeling sick. You know, like I've had too much cream with Nan's apple cake? That sorta way. You get it because I'm sure you've had times when you've overindulged on the biscuits.' A malodorous whiff reached Ava's nostrils, leaving her wondering if tonight was one of those nights. 'You're very smelly, so you are.'

Another put-out meow sounded, and Ava wasn't sure whether it was because she'd set the brush down on the bedside table or because she'd told him he was smelly. She scrunched up alongside the Persian, resting her back against the wall, and scratched behind his ear to compensate for the brushing.

'I feel like I have a shot at getting Shane back, which I want more than anything, but it could mean losing my sister. I don't understand why it has to be that way, Napoleon, but it's always been a competition where they're concerned. Why can't they see I love them both in different ways? Why do I have to choose?'

Napoleon offered up no comment. Ava closed her eyes, and imprinted on the inside of her lids was the look on Shane's face the day she'd said goodbye.

2021

Ava couldn't remember when the Egans' rambling house on the outskirts of Emerald Bay village hadn't looked unloved. She might have known Shane since she was small, but she'd not known him properly or started coming round to his house until they were both teenagers. After his mam died. And then, she'd been more interested in Shane than the state of the house. But today she was looking at it with fresh eyes because she didn't know when she'd see it next.

The lawn was always mowed thanks to the brothers taking turns with the push mower, but that was as far as their green fingers went – if you could even call it that. On either side of the front path, the flower beds were home to more weeds than blooms, and ahead of her, the house appeared weary and in need of TLC, starting with the parched front door desperate for a lick of paint. The Egan home had a mournful air that sometimes made her feel sad, and now the painful thought of never trudging up this path again made her limbs heavy, as though she were wading through water.

Mam had told her that Mona, Mrs Egan, had been a house-proud woman. 'She'd turn in her grave if she saw the way Rory and the lads kept the place these days.'

Nora Kelly had pursed her lips when Ava had asked what she'd been like. Shane didn't like talking about his mam, and curiosity had got the better of her. According to Mam, not only had Mona Egan run a ship-shape home, she'd loved her garden too, and her roses had taken home first prize in their category of the Kilticaneel horticultural show each year.

Ava didn't know much about gardens, even less about roses, but she knew they must be hardy, because every spring, the two bushes on either side of the entrance put on a gorgeous display lasting long into the summer months. Ava knew their beauty had a flipside, because she'd snagged her new sweater on a thorn thanks to the gnarly, long-reaching branch nobody had bothered to snip, creeping over the front steps just the other week. She'd have offered to have a go at the pruning and weeding for them if Mam hadn't said not to bother, because it was a thankless task. In the months after Mona Egan had passed, the villagers had organised a working bee to spruce the front entrance of the fisherman and his family's home in honour of his late wife's memory. Rory had scarcely acknowledged their hard work, and the garden had soon reverted to its overgrown state. It was very disheartening, Mam had said, adding that the spark had gone out of Rory Egan the day he'd lost Mona.

'He was grieving, Mam,' Ava had offered up simply.

The thorny branch was still waiting to snare her, and she was careful to stay out of its reach as she dragged her feet up the steps to stand on the porch. Her breath was ragged and her hand slippery on the tarnished knocker as she rapped on the door, not wanting to have to say goodbye.

Footsteps thudded down the hall, and Conor appeared, his muscular frame blocking the entrance.

'Shane's upstairs.' Conor's brow was hooded beneath the cap he was wearing back to front and his mouth set in a hard line as he guarded the door. 'You'd have heard Aunt Vonnie's down with the flu?'

She hadn't, as it happened, having been too caught up in packing, but she nodded anyway.

'Shane's supposed to be down at the fish and chip shop now getting ready to open, but he's up there saying he feels sick and isn't able for the chipper.' He jabbed overhead. 'So I've got to go instead, because Michael's not answering his phone, and Dad's working on boat repairs. Never mind that I had to cancel a date at the last minute.'

The girl had probably had a lucky escape, Ava thought, appraising Conor's rap-artist going-out look. The three Egan brothers were fine-looking men, but Conor's insistence on channelling gangsta vibes to head out on the town – aka Kilticaneel, not LA – made her wince. He wasn't the sort who'd welcome a spot of friendly advice from his younger brother's girlfriend. She'd long since made her mind up that she'd leave that task to a far braver woman than she.

Conor glowered. 'He's worse than useless sometimes.'

That wasn't fair, but Ava didn't dare say a word, because she fancied there was a hint of 'and it's your fault' in that glower. She was relieved when he finally stepped out onto the porch, leaving the way clear for her to skitter inside, but he wasn't finished yet.

'He says he's fine with you going, Ava, but he's not. You know that, don't you?' He gave her one last glower, then, hitching the back of his jeans up, slouched down the path she'd just wandered up without looking back.

Ava did know. Her heart was aching, and she was bewildered as to how she and Shane had reached this impasse. How had it led to her getting on a plane bound for London without him in the morning? Why couldn't she be happy with her lot, with Shane, and stay put in Emerald Bay? It was a question she'd asked herself repeatedly, always coming back to the same answer, because, as Grace and her sisters said, it wasn't enough. So, with a sigh, she stepped inside the house and closed the door.

Instead of heading upstairs, Ava stood immobilised in the hallway. The carpet under her feet was worn, the wallpaper was beginning to lift in the corners and the air smelled of stale cooking fat. But still, there were traces of the love that had once thrived within this house. She could see it in the portraits lining the wall. There was Rory and Mona on their wedding day. So young and happy, excited by what their future might hold. Then came the babies in short succession. Mona must have felt as though she was permanently pregnant, Ava mused, gazing at her standing on the hospital steps holding a shawl-wrapped baby.

Shane was the image of Rory when he was younger, she thought, taking a step closer to the wall on which the memories were hung. Her favourite was the family portrait snapped against a plain white studio background. Rory and Mona were sitting cross-legged, smiling broadly. Shane was a baby in his mam's arms, while their dad had his arms around Michael and Conor, cheeky toddlers with cowlicks that refused to be smoothed down. Not for the first time, Ava wished she could have known Mrs Egan with her warm smile. She gave the photograph one last lingering look before she made her way upstairs.

The light was dim on the landing, with all the doors leading to the three bedrooms and bathroom closed. Ava halted outside the room Shane shared with Conor. Michael, as the eldest, had his own. There was no response to her tapping on the door, but she opened it anyway and found Shane with his headphones on, lying on his back, staring up at the ceiling. He was wearing the T-shirt she'd bought him for his birthday.

He took the headphones off, tossing them aside. 'Hey, you.' He pulled himself up to sit but didn't pat the spot on the bed next to him as usual.

'Hi.' Ava hovered awkwardly in the doorway.

Shane's smile was sad. 'This is weird, right?'

'Weird,' Ava echoed. 'It's not goodbye, though.'

'No.' There was sadness in his eyes as he held his arm out toward her, and Ava curled up beside him.

But they both knew it was.

23

'Why did you sleep in here? And why's Grace tight-lipped about why she's flying back to London this afternoon?'

Ava groaned, squinting against the bright light as though she was in a cell with a single bright light bulb, being interrogated.

She wasn't, of course. She was in bed in Shannon and Imogen's room, the light had a pretty white shade over it and, instead of a CIA or KGB operative standing over her, Hannah loomed, her hands resting on her hips. She was clad in fleecy, smiley-emoji pyjamas as bright as the light hurting her eyes.

'Go away.'

'I'm not going anywhere until I get answers.'

Ava closed her eyes, mulling over her options. There was no point pulling the bedcovers over her head, because she'd only get in a tug of war over them with Hannah, and if they ripped them in the process, then there'd be murder. Maybe she could tell her sister there was a climate change protest taking place in Kilticaneel that would see her off.

Ava tried her luck.

'There's no protest in this country that I'm not privy to. Nice try, Ava.'

'Well, I'm not saying anything until I've had a brew. I know my rights.'

'I thought of that.'

Ava lifted her head off the pillow to see a mug on the bedside table. There was nothing else for it. She hauled herself up, rubbing her eyes before picking it up.

Satisfied there was action, Hannah flopped down on the end of the bed, pulling her knees to her chest as she began picking the fluff off her bed socks, waiting.

The tea worked its magic, seeing off the last vestiges of sleep, and when Ava had drained the mug, Hannah stopped picking, her amber eyes expectant. 'Well?'

'Nothing's going on with me and Grace.' Ava shrugged, hoping her nose wasn't growing. 'She doesn't need to stay on now we know everything's OK with Shane. Nor do you, for that matter.'

'Bollocks, Ava.'

'Charming.'

'Well, it is, and you know it. For your information, I'm heading back to Cork after breakfast. Dylan texted to say I'm needed at headquarters.'

Ava couldn't help the smile that twitched.

'What?'

'Headquarters?' She raised an eyebrow. 'And your face always goes gooey when you say Dylan.'

Hannah was unrepentant. 'My face does not go gooey when I say Dylan.' She repeated his name to prove her point. 'Dylan, Dylan, Dylan.'

'I'm sorry to have to tell you, but you have the same look on your face saying the "D" word as Shannon gets when she's told there's to be pudding after dinner.'

Hannah pulled a face. 'I don't. And I'm on to you. Stop

trying to change the subject. Grace is downstairs looking like she forgot to put her dentures in and she's trying to chew through a piece of overdone steak. Meanwhile, you're in here. C'mon, spill.'

Ava sighed. 'I needed some space, is all. Anyway, I saw you and Grace talking last night. She would have told you we were after having words on the way home from the hospital.'

'No, she didn't, as it happens. I had to put up with her thumping her pillow and huffing all night long.'

So Grace hadn't been spouting off, then. Ava was surprised and annoyed that it meant she would be the one that came clean about what had gone on between them. 'We had words, is all, about me not going back to London. It's no big deal. We'll get over it.' Would they, though? Because it was more than a difference of opinion. Much more.

'She doesn't think you should be hanging about for Shane,' Hannah stated.

It was a familiar tune.

'Yep. Grace seems to view it as a competition between them. She always has, and I'm sick of it. But I'm not just waiting to see if Shane and I can work things out. I've had enough of London, and she refuses to accept we want different things. And I told her I'd see her right for the rent until she can get a new flatmate in, so I don't get what the big deal is,' she added flippantly, aware it was her second fib since opening her eyes. She did understand what lay beneath her sister's reaction.

So did Hannah, it would appear. 'It's not about the rent, though, is it?'

Today should be a good day. A happy day. Shane should be up to having a proper conversation with her, and who knew, they might be able to sort things out between them. But instead of feeling hopeful about what lay ahead, her head was beginning to hurt, and Ava began massaging her temples.

'Grace doesn't get we're individuals. She's used to me going along with whatever she wants to do. We're twins, but that doesn't mean we're automatically going to want the same things. We have our own lives, and I told her as much.'

Hannah had her head tilted to one side, listening, and Ava wondered if the weight of those coiled locks of hair ever gave her neck ache.

'That's true, Aves, but you two have always been in each other's pockets. Think about things from Grace's perspective, because it's bound to not be easy for her.'

'It's not easy for me either,' Ava spluttered. 'But I'm trying to do what feels right for me.'

'No, I understand that. But the difference is you're making all the calls and changing things. Grace has never liked change, and I think she's scared.'

Was she? Ava wasn't so sure. Grace had always been fearless, but even if she was scared, it didn't change anything. 'I don't know about that, Hannah, but we could use some time apart.'

'OK, I get where you're coming from, but don't let her leave on a bad note. You'll only feel awful. Go and make things up with her.'

'No.' It wasn't like her to dig her heels in, and there was something gratifying about seeing the surprise on Hannah's face. Grace had pushed her to choose, and she'd done so.

'Ava.' Hannah pulled an exasperated face. 'Cop yourself on.'

'I've nothing to apologise for.'

'I didn't say apologise as such. I said make things up.'

'It's the same thing. I meant what I said about needing some time apart while I figure things out.' Ava had had enough. She didn't want to discuss it anymore because she should be getting ready to go to the hospital. Tossing the covers aside, she shut the conversation down. 'I'm going to have a shower.'

. . .

It was a boon that Imogen had forgotten to take her body moisturiser with her, Ava thought, catching a hint of cocoa butter fragrance as she finished applying her make-up. She smelled lovely but not in an overpowering way, inappropriate for a hospital visit. There was no harm in taking a few extra minutes to make herself presentable.

Today, she thought, puckering up, was a day for glossy pink lips.

Seeing her laptop abandoned on Imogen's bed sent a guilty pang through her as she put the cap back on her lipstick tube. She had deadlines to meet. Just because she'd had an emergency that had sent her running back home didn't mean finishing the projects in her own sweet time. She'd deal with the urgent stuff later. If it meant working tonight, then so be it.

Ava gave herself a once-over in the dressing-table mirror, deciding she'd do. Coat, bag and she was good to go.

Napoleon was snoozing again on his favourite pillow. 'No letting off on that pillow,' she instructed with a final pat. 'I've got to lay my head on that later.'

The Persian didn't so much as bat an eyelid.

As she ventured down the landing, she hesitated outside her bedroom, hearing someone thudding about inside the room. Downstairs, Hannah asked Mam to pass the milk, meaning Grace was the culprit. She was probably packing, Ava guessed. She could knock, try and put things right between them as Hannah had suggested, but her hands remained by her side. She was still too angry with Grace and didn't trust herself to stay civil. So she hurried down the stairs.

The conversation at the table between Nan, Mam, Dad and Hannah ceased the moment she stepped into the kitchen, letting her know she and Grace were likely the hot topic of discussion over the breakfast bowls this morning. Hannah's sheepish expression over the rim of her mug confirmed her suspicions, and Ava mouthed, 'Thanks a million, big mouth,' at her.

'There's porridge in the pot, Ava, and I've not long made a fresh brew.' Kitty Kelly was the first to speak up, keeping her tone light.

'Ah, Nan, thanks, but I'll grab something at the hospital.'

For once, there was no argument. A relief because she had no intention of sitting at the table while the three of them all got in her ear about patching things up with her sister. They could pick on Grace when she came down instead.

'Mam, can I borrow your car, please?'

Nora glanced at her husband, then got up from the table and fetched the keys off the hook by the back door, dangling them as she said, 'You're in luck. I was supposed to be heading to Kilticaneel this morning for my beauty treatment.' She unconsciously patted her chin. 'But Sandy's new girl's after double booking, and I've been bumped over to Friday instead.'

'I don't know why you don't just use an electric razor like myself,' Liam replied, a cheeky glint in his eyes as he ran his hand along his jawline. 'Smooth as a baby's bum, that is.'

'Oh, that would be grand, wouldn't it?' Nora shot her husband a look that told him she didn't appreciate his input. 'We'd both be behind the bar this evening with the six o'clock shadow if I took your advice.'

Hannah snorted into her tea at the picture painted, earning her a glare from Nan.

Ava swiped the keys from her mam. 'Thanks.' Then she took a step toward the back door.

'Give yourself plenty of room parking, Ava. I don't want you bringing Vera home with any dents or scratches.'

'Drive to the conditions, Ava,' Liam piped up.

'I will on both counts.'

'Not so fast, young lady. Did you stick your head around your bedroom door and say goodbye to your sister?' Nora asked.

'Mam.' Ava flung a dagger in Hannah's direction, but her sister was all but whistling and staring at the ceiling. 'I don't want to get into all of that again. I've got to go, or I'll miss the morning visiting hours.'

'Leave her, Nora. They'll sort it out. They always do,' she heard her dad say as she opened the door and stepped out into a frosty morning.

Would they this time? Ava wasn't so sure.

24

It had been a while since Ava had last driven. Tossing the windscreen cover on the back seat, she slipped behind the wheel. Sitting in the driver's seat of such a modern vehicle as her mam's was strange.

'Good morning Vera,' she said, half expecting the car to greet her back. Then, checking out what was where and adjusting the mirrors added, 'You might be new, but your brake and accelerator are in the same old spot, so don't be worrying. We'll get along grand, you and I. Oh, and if you could hurry up and do your magic seat-warming trick, I'd be grateful. It's freezing this morning.'

Seconds later, hunting for the ignition, Ava decided she'd spoken too soon and, muttering bad words, contemplated patting around to see if it was hidden under the seat. Then it dawned on her. *Of course! Keyless ignition. Duh.*

Ava pressed the starter button, and her foot pressed gently on the accelerator. 'Yes!' She fist-pumped the air when the engine purred over before wresting the gear stick into reverse. 'Right, Vera. We didn't get off to the best of starts, but we'll put that behind us, shall we?'

A surreptitious glance upstairs revealed no curtain twitching, which was just as well, she thought, bunny-hopping out of the parking area. She'd never hear the end of it if any family member observed her motoring skills.

As Ava slowed to indicate onto Main Street, she braked, blinking at the sight of the enormous Christmas tree overseeing life in Emerald Bay from the square. It was wrapped in a blanket of fairy lights, and she wondered if her dad had had a hand in popping the star atop this one, too. If so, he'd no broken bones to show for it.

As she continued on her way, she found herself smiling at the bonhomie of the villagers. It was as if the sight of the tree and shops with their windows now full of festive cheer had waved a magic wand of good spirits over the village. Sure, look, even Mr Kenny, tootling toward Heneghan's Pharmacy – who'd no doubt be having a run on the paracetamol and Alka-Seltzers today – had tinsel wrapped around the handlebars of his motorised scooter!

Oh, but there was no place like Emerald Bay this time of year, Ava thought silently. She was falling in love with her village all over again and didn't care that they were still weeks away from the big day itself. The idea that the novelty of being home would wear off in a few weeks was quickly squashed. But as another thought nudged her, she shivered despite the blasting heater and toasty seat. What would it be like for Grace returning to a cold, empty flat? She didn't like how the notion of that made her feel and, passing under the Christmas bunting, resolved to put her twin out of her mind. There was no point expending energy stewing over things and having a one-sided argument in her head. She'd only wind herself up again, which wouldn't help.

As Vera purred along, Ava began to relax. She'd a much better feel for the overly sensitive – in her opinion – brake and accelerator now and even allowed her eyes to dart off the road now and again. This morning's sugar-dusted scenery was a treat, with the sky seeming especially blue. Or maybe it was the same shade of blue it always was on a clear day, and it was just her. Hadn't she read somewhere that a near-death experience gave you a new perspective? Granted, it wasn't her near-death experience, but she was profoundly grateful to know Shane was safe and doing well at the UHG.

A camper van and a couple of cars were parked near the castle ruins as she whizzed past, although she doubted anyone other than hardy dog walkers would be down on the beach this morning. The tour bus that would make a pitstop in Emerald Bay before moving on to Westport was already pulled up opposite the thatched cottages. Ava tooted at the tourists, all kitted out for the cold, taking photographs from the roadside and waving as she passed. Hopefully, she wouldn't encounter any farmers herding their sheep down the road this morning – she was eager to get Galway.

Too keen, because five or so minutes later, as the vista on her right changed to blanket bog with the undulating expanse of ocean on her left, a siren sounded.

Ava's eyes flicked to her rear-view mirror to see a flashing blue light. Being pulled over wasn't part of the plan.

Ah no, she thought a moment later slowing then coming to a halt a safe distance off the road. It was Sergeant Badger, wearing aviator sunglasses no less, strolling casually toward Vera.

Ava scrambled out of the car to face the officer. 'I'm sorry for speeding, Sergeant Badger, but Vera's my mam's car, and she's got a very sensitive accelerator. Sure, my foot was barely touching it,' Ava babbled, barely registering the sergeant's raised eyebrow overtop his Top Gun glasses when she called the car Vera. 'It's a beautiful day, is it not?'

'Grace Kelly, isn't it?' Sergeant Badger cut to the chase, ignoring her weather remark.

Just for a second, as Ava saw her pale face reflected in Sergeant Badger's mirrored lenses, she contemplated pretending to be her sister but then realised he was asking for her licence. She wondered if the sunglasses were an intimidation tactic. If so, they were working a treat.

'Er, I'm Ava, and it's in my wallet on the passenger seat.' She held her hands up as she inched around Vera.

'There's no need for the dramatics, Ava,' Sergeant Badger said.

'Sorry.' She retrieved the necessary licence and handed it over.

He inspected it before addressing her. 'Do you know what speed you were doing just now?'

'One hundred and eight kilometres an hour,' she squeaked.

'And do you know the speed limit on a regional road in this country?'

'One hundred kilometres, Sergeant Badger, sir,' Ava replied meekly.

'So what I'd like to know – and what I'm sure your mam, given it's her car, is going to want to know – is why were you driving at one hundred and ten kilometres?'

'Er, eight – it was one hundred and eight, and as I said, Vera's got a very touchy accelerator.'

'I clocked you at one hundred and ten, and let me get this straight. Are you telling me it's the car's fault you're after speeding?' The sergeant's tone suggested he'd heard it all.

'Er, no – well, yes, sort of.'

'I can tell you're Nora Kelly's daughter,' Sergeant Badger huffed.

Time was ticking, and Ava decided to get things moving along. The situation was still salvageable, and the sergeant wasn't the only one who could use tactics. She'd try and tap into his soft side. And so, hoping he had one, she said, 'The thing is,

Sergeant Badger, you'll have heard what happened to Shane Egan?'

He nodded and, not looking up, began scribbling in his notebook.

'Well, it's been a terrible, stressful time, and I'm on my way to the hospital in Galway to see him now. In my eagerness to get there, I was a little lead-footed, like, but I can assure you it won't happen again.'

'I sympathise, Ava, but I will still have to issue you a ticket.' He tore a paper from the notebook and held it out to her.

Ava ignored his outstretched hand. 'Ah, c'mon now, Sergeant Badger. I am very sorry. My finances aren't in the best shape just now, and I can't be doing with a fine, so what do you say? Maybe we could come to a little arrangement instead?' She winked, thinking Nan's apple cake or a loaf of her brack might do the trick.

'What kind of officer of the law do you think I am, Ava Kelly?' Sergeant Badger spluttered, his eyebrows almost shooting off the top of his head at her suggestion.

Ava's face heated up like Vera's seat as she realised what he'd thought she was insinuating. 'I was thinking perhaps you'd like some of Nan's home-baking, is all.'

'A bribe! I see!'

The hole she was digging for herself was getting bigger by the second. 'No, not a bribe, baking. Nan's baking. You know she won the Great Emerald Bay Bake-off at the St Patrick's Day fete. Sure, you were one of the judges.'

'It was a tie-breaker, as I recall, and I will close my ears now, young lady, before you find yourself up to your neck in hot water.' He flapped the ticket at her. 'I suggest you take this and get on your way. Slowly.'

Ava grabbed the ticket. He'd get no further argument from her, and she turned, wanting to distance herself from the officer and the misunderstanding that had transpired. How would she explain to her mam and dad that not only had she been speeding, but Sergeant Badger thought she'd been offering him special favours to let her away with the ticket she'd been issued as a result?

'Ahem, Ava.'

What now? She spun around.

The sergeant was pointing at her boot. 'You've something trailing behind you.'

Ava frowned, unsure what he was talking about, and glanced down at her footwear, her eyes widening.

No!

Yesterday's knickers were wrapped around her boot like a forlorn leg warmer. They must have got caught up in her jeans leg when she climbed out of them last night and had been slowly working their way to freedom ever since. She vowed that no one would ever know about this, stepping out of the knickers with as much dignity as her flaming face would allow before picking them up and shoving them in her pocket.

Ava climbed back behind the wheel and drove sedately away without a backwards glance.

The journey to Galway's University Hospital passed without further incident, if you didn't count the eejit not indicating at the roundabout, and the gods were on her side for once when she pulled into a parking spot on her first circuit of the area reserved for the general public.

She braced for sensory overload as she walked under the canopy and through the hospital's main entrance, but today she was unaffected. Perhaps yesterday's visit had desensitised her, she thought, seeing a man stride past with a gift basket. Her own hands suddenly felt conspicuously empty. Was it rude to visit a patient empty-handed? She glanced about for a sign pointing to the gift shop. She hadn't thought about it in her haste to get here. Grapes, at the very least, might have been nice. Ah, well, it was too late now anyway. It wasn't likely the gift shop sold fruit and veg, so she went to the front desk to enquire whether Shane was still in the HDU.

He'd been moved first thing. Good news, Ava decided and, armed with the information of which ward she'd find him on, raced for the lift, stepping in behind a tracksuit-clad woman with a pink streak running through her hair. The smell of her takeaway coffee was enticing as they rode to the same floor in silence, though Ava wished she was alone in the lift so she could have checked her hair out in the mirrored back wall. Skittery nerves saw her stumble over two left feet as she stepped onto the floor, and steadying herself, she looked past the duty desk nurse to the corridor where she'd find the ward Shane was on now.

He'd been so out of it yesterday. Today would be a different story. Remembering how he'd said there was no going back if they broke up, Ava turned on her heel, facing the lift again. Was she setting herself up for rejection?

When Rory, followed by Conor and Michael, rounded the corner a few seconds later, Ava was still loitering by the lift. Shane's brothers' expressions were unreadable, but Rory smiled as he greeted her. His appearance was an improvement on yesterday, with the dark circles around his eyes having lessened and the beginnings of a beard gone. She couldn't be sure, but she thought she saw him elbow Conor, and to her surprise, he and Michael managed a cordial good morning.

She noted that Conor's fashion sense hadn't improved, and Michael was the poster boy for a wild and woolly Aran Man in his sweater. She returned their greeting, which was a step in the right direction and made her feel slightly more optimistic about what might lie ahead with Shane. 'How's the patient this morning?'

'He's loving the breakfast-in-bed service,' Rory deadpanned. 'I doubt he'll want to come home.'

Ava laughed, her shoulders relaxing to their normal position. Humour was a great icebreaker. 'Will I be OK to go in to see him? I know he's supposed to rest.'

'I think he'll be glad of the company, to be honest, Ava. His neighbours aren't up to much cop. They're both snoring.'

She nodded, remembering the man in HDU whose tonsils had been on display yesterday. 'Are you heading back to Emerald Bay now?'

'We are.'

'I'll swing by later and sort that food out for you if that works?'

'That would be much appreciated.'

Conor and Michael echoed the sentiment and then got side-tracked by a pretty nurse hurrying past.

'Second door on your left,' Rory informed her, inclining his head in the direction they'd just come.

'Thanks.' Ava said cheerio, leaving them to wait for the lift, and couldn't help but smile at hearing Rory tell his sons to stop gawping like a pair of yokels who'd never seen a woman before. She hoped the nurse that had caught their eye wasn't Shane's as she made her way to the first of the wards, pausing to check the names listed outside the door.

'Shane Egan' jumped out at her.

25

The ward Ava walked onto was bright, albeit sterile, with light streaming in the windows at the end. There was the same pretty nurse the Egan brothers had ogled, checking notes at the end of the bed of one of the snoring patients Rory had mentioned. Ava smiled at the nurse as she dragged her eyes up from her task questioningly.

'Good morning. I've come to see Shane Egan.'

The nurse's smile was warm as she said, 'Good morning. He's doing well if the breakfast he put away is anything to go by.' She pointed to the end bed.

Ava's eyes jumped hungrily down the ward to where Shane was, propped up in the trolley bed. His hair appeared black against the pillow, even though she knew it was dark brown. His eyes were closed, but she doubted he was sleeping, given Rory and co had only just left.

'That's brilliant to hear,' Ava said, smiling through her anxiety, which was now on high alert. Then, leaving the nurse to her rounds, she hurried past the other beds to stand alongside Shane's.

'Shane?' Her voice was barely above a whisper, but his eyes

opened instantly, and he stared at her for the longest second before slowly blinking.

Ava fidgeted with her hands, unsure what to do with them. She couldn't get a fix on what he was thinking other than he was struggling to comprehend she was there. Perhaps he had gone straight to sleep after his visitors left. He continued to stare at her, and after a few beats of excruciating silence passed, she jumped in with, 'Do you mind if I sit down?'

Shane licked his bottom lip, and she noticed it was chapped. When he spoke, his voice came out as a croak. 'Sorry, I forgot my manners. Of course. Sit down.' He cleared his throat before speaking again. 'Would you draw that curtain partition first? It might drown him out.' Pain flashed across his face as he gestured to the blue curtain.

Ava hastily pulled it across, blocking out the rest of the ward, and sat down as a honking snore from the bed next door shook the ward. 'Well, that worked,' she said, making her mind up that no matter how things panned out between them, she'd pick him up a lip balm tube and a set of earplugs from the pharmacy before heading home today. She was gratified to see Shane smile at her remark.

'I'm glad you're here, Ava.'

'I had to come.'

They held each other's gaze, only breaking apart as Mt Snore erupted again. Ava couldn't help the giggle that escaped, and Shane laughed too but winced.

'Don't make me laugh. It hurts. Cracked ribs.'

'Ouch.'

'Yep.' He shifted carefully.

'Do you want me to arrange those pillows for you?'

'Nurse Ava.' Humour flickered in those indigo eyes.

'I'd have made a good nurse, I'll have you know.'

'If you weren't prone to fainting at the sight of blood.'

'That's the only thing that stood between myself and Florence Nightingale status,' Ava bantered back.

This was her Shane, she thought. Not the off-hand fella who'd avoided meeting her eye each time she returned to Emerald Bay this last year or so.

'I'm sorry I've behaved like an arse.'

Like Grace, he'd always been able to read her mind, but she wouldn't let him off that easily. 'A right arse.'

'An *arse* arse.'

'Agreed.'

They exchanged a grin as the glacier between them began to melt.

'That was some ordeal you went through,' Ava murmured. There was no pointing in adding it was an ordeal they'd all gone through in their ways.

'Yeah, so I've heard, but it's a blur. Dad tells me I'm lucky to be here, though.'

Ava nodded. It was true, she thought, studying the hospital identification band around his wrist. 'Did your dad tell you Isla Mullins is on about you being Emerald Bay's walking, talking Christmas miracle?'

Shane pulled a face at the idea, his expression a cross between amused and horrified as Ava filled him in on the shop-keeper's grand plans for putting Emerald Bay on the map.

'There's no hope for me, then, because that woman's a force to be reckoned with when she gets an idea in her head.'

'That's true enough. Isla will be dragging you off to meet the Pope if you're not careful,' Ava said, only half joking. 'So, stupid question, but I've got to ask. How are you feeling?'

'I'm doing all right.'

'How are you *really* doing?' She searched his face for clues.

'Honest answer?'

'Honest answer.'

'Sore. And I'm knackered, but surprisingly OK.'

'Well, you look good aside from the nighty.'

Shane glanced down at his hospital nightgown. 'Speaking of arses.'

'No!'

'Yes. I'm hanging out in the breeze. I got up for the jacks while Dad and the lads were here. I don't think they'll ever let me hear the end of it.'

Ava's laugh was loud, and she clapped a hand over her mouth, not wanting to get a telling-off for being rowdy from Nurse Far-Too-Pretty, who was still buzzing about the ward.

Shane laughed with her, but it died in a grimace, and Ava, knowing he was in pain, desperately wanted to offer comfort. To make contact with his skin. She'd give anything to lay her head on his chest, but remembering his ribs modified her wish to wanting to hold his hand.

Jody sprang to mind with perfect timing to distract her from the physical tug toward him she was fighting. 'I'm sure you've heard, but Jody's been spoiled. She's had no shortage of volunteer dog walkers. Little Siobhan and Sinead Molloy are completely smitten with her. They've not given her a minute's peace, and I caught them sneaking her doggy treats.'

Shane's face softened at the mention of his best friend.

'Dad said everyone's been brilliant rallying around, like. Conor asked me if I'd had a coconut called Wilson to keep me company on the rock, and Michael says I should go MIA more often, because there's never been so much good food in the house. Not since Mam anyway.'

Ava's mouth curved at Conor's and Michael's typical comments, although she picked up on the undercurrent of sadness in Shane's words, which his grin attempted to mask. 'I'm calling by later to sort out what can be frozen and what needs to be eaten so nothing gets wasted.'

'That's good of you.'

'Not at all. Has the doctor given you any idea when you'll

be able to go home? Jody will be desperate to see you. It's not as if she understands what's happened.'

'She was there when I was brought in at the harbour.'

'She was.'

'You were, too.'

Ava chewed her cheek, nodding. Did he remember her making their sign?

'I didn't know for sure if I'd dreamed it. I've had the strangest dreams.' He shook his head.

'You didn't dream it.' Their eyes locked. 'I stuffed up, Shane. With leaving you, I mean.' Her voice was strained.

'No, you didn't. It wasn't a mistake, because you needed to go. I was wrong trying to hold you back,' he said quietly.

'Do you think we can fix things?' She clenched her teeth together hard, willing him to say yes.

Shane was silent, and his expression had closed.

Ava's insides lurched at the thought of it being too late to put things right between them. Grace may have had a point. Neither of them had compromised when they'd been pulled in different directions last time, no matter that, right now, Ava would stay in Emerald Bay for the rest of her days if it meant being with Shane. She snatched a tissue off the cabinet.

'I thought about you when I was on that rock,' Shane said, not meeting her gaze. His arms were by his sides again, and he clenched his hands and unfurled them.

Ava wiped her eyes, straining to hear him, then balled the damp tissue and shoved it up her sleeve, trying to catch the rest of his words.

'I couldn't believe I might not see you again and tell you how I feel. I saw something, too.'

'A selkie?' Ava sniffed, knowing her poor attempt at humour was a defence mechanism, because how did he feel about her? He hadn't said.

'My mam.'

'Your mam? In a dream, you mean?' She hadn't expected that.

'I don't know if it was a dream.' He made to shrug but grimaced as his ribs protested. 'I don't know what it was, Aves, but she kept me warm.'

'A guardian angel,' Ava murmured.

'Maybe, but it was Mam. How she was before she got sick. She told me things.' He twisted his head toward her, gauging her reaction.

Ava kept her expression neutral, not wanting him to clam up for fear she might think he was delusional from the hypothermia. She didn't. He believed in what he'd seen and felt. Shane was stoic, not prone to showing his emotions, but she could see on his face how whatever had happened out on that rock had affected him deeply. 'What things?' she probed gently.

'That she's at peace.'

He'd told her once how cancer had ravaged Mona Egan's body physically, and how much it had frightened him to see her in pain. She realised it had haunted him and picked up his hand, holding it in both of hers. It was calloused, the skin rough to the touch. He had strong, working hands. Fisherman's hands. 'I'm glad, Shane.' She hoped it meant he would be at peace from hereon in, too.

'I never told you or anyone this, but it wasn't just down to the business and Jody my refusing to leave Emerald Bay.'

Ava tilted her head to one side. She'd always felt there was more to his digging his heels in over heading off to see a bit of the world with her, but he'd remained tight-lipped on the subject, and it had become a wedge between them.

His voice was thick as he spoke. 'Leaving the village would have felt like leaving Mam behind. I couldn't bring myself to do that. I didn't want to say goodbye to her twice. But it meant losing you.'

The vulnerability on his face saw tears slide down Ava's

cheeks. 'Oh, Shane.' She freed her hand to rest her wet cheek next to his, and they breathed the same air for a few moments. 'You should have told me,' she whispered, the heat of his skin warming hers. 'I would have understood. I could have done things differently if I'd known.' Her lips brushed his cheek before she pulled herself upright and caught his watery smile.

'You had to go, Ava. You'd have wound up resenting me if you'd stayed. It was my baggage to unload. Not yours.'

Ava tossed that around, unsure if she agreed with him but aware she couldn't fix his pain over his mam's death. Shane had to learn to live with it himself.

'Seeing her, dreaming her, whatever, I understand now she's not in a place. She's in here.' He patted his chest. 'She's always with me in my heart. You are, too, and I won't lose you again.' A determined light shone in his eyes. 'Whatever it takes. I won't.'

'I'm not going anywhere.' Ava's hand snaked out and traced a line along his jaw, thick with stubble.

Shane reached up and caught hold of her hand, tugging her toward him.

Ava's mouth was so close to his, she could feel his breath warm on her face when she pulled back slightly.

Shane groaned his frustration, closing his eyes briefly.

'I don't want to hurt you.' Her eyes sought his for reassurance.

'Ava, how I feel now, I could stand on one of the tables at the Shamrock and do an Irish jig. Don't worry about hurting me. Just kiss me.'

The right side of his mouth curled up, and Ava caught sight of the dimple in his cheek as she giggled.

'Now that I'd like to see.'

'C'mere to me, woman, and stop talking.' Shane's hand slid around the back of Ava's head as he pulled her down toward him.

Her hair fell across her face in a red curtain, shielding them from the outside world as their lips, his rough and dry, brushed against each other's, gently seeking to get to know one another again. She wound her fingers into his hair, breathing the saltiness of him, tasting the peach from his breakfast as their mouths pressed hungrily against one another, lips parting slightly. She forgot where she was.

It didn't matter anyway, because she was back where she belonged.

26

'Now that would make a great front-page photograph,' a voice at the foot of the bed said.

Ava and Shane startled apart to see Jeremy Jones standing at the foot of the trolley bed with a camera in hand.

'What are you doing here?' Ava demanded, displeased at the interruption. Her eyes narrowed as she took advantage of her first opportunity to properly check out the man who kept springing up everywhere. She'd barely given him a second glance down at the harbour, and he'd been too far away at the pub for a close-up inspection.

Whippet and *weasel* were the words that sprang to mind once she'd finished her once-over. That was down to his pointy features, sly eyes and wiry build. She guessed he'd be in his early thirties, even though his sandy hair was already thin and receding. Her nose curled at the whiff of stale cigarette smoke clinging to his waterproof jacket with its *Galway Gazette* logo. Yer man looked like he should be selling dodgy insurance door to door, and she wondered how he ever managed to prise information out of people for his newspaper pieces.

'Charming.' Jeremy's eyes were two ice-blue chips as he surveyed her back. 'I'm here to ask Mr Egan a few questions.'

'Who are you?' Shane looked at Jeremy, bewildered, then twisted his head toward Ava, furrowing his brows questioningly.

Ava got in first. 'He's a journalist.' She tried to keep the distaste from her voice. 'Hannah had a run-in with him in Galway.'

'Jeremy Jones from the *Galway Gazette*, Mr Egan.'

'Er, Shane. You make me sound like my dad calling me Mr Egan.'

'Shane it is. Pleased to meet you. And with respect, I was doing my job.' He dipped his head toward Ava. 'If her sister chooses to go around breaking the law and chaining herself to trees scheduled for the chop, what does she expect?'

He did have a point when he worded it like that, Ava thought. Still and all, Shane was here to recuperate not be hounded for his story. The reporter had no business being here.

'Shane's supposed to be resting, not answering questions,' she said snippily. 'There'll be time for that when he's back home. If he chooses to.'

'Which was why you were snogging the face off him just now.' Jeremy smirked.

Ava blustered for a second but couldn't find a comeback.

Jeremy, sensing weakness, wasted no time getting down to business. 'Look, we seem to have got off on the wrong foot, Shane, thanks to your Rottweil— er, friend here.'

The pair scowled at one another before Ava pulled her gaze back to Shane. He appeared bewildered by the whole situation. But then it was only yesterday he'd been in the high dependency unit suffering dehydration and hypothermia, so was it any wonder he'd no clue what was going on?

'How about we start again?' Jeremy asked, not waiting for

Shane to reply. 'I'm here for a photograph and a few lines about your survival story.'

'He's not Bear Grylls,' Ava butted in.

Jeremy ignored her. 'I spoke to your father earlier, Shane, and he said he'd mention my swinging by to you. The public is desperate to know more about Emerald Bay's Christmas miracle man.'

Shane groaned at the mention of miracles.

Ava shook her head, half rising to escort the reporter off the ward as Shane's self-appointed bodyguard. Shane shook his head, though, telling her not so fast.

She sat back down, listening as he said to Jeremy, 'I'd forgotten – my brain's all over the show – but Dad did mention you might be calling up. He's also been telling me about the search and rescue effort that went into locating me. Not to mention the locals who've all been looking out for my family and dog. I want the chance to say thank you publicly to them all, but only if there's no mention of miracles.'

Ava nodded slowly, seeing the sense of it even if she disliked the whippet-weasel fella who'd invaded their personal space. 'Looks like you're getting your scoop.' She pulled a face at Jeremy.

Amusement flickered in Shane's eyes at her use of the word 'scoop'.

In contrast, Jeremy Jones shook his head and said, 'You're not guest-starring in an episode of *Murphy Brown*, you know. And I'm not making any promises, Shane, because miracles sell newspapers.'

'Murphy who?' Ava asked.

'Never mind,' Jeremy muttered.

Shane's sigh was resolved, and the reporter was already pressing record on his device, which he held toward him.

'Shane, how long were you in the water?'

Ava's breath caught as she waited to hear what he'd have to

say. But Shane's reply was vague, as were his responses to the rest of the questions being fired at him. Some things, like Shane's feelings about her or his mammy, were not newspaper fodder, she thought when Jeremy drilled him about what had gone through his mind while on that rock.

Voices murmured in the bay next door, and Ava realised at some point during her visit, the ground-shaking snores had subsided. Small mercies and all that.

'Excuse me. Our patient should be resting, not subjected to an interview.' The pretty nurse appeared around the curtain to reiterate Ava's earlier remark as she fixed a surprisingly stern gaze on Jeremy.

Ava glanced at her name tag – Jasmin Ahmadi – wanting to pat her back and say well done.

'I'm nearly done here, Nurse. A quick photograph, and I'll be on my way.' Jeremy didn't raise his gaze as he took the lens cap off. 'I'm not usually in charge of the photography side of the biz, but Frankie's off sick today. So I'm multi-tasking.'

Finally, he looked up from fiddling with the Sony camera and smiled to win over the nurse, who was now tapping her foot. His pupils doubled in size as he registered Nurse Ahmadi for the first time, and it took him a few seconds to gather himself as he leered in close to her badge. 'Nurse Jasmin. Pretty name.'

Her firm stare didn't falter. 'Nurse Ahmadi, and perhaps you didn't hear me?'

'I heard you,' Jeremy interjected, hurrying on. 'One quick photograph, and I'll be on my way. It would make a grand shot if you were to stand on the opposite side of the bed to the tree hugger's sister with an expression of grave concern. You know, life-and-death stuff.'

'My name's Ava,' Ava directed to the nurse, to be clear.

'No. I don't think so,' Nurse Ahmadi replied, her tone clipped.

She was well able to fend for herself where the likes of dubious journalists were concerned, Ava thought admiringly.

'I'm temping here, and I don't know the hospital policies on that sort of thing. I'll give you one minute to take your photograph when I've finished checking Mr Egan over. Then you're to be on your way.'

Jeremy nodded, love-struck, as he stepped aside to let her check the clipboard at the bottom of the bed.

Ava moved out of the way while the nurse asked Shane a few questions before taking his blood pressure. Then, satisfied all was as it should be, she repeated, 'One minute.' Her trainers squeaked on the lino as she exited the ward.

'I'll stand in for Nurse Jasmin.' A head covered in hair like tufts of white candyfloss bobbed around the curtain. 'Florrie Canavan's the name. I'm here seeing my Eddie, and we couldn't help overhearing you're from the newspapers.' Button-brown eyes pinned Jeremy in their line of sight, and then as quick as she'd appeared, Florrie was gone again.

'I'll be back in a jiffy, Eddie. How's my hair?' Florrie's voice rang out from behind the curtain.

Eddie's response was inaudible. A chair scraped, and then there she was, Florrie Canavan, a tiny woman in blue slacks and a striped blue-and-white sweater that gave her a nautical air.

Her size might be small, but her presence was enormous, Ava thought, watching as she pushed past Jeremy with a nod toward herself and Shane before perching on the side of his bed.

'Sorry about that, son – I didn't see your hand there,' she apologised as Shane freed his hand, flexing his fingers.

He and Ava exchanged an incredulous glance. Was this actually happening?

'Now then. I used to be in the amateur dramatic society,' Florrie directed at Jeremy, whose slack jaw suggested he was utterly unprepared for this photobomber. 'So don't be worrying. I know my stuff. I heard you saying you were after a grave, life-

and-death sorta face.' She arranged her features, and despite herself, Ava was impressed.

Florrie Canavan could pass for Shane's grieving granny. Then faster than you could click your fingers, she'd morphed back to the woman visiting her husband in the bed next door.

'Or are you thinking more along the lines of a "yer man here is lucky to be alive" look.'

Now she resembled a woman praising the Lord in the front pew about to burst into song.

'I can also do a joyous "he's come home to us" smile?'

This time Ava fancied her face mirrored a woman who'd unwrapped a pricey Christmas present she was chuffed with. A diamond ring, perhaps.

'But you're the professional. I'll leave it up to you,' Florrie finished.

Ava stifled the bubble of laughter that was rising in her throat at the ludicrousness of the situation and the frown on Jeremy's face as he tried to think of ways to tactfully remove the little woman around her nan's age determined to be a cover girl for the *Galway Gazette*. She didn't fancy his chances.

'Oh, and before you get clicking, I've got a story you might like to include in your paper about my Eddie there. You could get a two-for-one deal.' She chortled, chest-puffing at the idea.

Jeremy shot an anxious glance up the ward, and Ava supposed he was worried Nurse Ahmadi would return before he could get his front-page photograph.

Florrie chatted on, oblivious to the reporter's panic. 'He's after injuring himself by falling off a ladder, and if I had a penny piece for every time I've told him not to be climbing up the ladder to do the gutters, I'd be a rich woman. Why he won't pay someone to do it is akin to the sacred mysteries. It's an accident waiting to happen at his age. But sure, you know what men are like?' She clucked in Ava's direction, and Ava nodded, not daring to disagree. 'Do they listen?'

Ava dutifully shook her head.

'No. So up he goes, and there's me in the bedroom changing the sheets, still in my nightgown, when I see a face looming at the window. What's a woman to think when she sees a man's face staring back at her through her bedroom window? A peeping Tom is what, and I screamed blue murder. Of course, Eddie took fright and toppled backwards off the ladder. Now there he is' – she pointed to the curtain – 'with a spinal fracture. He's lucky to be alive is what he is, because he'll mend.'

'Er, great story, Mrs, er, Cavanagh, but I'm unsure of the angle I'd use,' Jeremy said warily.

'Canavan. C-A-N-A-V-A-N. Edward and Florence for your readers. And the angle is the moral of the story, young man.'

'Don't go climbing ladders when you're a pensioner?'

'No. Don't go peeping in women's bedrooms, no matter your age.'

Ava snickered and saw Shane's eyes had creased up, too. This was priceless.

'But he's your husband, and he was after doing the gutters.' Jeremy was lost.

'Janey Mack! Were you not listening to me, son? I didn't know that now, did I?'

The reporter was beginning to resemble a cornered wild animal as he attempted to expel Florrie with the promise of a photograph and exclusive on the dangers of being mistaken for a peeping Tom.

Shane and Ava watched as the little woman reluctantly disappeared behind the curtain, and then, with no further ado, Ava was told to shift her chair closer to the bed and lean in toward Shane. Her head rested next to his as Jeremy said, 'Smile,' before clicking. Then, hearing Nurse Ahmadi exclaim over his still being there from the entrance to the ward, he stuffed his camera away and beat a hasty exit.

'Thank goodness he's gone,' Ava said, righting herself.

A trolley rattled, and the smell of something soupy and meaty reached their end of the ward.

She held Shane's gaze. 'You still haven't told me.'

'Told you what?' Shane wrinkled his nose at the smell.

'How you feel.'

His eyes widened. 'It's obvious, isn't it?'

Ava shrugged. 'Maybe, maybe not, but I want to hear you say it.'

'I love you, Ava Kelly.'

Thousands of tiny bubbles fizzed inside her. 'And I love you, Shane Egan.'

'Do you love me enough to eat whatever they're serving up for lunch so I don't get in trouble with Nurse Ahmadi? She's quite scary when she wants to be.'

Ava laughed, sniffing the air. 'Er, can I get back to you on that?'

Shane reached out to her, and being careful not to bump him, Ava manoeuvred into a position where they could pick up where they'd left off before Jeremy Jones interrupted them.

So when the dietician rolled the trolley to a stop at the bottom of Shane's bed, she cleared her throat noisily and reminded them in no uncertain terms it was a hospital they were in, not a cheap motel.

By the time Ava left the hospital, she had a chin raw from Shane's stubble and a sore tummy from laughing.

27

The day awaiting Shane's discharge from the hospital was a mixed bag. The sun decided to break through the dark clouds one minute, and the heavens opened the next. Rainbows were around every bend in the road as Rory and Ava drove to Galway to bring Shane home. Ava was sitting in the front cab of Rory's battered four-wheel-drive workhorse, hoping she didn't smell like wild salmon when she got out to greet Shane. It was just as well he didn't have an aversion to fish.

Sergeant Badger's Gardai vehicle was tucked away down a laneway invisible until it was too late for passing motorists to slow down, and Ava's lips tightened seeing him parked up in his hidey-hole. Her mam and dad's response when she'd come clean about being pulled over by the sergeant had made her feel fourteen again, receiving a lecture she'd thought would never end. Fair play to them, though. She had been in the wrong. Still and all, it had crossed her mind that she was an adult capable of owning her mistakes, but would they ever see her like that? Probably not, given how Nan ran around after their dad. Your children were always your children, regardless of age. She wondered if that meant they might see their way to paying the fine for her. Ha! Dreams were free.

Rory's speed in the old four-wheel drive he got about in was sitting bang on the one hundred mark, which was a relief. Ava had no wish to meet and greet Sergeant Badger twice in one week. As for the rest of her mortifying encounter with the lawman, that would be taken to her grave. If her sisters ever caught wind of the sergeant having misunderstood her intentions, not to mention the knickers wrapped around her ankle, she might as well move to Timbuktu.

The conversation between her and Rory on the drive to Galway was minimal, but the silence was comfortable. It was so unlike her family, where someone was always talking and usually over the top of someone else. Rory spoke only when he had something to say; she felt no need to fill the gaps.

The relaxing, albeit juddering, trip gave her time to mull over the front-page article in the *Galway Gazette*.

The bold headline informed readers: 'Local Man's Survival at Sea a Christmas Miracle'. If anyone doubted whether she and Shane were a couple again, the proof was in the picture. What had made Ava smile, however, was the face peeping through the curtains spotted on closer inspection – Florrie Canavan had had the last laugh and photobombed Jeremy's picture!

The weasel-whippet reporter had relayed the facts as Shane laid out, but his article's slant as to a 'miraculous' survival would keep Isla Mullins happy, Ava had thought, scrolling through it earlier.

Isla had eyes and ears everywhere, it would seem. Somehow she'd found out about the cover piece in the *Galway Gazette* and had charged down to the Bus Stop corner shop to ensure they ordered a stack of copies, because it wasn't every day Emerald Bay locals were front-page news.

Ava's mood had been buoyant as she'd scoffed breakfast,

thinking that today was a fresh start for her and Shane, but then Mam had poured cold tea over her good spirits.

'Have you been in touch with Grace?' she'd enquired innocently while buttering her toast and keeping one eye on Liam to ensure he didn't dollop too much on his.

'No,' Ava had mumbled through her mouthful, the toast turning to sand in her mouth as her appetite vanished. Her anger was still simmering and she wasn't ready to speak to her, but that wasn't to say Grace hadn't been on her mind. The harder she tried to avoid thinking about what she was up to, the more she popped up in her thoughts.

'It might be nice to reach out to her,' Nora had pushed. 'It doesn't do any good to leave things festering, Ava.'

Ava had gritted her teeth. 'I'm not, Mam. I'm just doing my thing, and I've no time today. Rory will be here any minute. You know we're off to pick Shane up from the hospital, and then there's the party here,' she'd said overly brightly, leaving her crust unfinished to push back from the table. She hadn't turned around as she'd left the cosy warmth of the kitchen but knew if she had, she'd have spotted her mam and dad sharing one of those looks that spoke volumes.

Sometimes it was very annoying to be viewed as the compliant family member, Ava had thought, stomping up the stairs. She'd wished it was her with the reputation for being highly strung, because she doubted her mam was getting in Grace's ear about reaching out to her twin.

They were nearing the hospital now, and zipping all that away, Ava did as Rory suggested by texting Shane to let him know that they'd be pulling up outside the entrance in five minutes.

Today was a fresh start for them, and that was what she would concentrate on. Not Grace.

. . .

True to his word, Rory slowed to the mandatory speed as they entered the hospital grounds five minutes later, and a wide grin spread across Ava's face because there he was! Shane was standing with his bag by his feet to the side of the main entrance, and she waved.

Once Rory pulled into the designated pickup area, she jumped from the idling vehicle to hurry over and help Shane to the truck. His ribs would heal in their own sweet time, and until they did, he would have to listen to his body and not overdo things, she bossed, taking his bag and arm by the elbow. It was easier for her to squash in the middle of the cab and save Shane from having to shuffle over, and despite his passive expression as he buckled in, Ava could see the beads of sweat on his forehead and knew he was in discomfit.

'Dad, don't be haring off on any of your farm track shortcuts.' Shane leaned back against the headrest. 'I'm not able for that.'

Rory's mouth twitched. 'I'll stick to the main road, son, and give any potholes a wide berth.'

'Grand.' Shane reached for Ava's hand, and they sat with their fingers entwined for an uneventful journey back to the bay. The only point of interest other than the unfurling scenery was Sergeant Badger giving a young lad none of them recognised a talking-to on the side of the road. The teenager's clapped-out Honda Civic had an exhaust pipe like a fat sausage and almost scraped the asphalt. A boy racer, Ava thought with a prim shake of her head, then remembering she'd been in the same position the other day stopped shaking her head and slunk down in her seat, lest the sergeant spot her. She could feel Shane's curious gaze, but her lips were sealed.

Ava recalled how the sight of the holly wreaths adorning the doors of the tightly wedged houses leading into the village, along with blow-up Santa in the Brady family's window, had made her feel sad when she'd first arrived home. Today she was

full of the joys and smiled, seeing the Riordans' customary rein-
deer was also now keeping watch over the comings and goings
from their window.

'Look!' She jabbed a finger toward the windshield a short
while later as they reached Emerald Bay's Main Street. A
banner with 'Welcome Home, Shane!' was emblazoned in blue
against a white background and strewn across the street in place
of the Christmas bunting. 'I bet Isla Mullins organised that.'
Ava suspected the banner was part of her miracle-status quest.
Or perhaps she was being cynical, because it was a lovely touch
and made her proud to be part of such a tight-knit community.

The whole to-do was as big as when John F. Kennedy had
passed through the village on his 1963 Ireland trip, Kitty had
been saying over tea and toast that morning, thanks to Isla.

She had Carmel Brady on her side, too, Ava noted with a
grin, seeing her blackboard sign proclaiming the Shane Special
of a sultana scone and a pot of tea for only two euros. Shane
muttering something beginning with 'F' that rhymed with heck,
beside her, told her he'd seen it, too. It was a safe bet that any
tourist who popped into Isla's Irish shop or the Silver Spoon
cafe today would be privy to a detailed account of the 'miracle'
that had occurred not too far from Emerald Bay. Word of mouth
was the best advertising tool, Isla had often been heard to say.

Ava flicked a glance at Shane, seeing the stain flooding his
cheeks. She knew he hated being the centre of attention and
sometimes wished he didn't live somewhere so tight-knit. She
pumped his hand reassuringly.

'I don't want all this fuss,' he grumbled almost on cue.

'Shane Egan, you sound like Mrs Tattersall,' Ava tutted,
making him and Rory smile.

'Thanks a million.'

'Well, you do. People want to celebrate you being alive.'

Shane made to open his mouth, but Ava got in first.

'I know the last few days haven't been a picnic for you, but the village went through the wringer, too. Christmas was on hold for you. Remember that. They deserve a hooley to get them in the festive spirit.'

There was no doubt Emerald Bay's locals loved a celebration, what with the warm-up the other night when the news had come through Shane had been found.

'Ava's got a point, son. People want to raise a glass to you coming home, so we're heading to the Shamrock now.'

'Ah, Dad, let's just go home and see Jody.'

'Well, you know what the moral of the story is,' Ava said, mimicking Florrie Canavan's voice. 'Don't go falling off fishing boats again.'

Shane laughed despite his hooded brow. 'Very funny. I'll try not to.'

'Jody's waiting for you at the Shamrock. And we'll only stay an hour and then say you're to go home and rest, OK?' Rory kept his eyes on the road.

'OK,' Shane conceded.

The Shamrock wasn't to be left out when it came to welcoming their miracle fisherman home either. A fat holly wreath now hung over the door. The window boxes were bursting with red petunias, thanks to Nora Kelly's swift repotting of them, and in the windows, the stubby wax taper remains burned to keep watch for Shane had been replaced by gold Christmas candles.

'I feel like a fraud,' Shane said through clenched teeth, gingerly getting down from the four-wheel drive once Rory had parked.

Ava was quick to arrange herself by his side, eager not to stand outside discussing matters, because she didn't like the look of the heavy rain cloud that had settled overhead. 'Well, you're not,' she said brusquely, tugging him along as Rory strode ahead to hold the back door to the pub open. Today there were no hardy smokers in the beer garden, although there was evidence in the butts littering the pansy-filled beer barrel. They were the bane of Nora Kelly's life.

A cheer went up as the trio appeared, and Ava was aware of Shane stiffening beside her before slowly untensing at the sight of the people he'd known all his life. There were one or two interlopers, Ava noticed, seeing an older gent with a Houston cap raise his pint while the horsey blonde woman next to him, his wife presumably, held up her wine glass. *The more the merrier* was the motto for a hooley!

An excitable ruff-ruff-ruff sounded, and before either of them had time to locate its source, a black blur streaked toward them. Ava winced as Jody leaped up at Shane, but he wasn't letting on if his beloved dog's enthusiastic greeting pained him. She scrabbled her front paws against his chest, tongue lolling between barks.

'Hello, girl.' Shane grabbed hold of her head, ruffling behind her ears, and after waving over and mouthing, 'Thanks,' to little Siobhan and Sinead, who'd been keeping an eye on Jody, Ava joined in with the pats. She was just as pleased to see the Lab cross as she was them.

A table had been reserved for the guest of honour, and Michael and Conor were already seated at it. So with Jody dancing about by Shane's side, they steered their way toward it, making slow progress as Shane paused to thank whoever was reaching out to slap his back or shake his hand.

Dermot Molloy called out over the general din, 'What are you drinking, Shane, my boy, and you, too, Rory? Liam says it's a free house for youse two. I'm sure he'll stretch to one for his daughter, too,' he added with a wink.

Eagle-eared Liam shouted back, tongue-in-cheek, 'Don't be giving away my profits now, Dermot!'

Ava's attention had been caught by Michael and Conor nearly banging heads as they leaned toward one another at the mention of free houses. She fancied they were questioning the fairness of their dad getting on the house stout while they'd had to put their hands in their pockets. She could imagine the conversation between the brothers going along the lines of, 'Sure but weren't we out braving the conditions looking for him, too?'

Liam Kelly was a generous man, but he was also intelligent, and the two older Egan boys had hollow legs. He knew he'd go broke if he agreed to ply them with free ale for a night!

'A pint of Harp, thanks. What'll you have?' Shane angled his head to hear Ava's reply, adding, 'Are you still a pint of lager lass, or have you gone all fancy London cocktails on us?'

'Cheeky.' Ava elbowed him gently. 'And chance would be a fine thing. The price of them would make your eyes water. A pint of the Harp will do nicely.'

'And a Harp for Ava, too, Dermot, thanks,' Shane responded before carefully lowering himself into the seat Michael had pulled out for him. Jody sat by Shane's side, resting her head on his lap.

To Ava's surprise, Conor leaped up and saw to her chair. 'Er, thanks,' she said, sliding in beside him and Shane.

'It was good of you to sort the kitchen out for us, Ava.' Conor's voice was strained, and Michael nodded his agreement.

So it was to be a case of letting bygones be bygones, which was fine by her, Ava thought, telling the brothers it wasn't a bother. She didn't mention the hours it had taken, because she hadn't stopped at putting the food dropped around by the villagers to keep the Egan men going in the fridge or freezer; she'd wiped out and tidied the cupboards, too.

As two pints materialised in front of Shane and herself, she frowned, looking at him. He was still pale. 'Are you allowed to drink?'

Shane shrugged. 'I'm not on medication besides painkillers, so I don't see why not.'

Before Ava could argue, Michael piped up.

'What's he after doing?'

He was looking toward the bar, and they all twisted in their seats to see Rory standing on a chair near the door leading through to the Kellys' living quarters. Liam rang the last-orders bell to get the merry-making villagers' attention, and the chatter, like the roaring fire in the grate if it wasn't fed, slowly died down. Ava, Shane, Michael and Conor, along with the rest of those jammed inside the Shamrock, watched on with amazement as Rory, a self-contained man more apt to communicate with actions than words, cleared his throat before speaking.

'A parent's worst nightmare is to lose a child, no matter their age, and we've been fortunate to have the best possible outcome for Shane there.' He nodded toward his youngest son. 'Myself and the lads are so grateful to the Coastguard and the volunteers involved with the search, and we'll be donating a small token of our appreciation.' Rory paused to draw breath.

'I'll drink to that!' Enda Dunne exclaimed above the murmurings of agreement.

'Hold your horses there and let the man finish, Enda. You won't die of thirst.' Kitty Kelly flapped the cloth she was wiping the bar with at him.

'I won't take up much more of your time,' Rory said with a wry smile.

'You take as long as you like, Rory,' was bounced back.

Ava couldn't see who'd spoken up but thought it sounded like Ollie Quigley.

'It's high time I thanked you all, too, not just for looking out for the Egan family these last few days but for being there for myself and the lads when their mam, my Mona, passed on. I don't know how we'd have pulled through that dark time without your support, and I never told you how grateful I was to you for having our back. I believe Mona was with Shane on that rock, watching over him, and today's getting together here at the

Shamrock is to celebrate his safe return. So charge your glasses to each other and to Shane.'

'To Shane!' was roared.

Ava knew as she blinked furiously she wasn't the only one with wet lashes by the time Rory jumped down from the chair and Paddy McNamara, three sheets to the wind as usual, began to warble 'When Irish Eyes are Smiling'.

28

Ava and Shane were sitting at opposite ends of the sofa in the Kelly family television nook, topping and tailing with a throw rug draped over their legs. Jody was snuffling on the rug under the coffee table on which they'd each a mug of tea, under strict instructions not to shed any dog hair on it from Kitty Kelly. Her nan had ducked her head in earlier to ensure they'd found the leftover stew in the fridge. Ava suspected it was also to check there were no shenanigans going on between her and Shane. Fat chance of that with his ribs! They'd left the party in the pub in full swing, with Shane starting to flag as the afternoon wore on. It was easier to duck through to the Kellys than for Ava to drive him home to an empty house.

Shane had stuck to just the one pint, unlike his father and brothers, who were last spotted singing at the top of their lungs with their arms draped around each other. Ava had heated a warming bowl of the stew so he wouldn't swallow pain meds on an empty stomach. Now they were enjoying being alone together for the first time since he'd been rescued. No snoring patients or nurses buzzing in and out of the ward. No Mrs

Canavan poking her head around the curtain as she'd been apt to do for the duration of Shane's stay, keen for a chat. Aside from Nan, whom Ava doubted would spring any more stealth attacks, the only intrusion on the peace was a sporadic burst of loud laughter filtering through from the pub. That would be down to Nessie Doyle, hairdresser or butcher – however you chose to look at it – who sounded like a hyena when she got going.

'Did you see anything out on that rock there, Shane?' Ava mimicked Isla Mullins' voice, and Shane, laughing and pulling a face, nudged her with his sock-clad foot.

'Don't make me laugh. It hurts too much.'

'Sorry, but it was funny. The look on Isla's face – and that sweatshirt.'

Isla, resplendent in her newest piece of stock – a sweatshirt with the caption 'Go luck yourself' above the image of a lucky shamrock – had collared Shane as they'd quietly attempted to exit the hooley. Ava, seeing the sweatshirt, had done a double take to ensure it was an 'L' for luck, because the swirly lettering across Isla's bust could easily have been misread. It probably explained why Father Seamus had been so fixated on his church committee chairperson's chest.

'Did you have any visitors while you were on that rock, like, Shane? Any sense that you weren't alone?' Isla had probed, stepping into his path.

'I did see a seal,' Shane had told her, attempting to side-step around her.

Isla had danced back and forth like a boxer blocking his path, and Shane had given up eyeballing Ava for help – Isla was a formidable woman when she wanted to be, and Ava wasn't silly.

'No, that's not what I mean,' she'd said, impatient. 'I'm talking about anything unusual. A bright light – that sort of a thing.'

'And little green men?' Shane had tapped his chin with two fingers as though thinking deeply.

Isla's brows had knitted, the lines around her mouth turning to trenches as she pursed her lips. 'I was thinking more of a biblical rather than extra-terrestrial experience. Angels with wings and halos. Yes?'

'No.'

Ava had desperately tried to keep a straight face, especially when, quick as a flash, Shane had followed this up with, 'Although, Isla, I don't mind telling you I'd have been grateful to see the Ark cruise past. I'd have waved out to old Noah there, and I wouldn't have had a problem going steerage class with the zebras and giraffes either.'

Isla's eyes had narrowed as she'd studied him closely, unsure whether he was joking with her.

'This is of vital importance, Shane. Are you sure there was no kind of golden light, any light? An angel or two sighted near Emerald Bay by one of our own would be a tourism magnet. You know yourself with that family fish and chipper that tourists mean money. And it could be a nice little sideline for you running boat trips out to your rock. You know, like a pilgrimage to Lourdes, only on a fishing boat.' Isla had been warming to her theme, her eyes gleaming with euro signs.

'No.' Shane had shaken his head. 'I can't tell a lie to you now, Isla, but it was just me and the rock for the duration.'

Ava hadn't blamed him for a second for not telling Isla about feeling his mam's presence there. 'Shane's exhausted, Isla, so if you wouldn't mind.'

Isla's shoulders had slumped as she'd finally stepped aside and let them pass.

Ava was curious whether Shane had confided in his dad about what had happened while he'd waited for help, especially given Rory's comments when he'd addressed the pub earlier, and she asked him about it now.

Shane nodded slowly. 'I did, and Conor and Michael. They think I was delusional from drinking seawater, but Dad found it a comfort. Sure, look it, there he was tonight, public speaking no less. I think it helped him to know she's at peace and wants us to get on and live our lives.'

'Do you think your mam would have liked me, Shane?' Ava blurted. It mattered to her that Mona Egan would have approved of her son's choice of partner. 'Sorry, I know that's not fair.' She dipped her gaze, playing with the fringe on the rug. When she looked up, Shane's expression was thoughtful.

'She would have loved you, Ava.'

'You think?'

'I know.'

A smile flickered on Ava's face. 'I wish I could have met her.'

'Me too.'

Silence filled the room, and they sipped their tea before Shane put his mug down. 'After you left for London, Dad gave me a talking-to.'

Ava's head tilted to one side. She was unsure what Shane would say next. 'Oh yes?'

'Yeah. The gist was that I was an eejit not to check London out with you. He said the same thing to me at the hospital and that I'm not to worry about how he, Conor and Michael will manage the business without me if I want to go back with you, because they'll be OK. I told him as I told you – I dug my heels in over leaving because this is where I still felt Mam.'

'And I understand that. Emerald Bay's where your heart is, and you're where mine is. I want to be with you.'

They exchanged a lingering look. The heat of their bodies pressed against each other intensified, but Nessie Doyle's laugh ringing out broke the tension between them, and they grinned.

'If it's not Nessie and that awful laugh of hers, it's Nan. I'll bet you anything Dad will check up on us with some silly excuse, too.' Ava inclined her head toward the door, which was pulled to. There'd always been a rule that there were no closed doors when boyfriends called around, but Ava wanted to think it would have gone out the window as soon as she was of age. Her folks paid no heed to Shannon and James sharing a bed and didn't bat an eyelid over Imogen having moved in with Ryan, but when it came to the baby of the family, well, that was a different matter.

'What was London like?' Shane pulled his question from nowhere.

'I don't know. Big.'

He nudged her with his toe. 'I'm not that much of a culchie. I mean tell me what it was like living there.'

Ava swirled his question about in her head, thinking about her reply. 'The sights are grand, like. I mean all that history, it's something to see. It's buzzy and vibrant. Cosmopolitan. There's always something happening. I suppose it's everything you'd expect it to be.' She shrugged. 'I was lonely the whole time I was there, though, and you're not a culchie, but it was big.'

'I don't understand. Why were you lonely? Grace was there with you.'

'But you weren't.'

His eyes softened. 'No. And I was lonely, too.'

They reached out to one another, their fingers entwining.

'Describe London to me like you would if you were writing a scene for your novel,' Shane said, still not satisfied with her description.

He'd always believed in her, Ava thought, never doubting she'd write the book she had in her one of these days. But for whatever reason, she was suddenly shy.

'It's me, Ava,' Shane said gently.

He was right, and Ava closed her eyes, conjuring up the sights, sounds and smells of the city she'd spent the last year desperately trying to immerse herself in.

'London's past is part of its fabric. It's always there, mingling with the modern. Look up, and you'll marvel at the detail in the arches, spires, domes and stacks. Shade your eyes to see the sooty clay chimney pots or run your fingers across a mottled wall, and feel the hardship and toil in the stock bricks. History reminisces with the present – sometimes beautifully, sometimes not.' Her voice was growing in confidence as she warmed to her theme.

'The ebb and flow of the Thames is a constant to be relied upon – a watery testament to what's been and gone and what's still to come.' Ava's smile was wry. 'Even the pigeons have a look about them that says they've seen it all before. But underpinning it all is the sense of possibility. It comes from the melting pot of aromas – yeasty, fresh bread, fish 'n' chips and exotic spices signalling the cultural diversity with the common denominator of hope that's brought people here over the centuries.'

She paused for a breath, casting about for what else she wanted to say.

'London's grey but bright and glossy, too, and you know you could turn a corner at any moment and find something unexpected. The noise is constant, but there's an orderliness that tells you life is moving along as it should be.

'The city lures you in with its charm and promise of new horizons. But be warned, London will turn its back on you when you're down on your luck.'

Ava opened her eyes, looking at Shane expectantly. 'Too flowery?'

His eyes were shining as he shook his head, still absorbing her words, and she flushed with pleasure.

'And what about your dreams, Shane Egan? You know everything there is to know about me, but you've never told me what you want for yourself, not properly at least. And I'm not talking on a romantic level either. I mean your aspirations, and if Emerald Bay and working with your dad and brother is it, that's fine, but be honest, OK?'

Shane nodded, and thoughtfulness settled over his face as he stewed this over. 'Well, listening to you just now, I suppose I'd like to see things. I want to try something other than fishing, too. I don't know. Maybe construction. It would have to be something that involved working with my hands and being outdoors.'

He fell silent, but Ava didn't speak because she wasn't letting him off the hook, and he took his time before speaking again.

'Mam told me to be happy before she died, and I read somewhere that the definition of happiness is contentment. I don't want a lot, but I want to be happy, Ava.'

'I brought you through a bag of pork scratchings, Shane. I know you're partial to them.' Liam Kelly's sandy head appeared around the door, lightening the moment. A packet of salty snacks sailed through the air, landing on Shane's lap. 'Everything all right then?'

'Grand, Dad.' Ava twisted her neck in her father's direction, unsurprised that he'd proved her prediction correct.

Satisfied all was as it should be, Liam left them alone.

'I'm going to add to what I was saying,' Shane said, ripping open the pork scratchings.

Ava cocked an eyebrow waiting.

'I'd like a place of our own.'

'Me too.'

'No, Dad, Conor or Michael walking in on us.'

'Or Nan, Mam, Dad and whichever of my sisters happens to be about.'

'Your dad can still drop me round a bag of these whenever he feels like it, though.' Shane held the bag up and shook it.

Ava snatched it off him and helped herself.

'I think we'll have to establish some boundaries around

snack sharing when we're under the same roof, if things are going to work out.' Shane was tongue-in-cheek.

'I agree.' Ava's eyes twinkled. 'What's yours is mine and what's mine is mine is a grand house rule so far as I'm concerned.'

The pork scratchings were abandoned then as, forgetting his injuries, Shane lunged forward and tickled Ava until she was crying-laughing, begging him to stop. He did, still grinning even while groaning about his ribs hurting.

As she fell back against the arm of the sofa, Ava realised this was what Shane had been talking about.

This was happiness.

29

The Shamrock was quiet this evening, with Nora making the most of trade being slow by titivating the Christmas decorations and polishing the bric-a-brac behind the bar. Kitty was engrossed in a cut-throat game of gin rummy, keeping her cards tucked tightly to her chest, having made noises over dinner earlier that her opponent, Eileen Carroll, tended to cheat. Liam, meanwhile, was putting the world to rights with Enda and Mr Kenny. Reports had made it to the publican's ears that the rest of their regulars were still suffering for their sins at Shane's homecoming hooley two nights earlier.

Shane and Ava were warming their toes by the fire, Jody making contented snuffling sounds in her sleep at Shane's feet. Ava was unwinding after a frantic day trying to get the copy she'd been tasked with writing for a radio advertisement back to the ad agency before the close of business despite Shane's best efforts to distract her. She was feeling drowsy, unaware that her eyes were beginning to close, until his voice saw them flutter open.

'Ava, remember I told you when I was in the hospital how I finally understand that Mam's always with me here?' He laid his hand on his heart and looked at her, his expression serious as he put his pint glass down.

Ava nodded, wondering where he was heading.

'Well, I've been thinking about it. I do want to explore the world a little. You know, travel, like.'

'Shane, you don't have to pretend. It's me.'

'I'm not. I had plenty of time to mull things over in the hospital, and then listening to you describe London the other night got me thinking.'

'That's dangerous.'

Shane pulled a face. 'I'm being serious here.'

'Sorry.'

'You know I've got a cousin with a building company in New York. He'd take me on labouring. It would be a chance to try my hand at something different. And you can work anywhere. We could go for three months initially, see how it goes.'

'New York,' Ava repeated, wide awake now as her mind began to race. The Big Apple! City life in a metropolis like New York would be so different with Shane by her side. She pinched herself lightly. 'Are you serious?'

'I said I was.'

Amusement glittered in his eyes, seeing her face light up, but then Ava's smile vanished.

'But what about Jody? We can't leave her,' Ava whispered as the dog's ears twitched, hearing her name. She didn't stir, though.

'I've had an idea. I watched how little Sinead and Siobhan were with her in the pub the other day, and they've walked her after school the last two days. They love her, don't they?'

'I think they do.'

'I could speak with Dermot about taking her in for us. It's three months, and she'll be well cared for. If we decide to stay longer, we can assess things then.'

They could do this. Ava's heart was beating rapidly. They could go to America. But then the biggest obstacle of all reared its head. 'Shane, I've no money.'

'So? I have enough to set us up initially. It would be a working holiday.'

Ava's hand reached out for his, and she began humming the tune Frank Sinatra had made famous.

Shane's grin stretched from ear to ear. 'The Empire State Building.'

'Times Square.'

'The Statue of Liberty.'

'Central Park.'

Ava's phone ringing interrupted their bantering, and feeling like a shaken bottle of lemonade about to have the lid removed so she could gush her news, she snatched it up, hoping it was Grace momentarily, forgetting how things stood between. The number on the screen told her it wasn't her sister's but a client's, and the bubbles inside her went flat as she put the phone on the table again, letting it ring out.

'It's to do with work. I'll ring them back tomorrow,' she explained in response to Shane's raised eyebrow.

Once the ringing had stopped, Shane spoke up. 'What's going on, Aves?'

'Huh?'

'One minute you're buzzing, then your phone rings, and you're sad. You've not mentioned Grace to me either. Not once.'

Ava wished she could recapture the excitement of a few minutes ago. She gave a slight shake of her head and studied her fingernails. 'Grace and I had words after she followed me over here when we got news you were missing. Things were said that can't be taken back.'

'What things?'

Ava didn't want to get into all that, but under Shane's questioning gaze, she repeated parts of their fight, leaving out her sister's unkind words where he was concerned. She finished by raising her shoulders and letting them fall back down. 'She's back in London, and we haven't been in contact since.'

It was the longest she'd ever gone without speaking to her twin.

'Call her,' Shane said, simply seeing it as an easy fix.

'I'm not in the wrong.'

'Ava, Grace is a part of you. You know you'll be miserable if you don't sort things out between you.'

He was being more charitable about Grace than she had been about him. 'Since when did you become her champion?' She was irritated, because while she expected her mam to push her to make the first move toward patching things up, she hadn't expected Shane to do so.

Shane pulled a sheepish face. 'I'm not, and I do think, in the past at any rate, she has been overinvolved in your life. She's pushed you into things.'

'Like London.'

'Yes.' Shane thought about this. 'No. You wanted to go. I made it hard. Other things... I don't know, stupid kids' stuff. You do need each other, though, Ava – I recognise that.'

'Do we? Because I want to try life on my terms without her glued to my side. She's unwilling to accept or even try and understand that I might want different things from her. Going our separate ways is long overdue.' A terse finality in Ava's voice saw Shane offer no comeback, and the silence stretched between them.

The flames in the hearth flickered as Evan Kennedy strolled into the pub, bringing a whiff of the cigarette he'd undoubtedly ground out by the back door in with him.

'I want to look forward, Shane, not back.' Ava's voice was quiet.

Shane reached for her hand. 'I get that. I want you to be happy, though.'

That word again, Ava thought, placing her hand in his, and he folded his fingers around hers. 'And I will be. The Met,' she began again.

'The Brooklyn Bridge.'

'Broadway.'

As they batted to and forth, a little voice niggled at Ava. Would she be happy without Grace? She'd have to be, because she knew from experience she couldn't have them both.

It was Grace or Shane.

30

The waning moon was luminous, and the stars were pinpricks of light punctuating a blue-black ceiling as Shane led Ava by the hand down the coastal path. The phone torch gave enough of a glow to pick their way down the trail.

Shane was making a fast recovery. He was a quick healer the doctor had said at his check-up. It had been two weeks since he'd come home from the hospital, and they'd spent every minute they could together. Of course, work and real-life stuff intruded, but they'd settled into an easy routine with Shane happy to lie next to Ava on the sofa, either at his or the Kellys' place, while she tapped away on her laptop. The stand-off between herself and Grace was something Ava did her best not to dwell on, not wanting anything to spoil her reunion with Shane. It was a little like the proverbial elephant in the room, though. Hard to ignore.

Tonight, the evening was still with the promise of a frost in the morning, and the lack of breeze made the rustling in the grasses off to the side of the path all the more ominous. Ava was scrunched down inside her coat, glad of her hat, scarf and gloves. If it wasn't freezing, she would have had a sense of having been here before, only that had been a balmy night when the world had felt like it belonged to them to do what they wanted with.

'If you think I'm skinny-dipping tonight, Shane Egan, you can forget it,' Ava muttered.

'Don't worry. I won't be tearing my clothes off either.'

'Glad to hear it, given you've not long had hypothermia.'

Ava opened her mouth to ask what he was up to for the tenth time since he'd got up from the Kelly table after dinner with instructions for Ava to grab her warmest gear. He wouldn't say anything more on the subject other than he had a surprise for her. Nor would he be tempted to sit and enjoy a slice of Kitty Kelly's tea cake before they disappeared. That in itself had been enough to get Ava's antennae quivering. Instead of words, though, she squealed as something skittered across the path in front of them. 'What was that?'

'I don't know, but whatever it was, it was just as scared as you.'

'It looked like a stoat or a rat.' The distaste was evident in Ava's voice.

'Well, it's gone now.'

'But it could be watching us with its little stoaty eyes,' Ava persisted, quickening her pace to draw level with Shane instead of trotting a little behind him like a wayward child.

'I think it's probably got better things to do than spy on us,' Shane reassured her. 'Like hang out with its stoat crew having a stoat rave.'

'Not funny. Now I think hundreds of little stoaty eyes could be on us.'

The ocean's roar grew louder. She decided she'd have one more go at getting him to talk, her eyes straying off the path as she glanced up at his profile. It was unreadable.

'So, if we're not risking freezing our bits off by skinny-dipping, why are we heading down to the beach? Because if it was the stargazing you had in mind, we could have pinched my dad's binoculars, and if you'd cleaned your windscreen, we wouldn't have even had to get out of the car. We could be all cosy.'

'You're terrible when it comes to surprises, Ava. I'll put you out of your misery when we get to the beach.' Shane refused to be drawn further.

He was right. She'd always been the same when it came to surprises. She was the child that would search high and low for her Christmas presents once she'd recovered from the shock of finding out Father Christmas wasn't real! Shane wouldn't be budging, not now they were so close. There was nothing for it but to wait and see what he was up to and hope it was something nice!

Ava was impatient now to reach the shore.

'Watch your step there,' Shane said a few seconds later as the path led to the stretch of sand. The tide was ebbing, and their feet sank into the gritty ground-down shells. Ava surveyed the expanse of cove framed by rocks visible in the weak moonlight. At night, it had a mysterious quality illuminated like so, but she couldn't spot anything out of the ordinary.

'OK, close your eyes,' Shane bossed.

'Are you serious?'

'Very. And cover them with your hands, because I don't trust you not to peep.'

Ava sighed and shook her head – she'd come this far – and once she'd done as he'd said, he steered her forward.

'OK, you can look now.'

Dropping her hands and opening her eyes, all Ava could see was the inky water inching further away. She looked at Shane questioningly, seeing him shining his phone torch on the sand, so she tracked the ray's path. Her eyes widened upon seeing a collection of small pebbles laid out on the sand, and it took her a split second to register the pebbles' formed words.

'Ava,' she read the first word out, delight tingeing her voice at the thought of Shane coming down to the beach earlier to write secret messages for her. It must have taken him forever to collect the pebbles. The romantic gesture was out of character. He was many wonderful things, but a romantic wasn't one of them, and that's what made this, here, all the more special.

She scanned the rest of the words, saying them out loud as she read each one. 'Will you marry me?' She quickly traced her eyes over the pebbles once more in case she'd misread them.

Nope. It was definitely a proposal! And her hands flew to her mouth as she dragged her gaze from the pebbles to Shane, seeking confirmation. His face was half in shadow, but she saw the hope mingled with uncertainty in his eyes as he waited for her to say something. She couldn't speak, so she nodded, her eyes glistening.

'Is that a yes?' Shane asked.

Another bigger nod because her throat was too thick with emotion to speak.

'OK, let's be clear.' Shane dropped down on one knee and, taking her hands in his, trapped her with his eyes. 'Ava Kelly, will you do me the honour of becoming my wife?'

Ava swallowed, still trembling. 'I will.' Her eyes were brimming as she took a steadying breath. It was her turn to say her piece. 'Shane Egan, I would love nothing more than to marry you. You can't get clearer than that.'

Then she hauled him upright, flung her arms around his neck and showered his face with butterfly kisses between shouting, 'Yes!' over and over. She hadn't known it was possible to laugh and cry simultaneously.

Shane grinning broadly and cupped her face with his hands. 'I love you, Ava. I've loved you since that afternoon at the park when Jody jumped on you.'

'I love you, too,' she whispered through her tears.

'Happy tears?'

'The happiest.'

Shane's smile faded as his gaze grew tender, and he wiped her cheeks dry gently with the backs of his hands before brushing his lips over both her eyelids. When he kissed her properly, she could taste salty tears on his lips, which were at odds with her giddy joy. She would remember this moment for the rest of her life, stamping every scent, sound and sensation to memory before feeling him pull away.

Ava watched as he unzipped his jacket and patted around the inside pocket before producing a small velvet jewellery box. He opened it, and she stopped breathing, momentarily catching the glint of a diamond. Her left hand trembled as she held it out, waiting for him to slip the ring on her finger.

It fit perfectly, and Shane shone the torchlight for her to see it properly. The classic oval diamond solitaire glittered with hidden depth as she gazed at it, awestruck. 'It's beautiful, Shane.'

'It was my mam's. She wanted Dad to keep it for whichever of us lads got engaged first.' He spoke fast. 'I know some girls have firm ideas about their engagement rings, and you're not obligated to accept it. If you'd rather choose your own, that's fine.'

'It's on my finger now, Shane Egan, and it's not coming off. It's perfect, and I love the connection to your mam and dad. I'll be honoured to wear it.'

He looked pleased before saying almost shyly, 'I asked Liam and Nora for your hand in marriage. I wanted to do things properly.'

Ava stared up at him, wondering how he'd planned this all out while she'd been oblivious. She mentally shook her head, thinking over the last few days to see if there'd been any clues as to what was coming, but her parents hadn't given a thing away. 'They OKed it obviously?' God, she hoped there'd been no arguments on her parents' part about them being too young or only just having got back together. Her teeth hurt from clamping them together, waiting for Shane's reply.

'They did. They said we're made for one another. My dad said the same.'

Her parents' and Rory's approval meant a lot, and Ava relaxed her jaw.

Shane blinked, rallying himself. 'I almost forgot. Wait here one tick.' He strode off toward the rocks, disappearing briefly before emerging to return with a tote bag. Then, like a magician producing a rabbit from a hat, he plucked out a bottle of champagne.

'It's the real deal,' he said proudly, digging deep for a corkscrew. 'There are two flutes wrapped in a tea towel inside the bag, too. Could you grab those? I had to borrow them from the pub.'

Ava did so, unwrapping them and standing at the ready as the pop of the cork resounded like a firecracker. Shane sloshed the gold liquid into their glasses, and the fizz dripped over the sides. Then he carefully twisted the bottle into the sand to keep it upright before he straightened and took one of the flutes from Ava, raising it. 'To us.'

'To us.'

They clinked glasses and took a sip of the tart, fizzy liquid. Ava laughed at Shane's face. 'Champers is wasted on you. You'd have been happy with a bottle of Harp.'

He didn't deny it as he stoically got the contents of his flute down. Ava went in for seconds as Shane announced he still had one more surprise for her. She watched over the rim of her glass, curiosity pricking as he delved into his pocket again then held a plastic wallet out toward her with a flourish.

She took it, passing him her glass. 'What's this?'

'Open it and see.'

Ava did so, finding two air tickets inside. 'I don't understand?' She looked at him, wanting answers.

'Two one-way tickets to New York booked for the third of January.'

'Oh my God, Shane! We're going to do it?'

'We're going to do it.'

'What about Jody?'

'I spoke to Dermot, and the Molloys would love to look after her. The wee girls are so excited.'

Ava squealed and wrapped her arms around his neck again as he held the flute away.

'You have made me a very happy woman, Shane.'

'That was my intention.' He grinned, kissing her on the tip of her nose.

Now it was her turn to surprise him, Ava thought. 'I don't want to wait, Shane.'

'Er, it's Baltic down here, Aves. I don't know if I can do the biz.'

Ava tossed her head back, laughing. 'Not that! Jaysus, we'd freeze our arses off. I mean, I don't want to wait to get married. I want a Christmas wedding.'

Shane coughed, clearly thrown. 'This Christmas.'

Ava nodded. 'As in Christmas Day.'

'You do know that's like a handful of weeks away.'

Ava nodded.

'I won't be changing my mind if that's what the hurry is about.'

'I wouldn't let you. There's no backing out now, Shane. I will be Ava Kelly-Egan before Boxing Day.'

'You're serious?'

'Of course.'

'But isn't there like loads to organise?'

Ava shrugged. 'Not really. You don't like being the centre of attention, and nor do I. We can keep it simple.' She hadn't a clue what was involved in organising a wedding, even a simple one, but she knew she could make it happen.

'The sooner the better so far as I'm concerned,' Shane replied, and they refilled their glasses.

'To our Christmas wedding.' The chink of their glasses was barely audible over the tide.

'Shane, can we go home?' Ava downed the contents of her glass. 'I'm dying to tell everyone. And it's freezing.' Her teeth chattered to prove her point, and as he packed away the champers and flutes, she quickly snapped a photo of her pebble proposal, the flash from her camera a blinding blink.

As they trudged up the beach hand in hand, Ava thought about her Christmas wedding. It would be filled with the people that mattered most to her.

All except one.

May love and laughter light your days, and
*   warm your heart and home.*
May good and faithful friends be yours, wherever
*   you may roam.*
May peace and plenty bless your world, with joy
*   that long endures.*
May all life's passing seasons bring the best to
*   you and yours.*

— IRISH BLESSING

31

Nora pulled back the bedcovers and clambered in alongside her husband, whose glasses were slipping down his nose as he buried himself in the latest Lee Child. A toilet flushed in the distance as Shannon or James, now back from America and ensconced in the room she'd always shared with Imogen, went about their night-time ablutions. There'd been so many announcements these past weeks. They'd begun with Ava and Shane informing them they were engaged and planned on having a Christmas wedding before leaving for America. And, no, they'd not wanted an engagement party, saying there'd been enough fuss already, what with Shane's accident. Not only that, but the wedding was to be low-key. Low-key, indeed! The very idea made Nora want to snort. Did they not know there was no such thing in Emerald Bay?

Nora had barely had time to wrap her head around the wedding news and the short notice when Shannon, with James in tow, had arrived back in the village and told them of their plans. James was going to move to Ireland and set up practice in Kilticaneel.

Shannon hadn't breathed a word of his having been in

touch with the vet over in Kilticaneel. It had transpired her eldest daughter had visited Kilticaneel's only veterinary practice with Napoleon for his annual check-up. Upon learning of the sole practitioner's Spanish retirement plans having been put on hold because he couldn't find a suitable buyer for his business, she'd whispered in James's ear. The pair had kept all of this under their hats for fear of jinxing the sale, but now it was past the point of no return. James had told them he wanted to be with Shannon and close to his maternal grandmother, Maeve. His beloved dog, Harry, would be joining them soon.

All of the goings-on were delightful, but they'd put her in a spin, especially Ava's easy-breezy assumption a wedding organised in what amounted to weeks, rather than months, wouldn't be a bother. That one's head was in the clouds, Nora thought.

She leaned over and checked her phone alarm. A retired Canadian couple exploring their heritage were staying in the room overlooking Main Street. They were checking out in the morning and keen to hit the road early. This wasn't a bother, but it did mean she'd have to be up and about at the crack of dawn cooking up a storm, because guests of the Shamrock would only be leaving with a full Irish in their bellies. Sleep would be a luxury anyway, she thought, satisfied there was no risk of sleeping in before making a show of fluffing her pillow up. Then she flopped against it to stare up at the pool of light from Liam's bedside lamp on the ceiling, huffing a sigh.

Liam, lost in his book, continued to read, but when Nora sighed again, this time from the tips of her toes, he got the hint and slotted his bookmark into place, snapping the paperback shut and putting it aside. Then he turned and surveyed his wife over the top of his glasses. 'All right, Nora, you're not the big bad wolf blowing the house down with me inside it. Out with it.'

Nora didn't need a second invitation. 'It's Ava and Grace,

Liam.' Her face was drawn in the soft light as she faced her husband. 'What are we going to do about the pair of them?'

'This daft business of them not speaking to one another?'

This blasé manner was typical of her easy-going husband, and her lips tightened as she nodded.

He flapped his hand dismissively. 'Sure, it will blow over; I'll bang their heads together if it doesn't. That will make them see sense.' He flashed a cocky grin at his wife but quickly sobered on seeing her stony-eyed gaze back at him.

'That's not helpful.' Nora folded her arms across her chest. 'And that's the thing – it hasn't blown over. They've not spoken in over a month. Well, Grace texted her to say congratulations, but that's it, and only after I put the screws on when I rang to tell her the engagement news in the first place because Ava wouldn't. It's ridiculous, given how close they are. I thought they'd have patched things up within a few days, but then Grace took off back to London all in a tizz. And now, we've Ava and Shane's wedding looming. They're both hurting, and I can't believe Ava's entertaining saying her vows without her sisters standing behind her as bridesmaids.'

She barely paused to breathe as her worries poured forth like a gushing tap. 'The problem is the natural order between them has shifted. Ava's always been the malleable one who's more reliant on Grace, while Grace is the leader, but this time Ava's not bending, and she's determined to prove she's her own person. She feels she's had to choose between Shane and her sister. It shouldn't be a bloody choice!'

'But it's not a competition.' Liam frowned. 'Sure, they're not children. Ava needs her sister as much as she needs her fella.'

Nora studied her husband's perplexed expression, frustration surging. He could sometimes be so dense, yet sharp as a tack at others. She shook her head. 'Of course it's a competition, Liam. It always has been. Shane and Grace feel threatened by each other, where Ava is concerned. They've never been able to see she's room in her heart for them both. Or that she needs them both.'

'But that's stupid,' he spluttered, adding, 'Infantile is what it is.'

'Be that as it may, it's the way it is, and Ava's had enough. I can understand how she feels, but that doesn't mean I'll accept it.'

Nora had tried speaking to Grace after getting nowhere with Ava, but Grace had dug her heels in, saying Ava had made her feelings clear. She needed space from her twin, so that was what she would give her until she heard otherwise. Nora knew her daughters inside out and picked up on the deep hurt lurking beneath Grace's stubborn stance. Ava, too, had put a sticking plaster over not being able to bounce her wedding plans off Grace.

They'd all tried to talk some sense into the twins. Kitty had got nowhere, and neither had Shannon, and Imogen and Hannah had been given short shrift. A leaden weight bore down on Nora as she thought about when the twins were little. The girls had been double trouble, and at times they'd have her tearing her hair out, but the way she felt right now, she'd go back to those times in a heartbeat.

'It's not just that, Liam. I can't stand the thought of Ava and Grace not making up before Ava and Shane leave for America.' Her head was beginning to throb and threatened tears stung. 'This isn't how I thought it would be.'

'Ah, c'mere to me now, woman.' Liam, who couldn't bear to see his wife upset, draped an arm around her shoulders, pulling her to him. She leaned against him, grateful for his solidness.

'It will all work out – you'll see,' he soothed.

'I envisaged a big affair for the first wedding in the family,' Nora sniffed, tired of the smile she'd glued on since Ava and Shane had dropped their bombshell. 'I thought I'd spend days pouring over wedding catalogues with whichever of the girls was the first to decide to walk down the aisle.' She knew right enough that you shouldn't live your life vicariously through your children. Still, she'd always assumed her daughters' weddings would differ from her humble and hurried affair.

'And that's another thing, Liam. I thought it would be Shannon, being the oldest and all, not our baby you'd be after giving away first.'

Her voice had thickened thinking about how, in recent history, a hasty wedding would have had the villagers whispering behind their hands about speed being of the essence where saying 'I do' was concerned and watch this space because, sure as eggs, there'd be a baby born to the betrothed couple before they'd reached their seven-month anniversary. Condoms might be freely available in Ireland now, but accidents still happened. Happy accidents like Shannon, but that was hers and Liam's secret, and it hadn't meant attitudes had necessarily moved with the times.

'Ava's not us, Nora.' Liam had read his wife's mind. 'Don't go opening old wounds.'

'I'm not.' This was true, because the words her mam had spat at her when she'd told her parents she and Liam were getting married had cut deep. Too deep to ever heal. Ellen Nolan had not embraced the new, modern Ireland; nor had she approved of the circumstances surrounding Liam and Nora's small, no-fuss wedding or her daughter's choice of husband. She'd had Nora lined up to marry Mark Dorrance, who came from money, something that mattered to her mam, having come from a humble fishing cottage. So, too, did appearances. Nora had thought Mark was 'the one', but he wasn't who he'd appeared to be, and Liam had picked up the pieces. Only when she'd got to know Liam properly had she understood what it truly meant to fall in love.

She would have tried harder to let the hurt go sooner if she'd known her parents would pass away in short succession of one another before she could hold out an olive branch. But she hadn't known, and ties had been cut with her mam, who'd refused to warm to Liam, believing that when you made your bed, you had to lie in it. There was so much joy her parents had missed out on, because Nora had never once regretted her decision to marry Liam. They'd forged a good and happy life together, and her parents never being privy to any of that made her heart ache, but you couldn't change the past, only learn from it. Now she was terrified history would repeat itself between Ava and Grace.

She couldn't, wouldn't, let that happen.

Nora pulled away from Liam, her gaze decisive as she said, 'I'm going to get Grace and Shane together somehow. I'll make them see sense. When it comes down to it, they both want the same thing, for Ava to be happy.' Her mood lifted, having made a plan of sorts. She hadn't a clue how she would pull it off, but she would figure it out. She had to.

'Nora Kelly, you're a smart woman, and I've faith in you. This will all be sorted before Ava's big day, and just because her wedding's going to be —'

'Small,' Nora jumped in.

'Intimate,' Liam corrected, 'doesn't mean it won't be perfect. The most important thing is Ava and Shane have the day they want, isn't it?'

She knew he was right and reluctantly nodded, mulling things over, getting to the crux of what was bothering her aside from the stand-off between the twins. 'I suppose I want to feel needed.'

'Nora Kelly, that girl needs her mammy now more than ever. She needs to know you're there beside her as she embarks on her biggest life journey. Married life. And, sure, aren't you off to help her decide on her wedding gown in a couple of days?' Liam and Nora, who were footing the bill, had quietly decided on a reasonable budget.

'We are, and you're right.' Nora could always rely on Liam to pick her up, and she hoped Shane would do the same for Ava as they built their life together.

Liam's tone softened as he brushed the hair away from Nora's face. 'We might not have had the sort of wedding that makes the society pages, but it was the happiest day of my life.'

'Mine too.'

'And it will be the same for Ava and Shane.'

'You're a wise man, Liam Kelly.'

'And you're a beautiful woman,' Liam replied huskily.

'Don't be buttering me up now. You were more interested in your book than your wife a few minutes ago.' Nora mock-tutted at him.

'Ah well, now yer Jack Reacher man can wait.' Liam grinned, pulling his wife down under the covers with him.

32

'You're ganging up on me.' Ava slumped in her seat, folding her arms across her chest, a mutinous expression on her face as she glowered across the kitchen table at Shannon, Imogen and Hannah. She'd better things to be doing with her time, like working and cracking on with her wedding plans, than listening to her sisters go on. And she suspected there was nothing 'unexpected' about Hannah's arrival home for the weekend. It was a carefully organised coup between her, Shannon and Imogen, who'd bustled her into the kitchen this morning to debate her decision not to have bridesmaids. Mam, Dad and Nan had made themselves scarce, although Nan had left a calling card – a freshly baked test batch of mince pies.

So far as she could see, the only point of difference between being sat in an interrogation room was the pies and the pot of tea in front of them. The aroma of sweet pastry might be delicious, but she had no appetite, and if Nan had intended the Christmas staples as a sweetener between the sisters as they tried to sway her to change her mind, it wasn't working. It was her right as the bride to decide these matters.

'And you can all stop giving me the hairy eyeball, like. Intimidation tactics won't work.'

'But, Ava, you're cheating us out of our birthright to be your bridesmaids,' Hannah retorted.

'Not to mention you're the first Kelly girl to get married,' Imogen added.

She was bare-faced today, and Ava had found it hard not to stare. The pre-Ryan Imo would never have dreamed of going au naturel.

'I agree with what they both said,' Shannon added, inspecting a mince pie then making short work of it.

'It's not about you. This is mine and Shane's wedding, and we want a low-key do with no fuss or fanfare.'

'Cop yourself on, Ava.'

Hannah sat straighter in her chair, her hair piled on her head and secured with a scarf, wobbling triumphantly. She looked like she was about to play her winning card, and Ava braced herself.

'Weddings are never about the bride and groom. You might think they are, but when you get down to the nitty-gritty of saying "I do", it's about getting married life off to the best possible start by not annoying your family and friends. Weddings are a political minefield, and I know my politics.'

Ava opened her mouth, but Hannah was having none of it. Parliament was in session so far as she was concerned. She was a cabinet minister with icing sugar on her top lip and crumbs down her front.

'They're a carefully orchestrated exercise in public relations ensuring you don't forget to invite Cousin So-and-So and that you don't sit Aunty You-Know-Who next to Thingamabob, because they can't stand each other. And especially that you don't get offside with your sisters. Do you get my drift?'

'She's right,' Imogen piped up. 'I, for one, am hurt that you seem determined not to let us be a proper part of your day.'

'So am I,' Shannon chipped in, her hand sneaking toward the pies again.

Ava dropped her gaze and studied the contents of her mug. Hers and Shane's engagement announcement had been met with great excitement and then shocked surprise at how soon they intended to exchange vows. Eyes had flitted to her midriff, and she'd been quick to inform both her family and Shane's that their haste was down to having already wasted too much time and nothing more before dropping a further bombshell that they'd be winging their way to New York afterwards. Imogen had been quick to say it was the Gemini in Ava – she couldn't help but be spontaneous.

The look on Mam's face, however, had almost pierced her defiance that Grace had forfeited her right to share in her wedding news by making her thoughts around her settling down with Shane abundantly clear. There'd been a sadness permeating Mam's delight that she wasn't here, sharing it with them all. Of course, she'd been told there would be a Christmas wedding in the family, but Ava didn't doubt she'd been hurt to hear the news second-hand and not from her. She'd not heard a peep from Grace, though, other than a cursory congratulations text, and even though she slapped on a brave face, that had cut her to the core.

'Congratulations' was all her message had said. When Ava had gone to her mam about it, hoping for a sympathetic cuddle, Nora had given a sad shake of her head and said, 'Well, what did you expect, Ava? She'll be hurting just as much as you are, given she had to hear the news from me and not you. I wish one of you would be big enough to reach out to the other and patch things up.'

It wasn't what Ava had wanted to hear, so she'd vowed not to bring the topic of her twin up again around her mam. Nan hadn't been any better.

No one understood, because how could she ask Shannon,

Imogen and Hannah to be bridesmaids without Grace? Her family seemed to think it was a simple fix, not comprehending things had gone too far between them. There was no middle ground – they were in a stand-off where saying sorry was concerned. And the crux of the matter was that Ava wasn't even sure she *was* sorry.

It was easier not to go there and use the excuse that, given the timeframe, there weren't enough hours in the day to be faffing with bridesmaids' dresses. Not to mention the added cost. It was a cost she and Shane could ill afford given they would be heading off to the States shortly after the wedding and Mam, Dad and Rory were already generously contributing.

That was her story, and she was sticking to it.

Ava's chin jutted out as she looked her three sisters in the eye and told them no, softening her stance by adding she loved them dearly, but this was her day, and no bridesmaids would be trailing up the aisle behind her.

'End of,' she added with a finality that saw Shannon, Imogen and Hannah glance at one another, finally understanding that Ava meant business.

33

'So, we've got the cake and the catering sorted,' Ava said to Shane, putting a bold red tick next to where the two items were written under the heading 'Things to Do' in the notebook she'd bought to keep track of their wedding plans. Catering was a loose term, given Shane's father had offered to smoke a couple of Atlantic salmon sides for them, and her mam and nan were on board for roast beef with all the trimmings. It wasn't just their wedding after all; it was Christmas day, too, and the reception – or after-party as Ava preferred to think of it – would be held here, at the Shamrock. As such, there'd be the usual Christmas fare, like pud and trifle, along with their wedding cake.

The cake had been a stroke of luck with Carmel Brady, who'd done a cake-decorating course in Kilticaneel a few years back, offering to make the couple her speciality – a single-layer chocolate cake with white chocolate buttercream. It would cost them a fraction of what they'd pay in one of the fancy Galway shops. Rory and her folks might be generously footing the bill for her and Shane's do, but still, they were mindful of not taking advantage of their generosity.

It was all coming together nicely, Ava thought, not without a touch of smugness as she chewed on the clicky part of the pen. She'd get Mam to ask Grace to box her things up in London and send them home. In the interim, she managed with what she'd brought home with her fine, and she planned to travel light to New York. Between finishing out her contract with the London ad company, preparing for their trip to America and planning the wedding, she'd barely had a moment to think. And that was a good thing so far as Grace was concerned.

The reception was for a small circle of close friends and immediate family, with Ava having told her mam in no uncertain terms that her cousins, the Nolan brothers, weren't invited. The Kellys would also be hosting their regular extra Christmas guests. To ask those without family to share the day with them and enjoy Christmas dinner at the Shamrock Inn was a tradition Kitty Kelly and her late husband, Finbar, had established to ensure no one in Emerald Bay spent the day alone.

Ava plunged her hand into the open bag of crisps on the table and crunched down a salty handful before speaking. 'So that only leaves table arrangements, my dress and your suit, someone in charge of photographs, and flowers. I'll need a bouquet. Honestly, Shane, I don't know why everybody fusses about this wedding business because it's a doddle. If I ever get sick of copywriting, I could have a new career in wedding planning.'

Shane put his pint glass down on the coaster. They were tucked away in the snug overlooking Main Street. Ava eyed the table's timber top with its names etched into the varnish separated by hearts pierced by arrows. In Paris, the bridges were weighted by padlocks, love tokens with couples whose names and the date they were there were inscribed on them before the key was tossed in the Seine. Here at the Shamrock Inn, it was tradition for couples to etch their names on this table hidden from the publican's view. Ironically, her mam's and dad's names were inscribed on it, as were hers and Shane's. She spotted Imogen and Ryan's freshly etched names. She had a little grin seeing Shannon and James, because Shannon had had to scratch out that French eejit Julien's name first, like it was an unwanted tattoo.

'Hello there, you two young lovebirds. Congratulations on your upcoming nuptials.'

Neither Shane nor Ava had seen Nessie Doyle, Emerald Bay's resident hairdresser, sidle on over, although they should have. She was hard to miss with her tufts of multi-coloured orange, red and yellow hair, reminiscent of a rooster's plumage. They were both startled, and Ava wondered if Shane was also waiting for her to start strutting about cock-a-doodle-doing. Then, remembering her manners, she smiled politely, but it didn't reach her eyes. 'Thanks, Nessie.'

Ava hadn't forgiven her for hers and Grace's one and only childhood bowl cut. They'd been acceptable in her parents' era of the seventies, but then so had bibbed, flared overalls and belted vests, along with a multitude of other crimes against fashion. She'd seen the photographs. Ava and Grace, however, were millennium babies – Britney Spears' long tresses were coveted, not the pudding-bowl cut. The only silver lining was that all the other little children in Emerald Bay had sported the same cut. It was a rite of passage, Shannon, Imogen and Hannah had informed their little sisters, to spend your childhood in Emerald Bay looking like you and your classmates were secret cult members' children, and even though she and Grace hadn't suffered as much as their older sisters, once was more than enough.

'How're you, Nessie?' Shane enquired.

'I'm very well, thank you, Shane. I hope you're on the mend there.'

'I'm doing much better, thanks. How's business?'

'Glad to hear it. Brisk is what it is. People's hair doesn't stop growing no matter what world crisis is happening. Sure, look at yourself there. Your hair could do with a trim.'

'I've been a little busy of late,' Shane fibbed, and Ava didn't dare look at him, because she knew he'd be working overtime to keep a straight face.

'Well, it's your lucky day, because I was fully booked tomorrow, but I've had a cancellation at eleven. I could sort you out then.'

Ava nudged his foot with hers under the table, silently conveying she didn't want to be walking up the aisle to meet a newly shorn convict.

'That's very kind of you, Nessie, but I've, er, I've an appointment tomorrow. My ribs, you know,' he replied vaguely.

'Well, I hope you're not thinking about standing at the altar with hair curling around your collar like so.'

'No, sure, I'll get a trim before then.'

'It pays to book this time of year, because there'll be no spaces left the way my calendar's filling up.'

'I'll bear that in mind. Cheers, Nessie.'

'And what about yourself there, Ava?' Nessie swung so quickly toward Ava that for a moment there, she thought she might peck her.

'Er...'

'For the wedding – have you booked your stylist? At Nessie's Hair Salon, we specialise in bridal hair.'

Emerald Bay was hardly overcome with blushing brides, and Ava doubted brides-to-be travelled far and wide for a Nessie special. For one ludicrous moment, she pictured herself in a beautiful gown with the haircut of her childhood then, feeling Nessie's beady eyes on her, wracked her brains for an excuse to get out of this without upsetting the hairdresser whose beak was as sharp as her bite. 'Er, I've got Imogen doing my hair, Nessie, but thanks a million for asking.'

'I don't recall Imogen qualifying as a hairstylist.'

'No, she hasn't, but, sure, she's a dab hand with the messy bun, which is the look I'll be going for, and given it's Christmas Day and all, I didn't want to drag you out.'

Ava could have kissed Eileen Carroll when her strident tones rang across the pub.

'Nessie, I'm thinking about a new colour for Christmas. What do you think?'

It was music to Nessie's ears, and she forgot all about Ava and Shane as she waddled over to the bar.

Ava and Shane burst into laughter as soon as the hairdresser was a safe distance away, and when they'd sobered, they sipped their drinks for a moment before Ava remembered Nessie had a point. She opened her notebook and wrote 'Hair' down. It had been a fib just now, because her hair and how to wear it on the day hadn't crossed her mind. Grace usually fixed it in different styles for her.

Grace. What was she doing right now? Was she thinking about her?

She bit her lip to quell the pang of loss, and a sudden memory clouded her vision of her and Grace when they were younger, shopping with their mam in Kilticaneel for new school shoes. They'd watched a bride and her new husband posing for photographs on the steps of the big stone church near the town's square, and it had sparked an earnest discussion over the sort of dress they'd like to wear when they got married. Even then, Ava had known hers would be simple, while Grace theatrically announced she wanted an enormous dress to rival those from *My Big Fat Gypsy Wedding*. She'd forfeit the orange spray tan, though!

Shane's voice saw her blink away images of frothy meringue dresses, but an ache remained inside her. He was watching her intently as he asked, 'Can I have the notebook and pen?'

Ava slid it over to him, surprised. So far, he'd been happy to go along with whatever she'd suggested. She watched as he scribbled something in it before passing it back to her.

He'd added 'Sort things out with Grace' to her to-do list.

'Very clever.' Her mood plummeted. 'And that's easier said than done.'

'FaceTime her. It's not hard, Ava, and you know yourself you can't get married without her there. She's your twin.'

Ava squirmed in her seat. She'd never thought there'd ever be a time when she'd feel anxious about contacting someone who'd always been an extension of herself.

'Your sisters' noses are out of joint about not being bridesmaids, too, and I know the only reason they're not is because you're scared of asking Grace.'

'I'm not,' Ava protested feebly.

Shane's expression told her he didn't believe a word of it.

She didn't want to deal with Grace or the bridesmaid issue. She wanted to go back to happily ticking things off her list.

'Talk to her,' Shane urged as he picked up Ava's phone and held it out to her. 'You'll feel better.'

Ava knew he only wanted what was best for her, but still, she was reluctant.

'Ava, do it for me, please.'

That did it, and she snatched her phone off him, telling him not to go anywhere before she marched through the pub, pushing the door to the kitchen open.

Kitty Kelly was standing at the bench measuring flour into a bowl. 'There's tea in the pot, Ava,' she said, not looking up.

'No time for tea, Nan, thanks.' She took to the stairs, eager to get to the privacy of her bedroom before she changed her mind.

'Napoleon, drop it,' she ordered, seeing him dragging a sock, hers by the look of it, down the landing. He ignored her, tail in the air as he disappeared into her mam and dad's bedroom to deliver his present. She thought she'd fetch it back later, stepping into her room and closing the door.

Then, flopping down on the bed, she stared at the phone in her hand as though it were a grenade. Would Grace even answer when she saw who was calling?

Ava half hoped she wouldn't so she could go back downstairs and tell Shane she'd tried, but her sister wasn't prepared to meet her halfway. She decided it was better to get this over and done with, taking a deep breath and pushing the call button. Her hand shook, and she tried to still the trembling while it rang.

Then, there she was, filling Ava's screen.

Ava felt like a lump of dry bread had lodged in her throat as she tried to formulate everything she wanted to say, but all that came out was, 'Hi.'

'Hi.' Grace's tone was clipped as she looked back at her sister.

'Er, so, you know about the wedding being Christmas Day and all?'

Grace's red bob swished back and forth as she nodded.

'I'd like you to be there, Grace,' Ava blurted. There, she'd said it. The ball was in Grace's court now.

'I'll be there. It's Christmas, Ava. I want to spend it with my family.'

Ava flinched as though physically hit. Grace's eyes were cold and her face set like a marble statue. There was no mention of her wedding. 'Well, that's all I rang for – to check you'll be coming.'

'I'll be there.'

The screen died, and Ava dropped the phone on the bed, pulling her knees to her chest and wrapping her arms around them. A sick sensation mingled with her anger. Grace had slapped the olive branch she'd extended away with her indifference. More than sick or angry, though, she felt sad, and brides-to-be weren't supposed to be sad.

This was supposed to be one of the happiest times of her life, she thought, tears burning. She blinked furiously, unwilling to give Grace the satisfaction of knowing she'd got to her. Even if she was in London and so far as she knew, Ava could now be Irish dancing around her bedroom.

'You'll go downstairs, Ava, and tell Shane you tried, and then you'll forget about her and focus on the wedding and making it the best day of your life,' she said to the empty room.

And that's what she did.

34

Galway was a lovely city at the best of times, but come the festive season, it was truly magical, Nora thought. Her arm was firmly linked through her daughter's, and she felt like she'd been transported to wonderland. It was eleven thirty in the morning, but the intermittent snow flurries made it hard to guess what time of the day it was. The shops they'd passed were shoulder to shoulder with rugged-up residents from near and far, keen to get their Christmas shop done before the last-minute rush. It was busy now, but they'd be bedlam come 24 December.

'Here we are. I'll be glad to get in from the cold. The tip of my nose is frozen solid,' Nora said, thinking she probably looked like Rudolph as they reached their destination, McCambridge's. The windows on either side of the popular restaurant, deli and fine-food shop were a visual feast of gourmet delights, and mother and daughter eyed them hungrily before stepping off the cobblestones and under the red awning. Nobody was braving the elements dining outside this morning, and they didn't pause to read the specials on the blackboard.

The family-owned business had been serving treats at 38–39 Shop Street since the 1930s, and Nora had been sure to book ahead. Now she felt the rush of welcome heat as she stepped into the inviting glow of the shop. Hopefully, there'd be time to pick up a few treats after brunch, she thought, her eyes flitting over shelves full of interesting, unusual condiments and the nearby baskets full of freshly baked goods. Liam had begged her to bring home some of their specialty Butter Fudge. He'd been disciplined of late, if you didn't count her catching him with his hand in the biscuit jar the day before yesterday, and deserved a treat, and she wouldn't mind one herself. The aroma of freshly ground coffee beans led them up the stairs to the cafe.

'I'm starving,' Grace remarked once the waitress, menus tucked under her arm, had steered them toward their reserved table, and they'd ordered a latte bowl for Grace and a cappuccino for Nora. The table overlooked the shoppers hurrying about on the pedestrianised street below. 'And I need a wee,' she added, draping her coat over the back of her chair. If she wondered why they'd been taken to a table set for three, Grace didn't ask. She just slung a 'Back in a mo' to her mam and hurried across the cafe to the washrooms.

Nora watched her go, discarding her coat and hat before settling herself at the table to tug off her gloves. Grace looked drained, she'd thought when she'd met her and Hannah at Eyre Square in the city's centre as arranged. Perhaps she was anxious about seeing Ava later, she mused, picking up the salt grinder and inspecting it. Or it could be down to having slept on Hannah's lumpy old sofa.

Grace was here under false pretences, the planning of which had been more complicated than a Forbes 500 business takeover, but, touch wood, Nora tapped the table, things were falling into place.

The initial moves had involved a phone call to her daughter offering to foot the bill for her flights home for a long weekend. Nora had said it was a chance to catch up before the madness of Christmas and the wedding. Grace, however, had been reluctant to accept, saying work had gone ballistic and she'd be back for a week over Christmas anyway. Nora suspected it wasn't work holding her back but anxiety over seeing Ava, so she'd brought in the big guns – Hannah – confiding her plan to ensure Ava had the happiest day of her life.

Her crusading daughter could be very persuasive when she wanted to be – sure, hadn't they the beehives to prove it? She also never missed a beat, and Nora had agreed to cover her petrol expenses, given that Hannah would be collecting Grace from Shannon Airport and driving her to the meeting point here in Galway.

As Nora had hoped, Hannah had worked her magic, pulling enough of a guilt trip to get Grace to agree to the long weekend, picking her up last night and taking her back to her gaff to doss down. Then, this morning, with Hannah's car, Doris, full to the brim with petrol, they'd been up early to make the journey to Galway.

The second phase of Nora's plans had been put into play with the suggestion of a mammy-daughter brunch here, at McCambridge's. Hannah had pretended she was meeting a colleague to distribute Feed the World with Bees pamphlets for a couple of hours. She couldn't join them but promised to meet up with them later. And right there was where things got complicated, because Hannah was, in fact, off to meet Ava and Imogen, whom Nora had driven into Galway with her.

Imogen was also privy to what was happening, whereas Ava was in the dark. She'd offloaded the twosome close to Brown Thomas on Eglinton Street upon Imogen's insistence she wanted to look for something to wear to the wedding before parking and hurrying to meet Hannah and Grace in the square. Shannon's patients needed her, so she couldn't get away that morning, but she would do her best to be in Galway in time for the wedding-dress shopping planned for the afternoon. Grace knew nothing of this and thought they'd be homeward bound for the Shamrock after brunch.

Janey Mack! Nora's head spun just thinking about it all. If it all went smoothly, she and Grace would join the others at the Galway Wedding Centre at one o'clock. She checked her watch, hoping Shane would be on time. She didn't need any spanners thrown in the works, thank you very much.

A woman at a nearby table was tucking into poached eggs from which bright yellow yolk pooled on seedy, thick toast. She'd a side serving of avocado. It looked scrumptious, but right now, Nora didn't think she'd manage much more than a cup of coffee. Her insides were churning as she pondered how this morning's rendezvous would pan out. She wasn't used to such subterfuge.

The woman looked up from her brunch, and Nora, realising she was staring, flashed her a smile before turning her head toward the window, watching the foot traffic below, hoping to spot Shane.

She'd never told so many fibs in such a short time, but she was trying to think of them as little white lies that didn't need to be mentioned to Father Seamus in the confessional.

Shane was under the impression he was meeting his soon-to-be mother-in-law for a one-on-one heart-to-heart about him becoming part of the Kelly family. She'd insisted on the Galway location, telling him tongues would wag in Emerald Bay. Besides, nobody did brunch quite like McCambridge's – not that Nora would be brave enough to say that within earshot of Carmel Brady! And Ava thought Nora couldn't join her and Imogen at Brown Thomas because she had a chiropodist appointment. Nothing was wrong with her feet, but as Nora had planned, Ava hadn't pressed for further information over her porridge earlier that morning.

Grace was a distraction from her racing thoughts as she breezed over and sank into her chair before flipping open the menu. Her daughter made appreciative noises over the offerings while Nora, still scanning the street, marvelled over the friendly smiles people exchanged as they passed one another below. Christmas brought out the best in people. She wondered if the spiced mulled wine, roasting chestnuts and gingerbread smells wafting off the various stalls on the labyrinth of inner-city streets had anything to do with it.

Oh, there he was! Her stomach lurched as she spotted Shane weaving his way through the crowds, hands shoved in his jacket pockets, a woollen hat pulled down over his ears. His form was instantly recognisable. It was strange and wonderful to think that lad confidently making his way toward McCambridge's would soon be hers and Liam's son-in-law.

Oblivious to her mother's reaction, Grace wondered out loud whether to have mushrooms on sourdough or to go all out with the McCambridge's full Irish.

Shane reached the top of the stairs and whipped his hat off, stuffing it in his jacket pocket just as the waitress approached to ask them if they were ready to order. Grace opened her mouth to place hers, but Nora jumped in and asked if they could have five more minutes.

'Mam, could you not have made up your mind while I was in the jacks?' Grace muttered irritably, dolloping a spoonful of sugar into her latte.

She'd always had a sweet tooth, Nora mused. 'I was too busy people-watching. I haven't even picked up the menu.' She stared past her daughter to where Shane had faltered upon scanning the tables, locating Nora and realising she wasn't alone. She waved vigorously, not letting him think about turning on his heel and disappearing back down the stairs.

Grace twisted in her seat to see what had her mam waving like she was trying to get a pop star on stage to notice her. She groaned on seeing Shane, slouching in her seat as though that would make her invisible.

Her eyes flashed as she fixed them on Nora. 'How could you, Mam?'

Nora steeled herself. She'd known this meeting between Shane and Grace wouldn't be easy when she'd begun organising it, but there was no point doubting her actions now. Neither of them would be leaving McCambridge's until their ongoing animosity was resolved.

As Shane drew closer to the table, dragging his feet, she took a slow, deep breath and thought, *Here we go*.

35

Nora patted the empty seat at their table in the busy cafe area. 'Come and join us, Shane.'

'Grace, Nora,' Shane greeted them before sitting down. 'You didn't mention Grace was in town, Nora.' His expression matched Grace's from a few moments earlier.

'No. I thought it best not to.'

Grace thrust a menu at him. 'I had no idea you were coming either. But since you are, can you make up your mind about what you're having so we can order, eat and say goodbye.'

Nora nudged her daughter's leg under the table at her rudeness, but Shane took the menu without comment. She supposed he was glad of an excuse not to have to make eye contact or conversation with either woman.

'Have whatever you fancy, both of you,' she piped up brightly. 'Brunch is my treat.'

Shane was too polite not to thank her as he scanned the menu, even though his expression said he'd rather chew his arm off than have eggs of any description with Grace.

When the waitress approached them this time, they ordered, and once she'd departed, an awkward silence

descended over their table. Shane picked up his knife as
though inspecting it for watermarks while Grace picked at
her nail polish, and Nora looked from one to the other,
pondered where to start. She moved her pursed lips from
side to side and decided there was no point in pussyfooting
around.

'In case you were wondering, I've engineered you both
being here together because someone had to do something
about the state of affairs between you and Ava, Grace,' she
began. Then, fixing first Grace and then Shane with her
sternest gaze, the one that would see the wooden spoon come
out of the drawer to be waved about when Grace was small, she
added, 'The only way I can see to do that is by you two clearing
the air between you, and I can tell you right now, neither of you
is leaving here today until you're on the same page.
Understood?'

Shane wasn't about to go head-to-head with the woman
who'd be his mammy-in-law in a couple of weeks, so he nodded
while Grace squirmed in her seat before mumbling,
'Understood.'

'Right then, Grace, you can start. I want you to tell Shane
why you've always felt threatened by him.'

'But I haven't, and I don't. Where did you get that from,
Mam?' Grace had pressed herself back in her seat on the
defence.

Nora raised her eyebrows but didn't say a word, and the
longer the silence stretched around the table, the more uncomfortable Grace became. She picked up a napkin and began
folding it into a fan, not looking at either Nora or Shane as she
finally spoke up.

'All right. I wouldn't say I felt threatened, but it was always
me and Ava. Then you came along.' She side-eyed Shane under
her lashes. He stayed silent. 'You took up all her time, and I felt
pushed out.' Her voice was small. 'It sounds childish saying it

out loud.' She shot her mother a look that said, *There. Are you happy now?*

Shane, equally uneasy, mumbled, 'I never meant for you to feel like that, and so as you know, I've pushed Ava to sort things out between you.'

Grace shrugged. 'Well, I did feel like that, and she hasn't.'

'Because you wouldn't meet her halfway.'

Grace glowered but didn't say anything as they both lapsed into a silent stand-off.

Beginning to feel like a maternal Judge Judy, Nora turned to Shane. 'I know you don't want this animosity between the girls, but to be fair with you now, Grace has been honest about her feelings. I think it's time you opened up, too.'

'God, Mam, this is like a bad reality TV show.' Grace's eyes darted about the dining area as though she expected to see cameras pointing their way.

'I don't know what you want from me, Nora?' A frown was embedded between Shane's dark brows, and he turned his gaze on Grace. 'I told you I've done what I can to get Ava to make things right between herself and you, Grace. And I apologised for making you feel pushed out when I came on the scene.'

'Er, no, you didn't.' Grace bristled as she sat up straighter in her chair, 'You said you didn't mean to make me feel like that. I didn't hear an apology in there.'

'I'm sorry. It was never my intention. Does that make you feel better?' Shane's voice was churlish.

Grace didn't appear to be appeased, and Shane, rigid in his chair, picked up his fork this time for inspection, obviously irked by her reaction to his apology.

Nora sighed. She would have to hold their hands and walk them through this.

'C'mon now, Shane, it wasn't one-sided.' Shane didn't meet Nora's gaze, but she continued nevertheless. 'I think you felt threatened by Grace's relationship with Ava.'

'Jaysus wept, Doctor Phil!'

'Grace, would you stop butting in? Shane let you have your say. Allow him the courtesy of the same.'

'I didn't feel threatened.' Shane finally put the fork down and raised his eyes, looking from one to the other. 'That's school playground stuff.'

'Yes you did. Don't make out I'm the child here.' Grace's eyes flashed as she ignored her mam's glare.

Shane fired back, 'Well, if I came across that way, it's because you were always trying to split us up.'

Nora's head swung between the two like she was watching a nail-biting match at Wimbledon.

'Ava had big plans, but you weren't interested. You wanted her under the thumb in Emerald Bay. I wanted her to follow her dreams.' Grace leaned back into her chair with a self-satisfied air at having painted him as the villain and herself the good guy.

'Is that what you think?'

'It's what I know. You wouldn't entertain coming to London with her even though you knew she was suffocating in Emerald Bay. Now you're suddenly getting married and going to America, which puts me out of the picture.' Grace's voice had risen a notch, her eyes were overly bright and a flush had spread across her cheeks.

Shane's shoulders slumped. 'That's not why we're going, Grace, and I never meant to hold her back.'

Nora reached over and patted his hand. 'I know you didn't. Grace does, too, deep down.' She held up her hand to silence her daughter. 'You want what's best for Ava. Of course you do.'

'I didn't want Ava to leave, because I couldn't,' Shane blurted.

Grace jumped in. 'Why not? Your dad's got Conor and Michael. It's not as if the fishing business would collapse if you weren't there, and you've your aunt running the fish and chipper.'

Nora kept her hand on Shane's this time. 'What was holding you back, Shane?' She could see the uncertainty on his face and sensed she was getting somewhere. Grace, to her relief, seemingly understood she needed to listen to what he would say next.

Shane cleared his throat but didn't speak.

'It's all right, love. We're as good as family.' Nora nodded encouragingly.

Shane's blue eyes searched hers for a moment, and then he said, 'My mam.'

His voice was so soft both women had to strain to hear him.

'I didn't understand it myself, not properly until the accident, and it sounds screwed up, but I'd stopped seeing her clearly like I used to be able to whenever I thought about her. She was beginning to blur around the edges, and I was scared if I left Emerald Bay, she'd fade from my memory for good.'

Both women stared at him, and then Nora spoke. 'Oh, Shane, you poor love.' Her voice was choked, and her heart ached for the young boy who'd lost the most important person in his life and never come to terms with it.

The fight had gone out of Grace. Her daughter's face had softened as she digested what she'd just heard.

'Did you tell Ava any of that?' Grace asked gently.

'Not at the time.'

'If you had, she would have told me; maybe I'd have understood.'

'But it would have stopped her going, and I didn't want that either.' Shane dipped his head.

'You have told her now, though?' Nora asked.

'At the hospital. When I was on that rock, not sure if I'd make it home or not, I realised that Mam's always with me wherever I go, and I don't have to choose between her, Emerald Bay and Ava.' His voice was throaty as he said, 'I don't want Ava to have to choose between you and me, Grace.'

'She loves you,' Grace stated matter-of-factly.

Shane nodded. 'And I love her.'

'I mean, she *really* loves you.'

'I've tried life without her in it, and I don't want to experience it again. I won't ever hurt her. I promise. And she loves you, too.'

Given life's unexpected curveballs, Nora thought that was a hard promise to keep, but she didn't doubt he'd try his hardest to keep his word.

'I want her to be happy, and you make her happy,' Grace said after a second or two had passed.

Nora's spare hand reached for her daughter's, squeezing it. 'That doesn't mean you're going to lose her, Grace,' she said softly. 'You're her twin. Her other half.'

Grace nodded slowly. 'Mam, do not say "the yin to her yang".'

'I wasn't going to.' That wasn't true, but Grace didn't need to know that.

'I never wanted to come between you and Ava, Grace. It would be impossible even if I'd tried. The bond between you is too deep, and the last thing I've wanted is for you and her to be out of sorts with one another during all this wedding stuff. She needs you by her side.'

His use of 'stuff' – such a typically male way of referring to wedding arrangements – made Nora smile. She could feel the warmth of both their hands in hers. 'It seems mad, doesn't it?' she said. 'When all either of you wants is what's best for Ava, yet there you've been pulling her in two different directions all this time.'

'What she needs, what she's needed all along, is both of us,' Grace finished for her mam.

Nora gently pressed their hands before releasing them. She felt lighter, and it was only now she realised the extent of the weight she'd been dragging about with her this last while, worrying about her daughters.

Shane held his hand out toward Grace. 'Can we start over?'

The curve of Grace's lips spread to a smile. 'A do-over?'

'A do-over.'

Grace grasped his hand, and they shook on it.

Nora hoped the waitress didn't notice the tear sliding down her cheek as she presented her with her smoked salmon brekkie.

36

Brown Thomas curved around a corner site in a prime location on Galway's energetic Eglinton Street. Ava had always loved the regal old building with its display windows on the ground floor, arched windows on the second floor and rectangle windows on the top floor. Today it had been transformed from a high-end department store to a Christmas palace with an abundance of holly wreaths, red bows, evergreen garlands and twinkling golden fairy lights.

'Slow down, Imo, I want to look at the Christmas windows first,' she urged, reaching for her sister's arm to haul her back as she strode ahead. Imogen was honing in on the entrance to her happy place. Ava didn't blame her, given the store was lit from within by a welcoming glow that promised warmth and a festive vibe.

Imogen halted, her frown unimpressed and her hair, carefully curled for today's outing, beginning to straighten under her beanie in the damp air. 'But it's freezing, Ava. And you know yourself, you've seen one Christmas window, you've seen them all. You can only put so many spins on the babby Jesus manger scene. Besides, I told Hannah we'd meet her by the services desk. We should have been there five minutes ago.'

Ava wasn't to be swayed. 'Just a quick look, I promise.'

She tugged Imogen over glistening cobblestones toward the clusters of tourists and shoppers wrapped up against the elements as they admired the store's iconic window displays. Then, teetering on the balls of her feet to get a proper look over the top of the woolly-hatted heads, she exclaimed, 'Oh, look, Imo! It's gorgeous, so it is. And it's not a manger scene – sure, there are penguins and Santa in there.' She thought someone was eating roasted chestnuts, too, her nose twitching.

Imogen was about to nudge Ava out of the way so she could have a look when Hannah materialised alongside them, stomping her feet and rubbing her hands. 'Hello, you two. I was worried I was going to be late. C'mon, let's get inside. It's freezing out here. Sure, I don't know what the fuss is about. If you've seen one Christmas window, you've seen them all.'

Imogen shot Ava an 'I told you so' look before giving Hannah a quick hello hug.

Ava stepped up next, hoping Hannah's coat, a relic from the seventies, had been to the dry-cleaners between then and now. It was two against one, and breaking away from her sister, she reluctantly followed Imogen's lead into the store.

'Hannah, so as you know, I don't want to hear a word about sustainability or consumerism today. I just want to find a dress for the wedding, OK?' Imogen tossed over her shoulder. 'And, Ava, FYI, I'm still not over the bridesmaid thing.'

'I can't promise anything, but I'll make a concerted effort not to remark on your fashion choices so long as we can go to a thrift shop afterwards. I need to find a dress, too. And neither am I. Over the bridesmaid thing, I mean,' was Hannah's reply. It was almost swallowed up by the piped Christmas music, chattering buzz and the odd squeal from an overwrought child that enveloped them as the doors closed in their wake.

Ava sighed. She was doing her best to be upbeat and excited. After all, today was a big day. She was going to choose her wedding dress and should be excited. Instead, it all felt muted. Finding the perfect dress to walk down the aisle in to meet the man she was about to marry was momentous, and she couldn't believe Grace wasn't here to help her.

How had things got to this point? And she could do without being offside with Imogen, Hannah and Shannon, who would show up as soon as she'd finished her rounds. So, injecting a brightness she didn't feel into her tone, she said, 'I'm sorry, but you know my stance on that, but it doesn't mean you can't both look gorgeous on the day.' Then sounding a little like a Girl Guide leader trying to instil enthusiasm in her troops, she rubbed her hands together, 'Let's go find the perfect dresses. Hannah, if you find something you like here, I'm sure we can sort something out.' *Or Mam could*, she added silently.

Imogen and Hannah exchanged a look that said Ava was missing their point and that it wasn't just about the dresses. Then Hannah paused beside a perfume counter, and her chest swelled sanctimoniously beneath her coat.

Here we go, Ava thought, knowing that look well.

'Ava, how long have you known me?'

'Er, since I was born, obviously.'

'Exactly, so you know my sentiments on—

'No!' Imogen made a stop sign with her hand. 'No talk about sustainability or consumerism, remember?' Then, side-tracked by a shiny perfume bottle, she picked it up and squirted her wrists.

Hannah's expression was comical as she attempted to swallow the lecture on the tip of her tongue. But then, salvation! She spotted someone she knew across the shop floor. 'Oh, there's Paula. I haven't seen her in forever. 'Paula!' She waved to a woman with her credit card out at the counter.

The woman's face broke into a wide smile when she noticed Hannah.

'We used to work together. I'm just going to say hello properly. I'll find youse both in a bit.' Hannah took off.

Ava and Imogen shrugged at one another, and Imogen brought her wrist to her nose and sniffed before holding it out for Ava to do the same. 'What do you think?' she asked. 'Toilet freshener?'

Ava dutifully inhaled and then coughed. 'It's not as bad as the peach one Dad's so fond of gassing us all with, but it's a close second.'

'I agree. I wish I hadn't been so heavy-handed spraying it now, but the bottle's gorgeous.' Imogen wrinkled her nose. 'Ah, well, never mind. Let's make the most of the peace without Officer Sustainability on the case.'

She didn't hang about, fast-tracking her way to womenswear. With an expert shopper's eye, she was soon plucking dresses off the racks, holding them out to either approve of or shove back.

Ava stood scarecrow-like, a human clothes rack, as Imogen draped various styles that passed muster over her arm. A mammy and her entourage of little ones hurried past them. The children's chatter was excited, and she drifted back to outings when she and Grace had been that size. To visit Galway around this time of year was an annual treat. They'd be in awe of the Christmas lights decorating the city, and popping up to the Brown Thomas Christmas shop had been a must. Seeing Santa Claus as well had been the icing on the cake. The tears that welled at the memory surprised her, and she blinked them back as fast as they'd arrived.

'You know you don't have to be a traditional bride, Ava. There are some gorgeous dresses here. Why don't you have a browse while I go and try these on?' Imogen was oblivious to

Ava's low mood or overbright eyes as she relieved her of the load of dresses. 'I'll sing out if I want a second opinion.'

With that, she marched purposefully toward the fitting rooms.

Ava nodded mutely, watching Imogen until she couldn't see her anymore. On automatic pilot, she pulled out a dress at random, the silken fabric running through her fingers. However, it could have been a hessian sack so far as she was concerned because all Ava wanted was Grace.

Not giving pride a chance to get in her way, she dug out her phone and rang her twin.

It rang and rang then went through to voicemail.

Ava disconnected the call, not bothering to leave a message. What was the point? Grace not picking up was a loud-enough message all on its own.

37

Nora stared at her phone with a frown. She and Grace were en route to the Galway Wedding Centre as arranged, having said goodbye to Shane outside McCambridge's, but there'd been a change of plan.

'Hannah met up with your sisters earlier and she's dragged them to a vintage bridal shop off the beaten track that her friend Paula told her about, and they want us to meet them there instead. Remind me to let Shannon know where we'll be.'

Grace nodded, stepping out of the way of a hurrying, suited man toting a brown paper bag beginning to soak through with grease.

'I'll google it and get directions, because I wasn't familiar with the street Hannah said the lane ran off.'

'Hurry up, Mam.' Grace's breath was plumes of white on the air.

Nora stabbed at her smartphone, sighing at her sausage fingers before announcing after several tries, 'OK, so we take a left at the end of the street, then the first right and then another left, which should lead us onto Longfort Lane. Have you got that?'

Grace was already striding off.

The wedding shop was simply called Second Time Around Sweethearts. It was rather cute, Nora thought as she and Grace eyed the gorgeous froth of white on display in the window before pushing the door open.

Inside was warm and toasty and tastefully done with polished floorboards, strategically placed Regency-style one- and two-seater velvet-covered chairs, and racks and racks of pre-loved wedding dresses lining the walls, illuminated by spotlights. Down the back of the shop, to the left of the counter area, was a red carpet leading from the curtained-off fitting room area.

Nora swiftly appraised the scene, noting Imogen's mouth was puckered, signalling things weren't running smoothly, while Hannah was inspecting the label on a dress, no doubt checking to see whether she approved of the fabric. A woman in varying shades of russet from the head down stood behind the counter, keeping a wary eye on Hannah while dealing with someone over the telephone.

Nora held her fingers to her lips, signalling Imogen to be quiet, not wanting Ava to know her twin was here until she'd had a chance to see how the land lay behind the fitting-room curtain.

Imogen embraced Grace, whispering over her shoulder, 'Shannon's not far away, Mam. She texted to say she'll be here in half an hour.'

Grand – this was more like it, Nora thought. All her girls together to help Ava choose her gown was as it should be. She reminded herself to pop into the milliners she'd found online before they left Galway, because she wouldn't be cheated out of a hat on her daughter's wedding day, no matter how zero fuss Ava said it would be.

'Our bride-to-be is in the dressing room, I take it?' Nora dipped her head in that direction.

Imogen rolled her eyes, as did Hannah, who'd put the dress she'd been checking out back, but Imogen was the one who spoke up. 'Honestly, for someone who supposedly wants a simple, low-key wedding, Ava turned into a bridezilla the moment she stepped inside the shop. Four different styles she's after trying on and not one of them right. Hopefully, you can sort her out, Grace. She tends to listen to your suggestions when it comes to fashion.'

Grace raised a smile while she fidgeted with her hands. 'I don't know about that, or if she'll be pleased to see me, but I'll do my best to find the right dress.'

'Of course she'll be pleased to see you. She thinks Hannah and I are fooled by her gung-ho gym instructor "we're gonna nail this" act, but we're not. She's miserable, and it's down to you not being here.'

'She does like the shrug, so that's something.' Hannah fetched a white faux-fur wrap with a diamante clasp.

'It's divine.' Grace admired it, stroking the fur.

Nora agreed. Although Ava couldn't very well walk up the aisle in nothing but a shrug, and time wasn't on their side when it came to finding a suitable gown. What if it needed alterations?

Hannah swivelled her eyes toward the woman behind the counter, still on her call. 'Yer woman over there couldn't do enough for us when we first came in, but now she's all bared teeth like an angry grizzly bear. Not many gowns qualify as eco-friendly from what I can see either.'

With her reddish-brown shaggy hair and similarly toned outfit, Nora could see the grizzly correlation. 'Surely vintage is a good-enough compromise, Hannah, given the dresses are getting a second inning.'

'Hmm.' Hannah didn't look convinced. 'And I'm telling you, Mam, there'll be no free glass of fizz like my friend Lottie and her crew were after getting when they went wedding-dress shopping. Not at this rate.'

'Leave it with me.' Nora smiled at the grizzly bear, who was now inspecting her fingernails – coloured to match her outfit – and explaining to whoever was on the other end of the phone that she couldn't guarantee sizes, being a stockist of vintage gowns, which meant she was reliant on second-hand dresses coming her way. Her tone grew pointed as she added, 'Hence the name of my shop and why my dresses are priced considerably lower than the competition.' She didn't return Nora's smile.

When Nora stuck her head through the fitting-room curtain a split second later, she was confronted with the sight of her daughter in an eighties-style white monstrosity with leg-o'-mutton sleeves. She was wrestling with the back zipper. Fashion might go around in circles – sure, her girls had often bemoaned her not having kept any of the eighties and nineties fashions – but some styles should never have got an airing the first time, let alone a second.

'What took you so long, Mam? Help me get out of this, would you? I look ridiculous,' Ava sniffed. Her face was a picture of frustration and despondency.

Nora stepped into the spacious fitting-room area, pulling the curtain closed before she wiggled the zip carefully down.

Ava stepped out of the dress, standing in her bra and knickers while her mam picked it up, slid it on the coat hanger and hung it up.

'I thought retro might work,' she said glumly.

This called for sugar, Nora thought, digging around in her handbag to produce a Jacob's club orange bar. 'Here – have this, Ava.' She thrust it at her flustered daughter.

'Thanks, Mam.' Ava snatched the bar from her gratefully. 'Everything always feels better with chocolate. What are you doing with a Club bar in your bag anyway?' she asked, unwrapping it. 'I thought you were off sugar between now and the wedding?'

'I always keep a Club orange on hand for emergencies, and your expression fits the criteria.'

'Oh, it is an emergency, Mammy.' Ava took a bite, mumbling through her mouthful, 'A great big one. I feel like calling the whole thing off.'

38

An enormous glass of wine would go down well about now, too, Ava thought wistfully, only half listening to her mam telling her there was to be none of this nonsense about calling the wedding off. She popped what was left of the orange-flavoured chocolate biscuit in her mouth. She'd best get it down before the boutique's owner returned with yet another dress in her size for her to try. It was doubtful she'd approve of chocolate being consumed near all this white.

She'd been keen to take up Hannah's suggestion to call in here because the prices would be less exorbitant, and she was mindful that her mam and dad were the ones springing for her gown. Besides that, she loved the word 'vintage', because it conjured up a bygone elegance. Of course, the other bonus of going vintage was it would keep her principled-to-the-point-of-being-a-pain-in-the-arse sister from going on at her. She'd thought it a win-win, but so far it was a lose-lose.

Mind, there'd been nothing elegant about that thing. She glared at the dress her mam had just hung up. Oh, how she wished Grace was here. She'd think the situation was gas and would have said between fits of laughter that all Ava needed was a bonnet and a crook to top off that monstrosity. Then she'd look like Little Bo Peep off to find her sheep instead of a radiant bride!

Ava was going goosy, standing about in next to nothing, but made no move to get dressed. She'd thought finding the perfect dress would be a doddle. Turns out it wasn't. The most surprising thing about shopping for her wedding dress was how exhausting all that clambering in and out of flouncy white gowns was, and she'd had enough.

Hearing the curtain rustle, she swallowed the last of the bar down in haste, feeling it scrape her throat on the way down.

It was only Imogen, though. She zeroed in on the wrapper in her sister's hand. 'Where'd you get that?'

'Mam's handbag.'

'You never told me you carried a secret snack stash with you. I'm starving, so I am, Mam. You don't have a bag of Tayto's cheese and onion in there, do you?' Imogen made a grab for her mam's bag, but Nora hugged it to her side.

'Get off. I'm not a one-stop supermarket shop, Imogen. You should have had something to eat before you left home.'

Imogen pulled a face and muttered something about Nora having favourites, adding, 'You know I had a Zoom with a client first thing. I'd no time for breakfast before you picked me up.'

They all knew Nan's ears were probably burning back in Kilticaneel. No breakfast was a cardinal sin in her book.

'How was it?' Imogen changed the subject, nodding toward the dress.

'I looked like I should be on an eighties soap opera. That or in panto, playing a character from a children's nursery rhyme.'

'Not good, then.'

'No.' Ava rubbed her arms, her bottom lip trembling. 'I think we might as well give up and go home. I'll borrow one of Nan's up-to-the-neck white flannelette nighties and be done with it.'

'What about this one? It's definitely you,' a familiar voice said. 'The champagne toning will work with our colouring, and the slip-dress style will suit your shape. I love this lace overlay, too. It adds a romantic, bohemian vibe. And, it's the right size.'

Ava's eyes popped as the curtain was pulled open to reveal Grace holding a dress up. Her eyes swung to her mam, who was giving nothing away, but Ava had no doubt she'd had a hand in her sister being here today.

What happened next surprised them all, including Hannah, who'd mooched up with Shannon. The eldest Kelly girl had just arrived, breathless and muttering about spending ten minutes trying to find the place.

Ava looked at her sisters, all there to support her, and burst into noisy sobs, because it dawned on her that the root of the problem today didn't lie with the dresses she was trying on. Well, a little where the one with the leg-o'-mutton sleeves was concerned. No dress would fit the bill because Grace should have been here with her. Now, as though she'd conjured her up, here she was, offering her the peace pipe in the form of a dress. A dress Ava could already see through her watery eyes was going to be the one.

Grace thrust the gown at their mam and stepped toward her twin, uncertainty flickering across her mirror-image features. 'I'm sorry, Aves. For everything.'

'Me too,' Ava spluttered, feeling how she imagined those who'd witnessed the Berlin Wall falling must have felt – an overwhelming, elated relief. She plucked a handful of tissues from the box the lady in russet had rushed over, burbling, 'Thank you.' Then, having dabbed her eyes and blown her nose, she flung her arms around her sister.

Nora herded the others away from the fitting room, pulling the curtain behind her. 'Let them clear the air on their own,' she bossed.

Inside the changing room, Ava and Grace were still embracing, half laughing, half crying over Ava's state of undress as they apologised over the top of one another.

'I didn't mean those things I said.'

'I shouldn't have always pushed you into doing what I wanted.'

'I kind of wanted you to.'

And so it went until they broke apart, and Ava, her lashes wet, wiped her eyes and gave her nose a good blow.

'Right.' Grace, too, composed herself. 'Let's do this.' She held out the dress for Ava.

The satin material felt like water rippling over her body as Ava pulled it up carefully, sliding an arm into each of the lace sleeves before standing with her back to Grace so she could zip her up.

Grace eased the zipper into place and rested her hands on her sister's shoulder as they gazed toward the mirror. Their silence was reverential until Ava breathed, 'I love it.'

Grace puffed up. 'I'm thinking of offering my services as a stylist part-time.'

'Oh, you definitely should.'

'Did Mam tell you she wants to go hat shopping, too?'

'Ah, no.' Ava grimaced.

'Ah, yes.'

'You know what she's like with her Francophile tendencies. It will probably be a flipping beret with flowers stuck to the side.'

They were still in fits when they stepped out of the fitting room.

'Ladies, we have a winner!' Grace announced.

Ava struck a pose on the strip of red carpet, and there was much exclaiming and orders to turn this way and that.

Nora began to weep, overwhelmed by the sight of her child, grown up and soon to be married. 'Seeing you like this, so beautiful, it's all just become real,' she said as Shannon put an arm around her mam's shoulder. 'They're happy tears,' she blubbed.

'It's fabulous.' Imogen clapped her hands. 'You look gorgeous.'

'You'll be the most beautiful bride the West Coast of Ireland's ever seen.' Shannon smiled. 'Won't she, Mam?'

Nora's nod was emphatic. 'Wait till your father sees you. He'll be a mess, so he will.'

'Can I see the label? I want to check the fabric.'

'Feck off, Hannah,' all four sisters chimed.

Hannah looked affronted, but then her eyes lit up at seeing champagne flutes arranged on the counter.

A cork popped, and the grizzly bear filled the glasses before offering them round.

Nora waited until all the glasses had been passed out and then announced, 'I'd like to propose a toast.'

Six glasses were raised.

'To my beautiful daughters.'

'To us.'

The sound of clinking glasses echoed off the polished timber boards.

'And to you, Mam,' Ava said, mouthing, 'Thank you,' over her champagne flute before taking a sip.

For the first time since the wheels had been put in motion for her wedding day, Ava was filled with happiness as bubbly as the cheap plonk tickling her nose.

39

Grace and Ava were sitting cross-legged on their beds in their pyjamas as they had when they were teenagers, comparing notes on make-up, fashion and boys. A packet of chocolate digestives found unopened in the pantry had been sneaked up the stairs as an illicit snack, and the bedroom door was closed. Unimpressed by all the girly giggling, Napoleon had curled up in a ball down the bottom of Hannah's bed and was making snuffling sounds in his sleep. It had been tempting to hang a 'Keep Out' sign on their bedroom door just like when they were younger, given this was their first opportunity to talk properly, but that would have been taking things a tad too far!

A slap-up lunch at their mam's insistence had followed the bubbly at the bridal shop, and time had got away from them. So it was that when they waved off Hannah, who was heading back to Cork, the only person going home that day with a dress for the wedding was Ava.

Dad had been waiting to hear what the dress had set him back when they filed back into the Shamrock, and Shane had been sitting with his brothers, supping pints. A second round of celebrations had ensued, which Kitty had ensured wasn't entirely liquid by doling out bowls of steaming, creamy seafood chowder with crusty bread for dunking. The recipe was a closely guarded secret; she'd joked she'd only reveal it on her deathbed.

It had been a wonder to see Shane and Grace being cordial with one another, and it had warmed Ava inside even more than the chowder. She'd blinked seeing Grace laughing over something Shane had said, and that was when she'd decided she'd been blessed with a second Christmas miracle. That or the best Christmas present she was ever likely to receive.

Now she and Grace kept laughing between bites of biscuits because, in their haste to fill the other in on all that had been happening these last few weeks, they kept talking over each other.

'OK, you go,' Ava said, flicking crumbs off her PJ bottoms onto the carpet.

'I've found a flatmate,' Grace said, her hand held out, fingers waggling, for the packet of biscuits.

Ava leaned across and passed them over. 'Sophie?'

'No.'

'Who, then? And more importantly, does she pick up after you like I used to?'

'*He*, actually.'

Ava hadn't expected that. 'He?'

'Christopher – Chris for short. He'd put a note on the board at the pub to say he was looking for a room. He's nice, even if he doesn't pick up after me.'

'Christopher.' Ava sounded his name out slowly. 'And what does he look like, this Christopher, then.'

Grace shrugged, digging around for a digestive. 'I don't know.'

'Not good enough. Give me a celebratory match.'

There was the sound of biscuit nibbling before Grace spoke up. 'OK, well, I suppose he's got a look of your Hemsworth one.'

'Fit, then. Which one – Liam or Chris?'

'Liam.'

'Aha! I see.'

'You see what?'

'Christopher and Grace, Chris and Grace.' Then in a lousy attempt at a seductive Italian accent: 'Christoph and Grace.'

'Ava!'

Ava grinned. 'I think they all have a nice ring to them.'

'Ha ha! You're hilarious, and don't go getting ideas. He's my flatmate, is all. Besides, he's got a girlfriend.'

'Oh.' Ava deflated as her bubble popped. 'So, there's to be no screwing the crew?'

Grace spluttered, sending biscuits crumbs flying. 'No!'

'But you'd like to. I can tell.'

'I would not.' Grace flapped her hand dismissively. 'Anyway, enough about that. Tell me more about your New York plans. It's so exciting. It's all so exciting – the wedding, everything!'

It was a clever change of subject on her sister's part, Ava thought, filling her in before getting around to the burning question of how Grace and Shane had come to declare a truce. She began at the beginning. 'What made you come home?'

Grace spoke through her mouthful. 'Mam, of course. She orchestrated a meeting with Shane and me earlier. Neither of us knew anything about it.'

Ava nodded. 'I thought she must have had a hand in things. Mam kept very quiet about it. I hadn't a clue she was meeting up with Shane either.'

'She was very sneaky, so. We had no choice but to hash out our issues with each other. You want to have seen her, Aves. She thought she was Judge flipping Judy preceding over her courtroom, only it was McCambridge's we were sitting in.'

'McCambridge's. I haven't been there for ages.'

'The brunch was as good as ever. I had the full Irish, and I could hardly move after.'

Ava pushed aside the image of rashers, eggs, sausage and black and white pudding. 'Was it like that time Imogen helped herself to the cooking sherry, and Mam lined us all up in the kitchen for an interrogation?' Ava nipped her bottom lip, nervous about what had happened between Shane and Grace, even though she knew it had all worked out.

'It was. Only add a little Doctor Phil to the mix, and you'll get the idea.'

'At least it wasn't Jeremy Kyle,' Ava said, making Grace grin.

'True.'

'Are you going to tell me what you said to each other?'

Grace shrugged. 'In summary, we both realised we've been eejits where the other is concerned. It dawned on us that you need us both, and we need you. For your information, Shane and I even had a hug today.'

That made Ava's eyes widen. 'Really?'

'Really. Things are going to be OK from hereon in, Aves. I promise.' Grace held out her hand, and Ava grasped it. Her twin held it tight before letting it go as she donned a vexed expression. 'And what's all this rubbish about you not having bridesmaids?'

Ava squirmed under Grace's piercing stare. 'I didn't want bridesmaids. Not if you weren't going to be maid of honour.' She cleared her throat. 'Will you be?'

'Your maid of honour?'

Ava nodded and then unfolded herself as Grace promptly burst into tears. 'Is that a yes?' she asked, wrapping her arms around her twin.

'Yes!' Grace sniffed.

'Shall we FaceTime the others and tell them they'll be bridesmaids after all?'

Grace swiped the tears away with the back of her hands and nodded.

Five minutes later, Shannon, Imogen, Grace and Ava were giving Hannah short shrift over her request for bridesmaid gowns made from hemp.

A glowing moon and a full tide are a good time to marry

— IRISH PROVERB

40

'Imogen, my false eyelash keeps pinging off! You didn't glue it on properly.' Hannah wasn't a false eyelash sort of a girl, and Ava was sure she'd been fiddling around with them when no one was looking.

The Kelly girls were gathered on this extra special Christmas morning in Hannah, Grace and Ava's bedroom. They'd been up since dawn enjoying a champagne breakfast followed by present opening before trooping upstairs to make themselves beautiful. The room smelled of hairspray and the light floral scent from Heneghan's Pharmacy that Ava had chosen to wear on this, her wedding day.

Ava was perched on the stool in front of their dressing table. Imogen had styled her hair into a tumble of loose waves and Grace was primping about with them. She put the finishing touch to Ava's half updo by sliding in dainty, gold flower pins with pearl centres. The sisters had clubbed together to buy her antique hair pins and the delicate baroque pearl pendant necklace resting against her décolletage as her 'something new'. Nan had given her pearl stud earrings to match.

'I did glue it on properly. Don't blame me. I saw you fiddling with it.'

Imogen had volunteered to do her sisters' hair and make-up this morning, but the sigh and shake of her head as she twirled the curling wand through Shannon's hair suggested she might be regretting it as her older sister piped up with, 'Not too curly, Imo. I don't want to look like a thirty-something Shirley Temple, thanks very much.'

'Hannah, don't be crawling about like so in your dress. You're such a heathen!' Grace exclaimed, horrified by the sight of her on all fours in her wine-coloured, flutter-sleeved velvet gown.

It had been no small feat to find a colour and style of dress, not to mention fabric, the four Kelly girls could all agree on, and now here, Hannah was getting hers covered in cat fur!

Hannah scowled up at Grace. 'Cop yourself on. I can't very well have one eye with long lashes and the other with little short stubby ones now, can I?'

Imogen turned, and Ava realised she'd seen something moving by the bed. 'What's Napoleon after batting about there?'

Hannah shrieked as she crawled closer to the Persian to see what he was playing with. 'Spider!' She might love bees, but she wasn't keen on creepy crawlies, and she shuffled away, eager to put distance between herself and Napoleon's hairy plaything.

'What's all the shouting?' Nora Kelly rustled into the room clad in her long-sleeved teal taffeta dress. She'd fallen in love with the sash, which the boutique owner said nipped in her waist. Matching pumps and hat completed the outfit as she took in the tableau.

'Hannah's being a drama queen,' Shannon supplied.

'Mam! You look beautiful!' Ava exclaimed, relieved that she wasn't wearing a beret on her head but rather a stylish wide-brimmed hat in the same teal as her dress. The colour was gorgeous on her. In the end, she'd found it in Kilticaneel, and this was Ava's first glimpse.

Nora was silent for a moment as she soaked in the sight of her daughter in her wedding dress, pride shining on her face. 'Oh, Ava.' Her voice was thick. 'You look so lovely.'

'Thanks, Mammy.' Ava got up to embrace her. 'For everything.' Her mam had been her rock from the moment she'd arrived back in Emerald Bay to wait for news of Shane. Today was down to her, too. For all her talk of it being a doddle to put together, Ava knew that without her in the background organising everything, she'd have been pushed to pull a wedding off in such a short timeframe. Mam had made it look easy. Grace and her being back on track, and Shane and Grace making their peace with one another, wouldn't have happened if she hadn't brought it about either. 'I love you, Mam.' There was a tell-tale wobble in her voice.

'Don't cry, or you'll ruin your make-up,' Grace bossed them both.

'Mam, there's a spider,' Hannah interrupted the mother–daughter moment by pointing to Napoleon.

Nora and Ava broke apart, and Nora rolled her eyes, going into business mode. 'Would you get off the floor before you wind up covered in cat hair. And did none of you think to take the poor thing off him?' She'd been a huge fan of *Charlotte's Web*. 'You all look beautiful, by the way.' Her eyes flitted over the bridesmaids and maid of honour. 'The wine colour's fabulous.'

'Thanks, Mam. But I'm busy. No time for spiders.' Imogen brandished the tongs.

'And I'm not to move. She said so,' Shannon replied, pointing her index finger over her shoulder to where Imogen stood. 'You know how bossy she can be, Mam.'

'Well, I shouldn't have to get involved in spider removal

because I'm the bride,' Ava stated, imperiously sitting back on her stool.

'I rank higher than them as maid of honour, which means it's their job.' Grace gestured at her sisters.

'And I've arachnophobia.' Hannah cowered in the corner.

'You've no such thing. Now get up.' Nora crossed the floor briskly to where Napoleon had a paw firmly over his new pal. She picked up his furry appendage and plucked the black spider between her thumb and forefinger. Only it wasn't a spider at all.

'What's this?' She held it out, frowning.

Hannah scrambled to her feet. 'My eyelashes! Oh, thanks, Mam, you've saved the day.'

'Drama queen,' Grace reiterated under her breath.

'Eww, you can't put that back on. You don't know where his paw's been.' Imogen curled her nose up.

The eyelashes were momentarily forgotten as Kitty popped her head around the door. 'Nora, James said to tell you we're leaving in five minutes. Shane, Conor and Michael will be off to the church in another ten minutes – Rory just rang.'

Shane had broken from tradition by having both his brothers as best men. Grace wasn't overly impressed given it meant she'd have to dance with not one but two Egan brothers, if anybody had the energy to break out the moves after the feast to be laid on later.

'Come in, Nan. Let's get a look at your outfit.' Shannon waved her in. 'Don't you look lovely.' She voiced what they were all surely thinking after Kitty stepped into the room and struck a pose.

'Will I do, then?'

'You'll want to watch out for Enda, Nan.' Imogen smirked but swiftly wiped it off her face upon receiving a fearsome bright-blue-eyed glare.

'Ignore her, Nan. You look beautiful, so you do,' Ava said,

admiring her floral jacquard jacket and matching skirt. She had a fascinator perched on the side of her head and a tissue-wrapped package in her hand.

Kitty turned to Ava, her expression soft as she appraised her lastborn grandchild, who was about to be her first grand-daughter to wed. Her eyes glowed, and her mouth trembled as she told her she'd never seen such a pretty bride.

Nora smiled, a faraway look in her eye, and Ava was sure she'd said the same thing to her the day she'd married their dad.

'I've something for you.'

Ava took the parcel with a curious smile and unwrapped it. 'A garter!' She held it up, giggling for her sisters to see.

'A blue garter, handsewn by yours truly.'

'Oh, Nan, I love it – thank you!'

She stood up, lifting the hem of her dress high before she placed a foot on the stool and bent down to slide the garter up her leg.

'And I'll have no smart-arse rude remarks.' Kitty eyed each of her granddaughters, who hastily closed their mouths.

'So now I'm only missing something borrowed,' Ava said, placing her stockinged foot back on the floor then letting her dress drop around her ankles.

'That's my domain,' Nora said. 'Back in a tick.'

True to her word, Nora reappeared with a silver-coloured box in her hand. She removed the lid and held it out to Ava. 'Your father gave me this for our twenty-fifth wedding anniversary.'

'I remember,' Ava said, holding her wrist out so her mam could affix the rose-gold heart charm bracelet around it. 'I'll look after it, I promise.'

Nora closed the clasp. 'It could have been made for you,' she said, admiring her slender wrist before stroking her cheek gently. 'I love you very much, Ava.'

'Don't make her cry, Mam,' Grace commanded.

'I love you, too.' Her tone became efficient as they broke apart, and she checked her sister over with a critical eye. 'Imo will go mad when she sees you've smudged your eyeliner. We'd best sort that out. There's bound to be a cotton bud in the drawer I can work some magic with.'

'Not as mad as when she realises she left her Kiehl's Creme de Corps body moisturiser here, and I've used it all up.'

They were still laughing when Liam Kelly's voice boomed up the stairs. 'Are you girls ready? It's time we were on our way.'

41

Five minutes of pandemonium ensued after Liam's announcement while shrugs and shoes were located. Finally, the five sisters, led by the bride, took to the stairs where their father, resplendent in his grey-and-black morning suit, was waiting at the bottom.

'Ah, Jaysus, would you look at you, Marigold. You'd break a man's heart, so you would. Why'd you have to grow up so fast?' Liam choked, using his pet name for her before wrapping her in an Old Spice hug. 'He's a lucky fella, your Shane.'

'Thanks, Dad.' Ava hugged him back hard. 'I think I'm lucky, too. To have Shane, you and Mam, Nan, even that lot.'

He rustled up a smile as she pulled away from the embrace to point at her sisters.

'And you look beautiful, Honey, Rose, Penny and Pearl.' Liam beamed, his eyes filling as he called them by their Connemara wildflower nicknames.

'Don't cry, Dad,' the four Kelly girls chimed, kissing him on the cheek as they filed past into the kitchen, where the smell of roasting beef filled the air.

Ava's bouquet of snowy white florals interspersed with deep

green foliage awaited her on the table, and she picked it up. She was getting married today. Her previous jitters were forgotten as happiness surged, and she breathed in their sweet scent deeply, holding the flowers to her nose.

'I'm not. My eyes are leaking, is all,' Liam muttered. Then, rallying himself, he hurried through to the pub after the girls, announcing, 'I've a surprise waiting for you outside. But hold up just a moment.'

The tables in the pub were laid in preparation for the festivities later, and the fire crackling in the grate bathed the festive decor in an amber glow. He tossed a fat log onto it to ensure the flames continued to burn in their absence, then strode importantly to the door before opening it. Outside, flurries of snow were beginning to fall.

'Milady, your horse and carriage await,' he said, holding his arm out for Ava to take.

'Dad, this is perfect!' Ava gushed, her excitement palpable as she gazed at Lorcan McGrath, who looked suspiciously like a funeral director in his coachman's livery, complete with a black top hat perched in the driving seat of the open-topped carriage. Blarney, his docile Clydesdale, was attached to it, waiting to do the honours. Behind her, her sisters were clamouring for a look.

'I recalled Lorcan telling me he'd picked up a carriage in relatively good condition at an antiques fair with a view on polishing it up and offering his services for weddings. He'd never got around to tidying it up, so I gave him a hand, and he offered a free test drive today. So here we are. Voila! As your Mam would say.'

Lorcan tipped his hat at Ava as Liam led her to the carriage, helping her and her sisters up.

'Will we all fit?' Ava asked anxiously as Grace crammed in alongside her, because it was only designed for four.

'Sure, there's nothing of youse. You'll be grand, and you'll keep each other warm. I'll ride up front with Lorcan.' Liam closed the door of the carriage and left them to squish up.

Main Street was like a ghost town as they clip-clopped around to the church, where the villagers had abandoned their slow-roasting dinners to witness two of their own being wed. The snow whispered around them, and Hannah poked her tongue out, catching a flake on it and making the others laugh. Their hair was flecked with white crystals.

The journey didn't take long, but it was just long enough for Ava to begin feeling anxious once more at the thought of the full church and saying her vows in front of all those people.

Grace nudged her gently, repeating her earlier sentiment. 'You've known them all your life. You've no need to be nervous. Remember one, two, three.'

She'd read her mind, and Ava flashed her a grateful grin, feeling the jumping crickets in her stomach settle down as a thrill coursed through her at the thought of soon becoming Shane's wife.

The little stone church they pulled up in front of looked as though it was trapped inside one of those snow globes Isla Mullins was after selling in her Irish shop, Ava thought, doing her best to elegantly step down from the carriage with a bit of help from her dad. She thanked Lorcan and petted Blarney before lining up behind her sisters, firmly attaching herself to her father's right arm on the church steps.

Inside the church, the ring-warming prayer would conclude with the Celtic gold bands she and Shane had picked out – tied together with a piece of ribbon and placed along with a bunch of shamrock on a bridal cushion – making their way back to Michael. Their rings would have been passed from one guest to another to be warmed in their hands while they asked for God's blessing of the couple and their marriage. Meanwhile, Mrs Rae, Father Seamus's housekeeper, who moonlighted as the church's organist, was playing a classical melody in the background. At the signal, she switched to Mendelssohn's 'Wedding March', which Father Seamus had conceded to allow, given it was a modern service and not a nuptial wedding Mass Shane and Ava were after having.

Ava knew that Father Seamus would now proceed from the vestibule to the altar and that Michael would follow with the rings secure on the bridal cushion. Then Conor and Shane, escorted by Rory, would walk forward to join him. Was Shane nervous? she wondered, and more to the point, had Michael made sure to keep a firm eye on those handling the rings during the ring-warming ceremony? These thoughts filtered away as she watched Shannon, Imogen and Hannah be enveloped into the welcoming inner glow of the church to glide down the aisle, followed by Grace as maid of honour.

'Ready, Marigold?' Liam turned toward his daughter, his eyes shining.

'Ready, Dad.' Ava smiled up at him, and together they walked or, in Ava's case, floated into the light to where her future husband was waiting.

Shane was flanked by his brothers, who were fidgeting anxiously. Ava noticed they'd scrubbed up well, shooting them what she hoped was a reassuring smile.

Her dad let go of her arm, leaving her to stand opposite Shane while he slipped away to join her mam and nan in the front pews. Ava was suddenly shy. Perhaps it was because she couldn't recall ever having seen Shane in a suit like so before. Her eyes ran over the tailored lines. Even though she guessed he'd be dying to ditch the tie and loosen his collar, he wore it well.

She raised her eyes to meet his. His hair had been neatly trimmed and shone under the lights, the smattering of stubble he'd sported of late was gone, and her nose was teased by the woody scent of the aftershave he knew she loved. Ava had all but forgotten she was standing in a church fit to burst as their eyes communicated a myriad of emotions without the need for words.

Father Seamus cleared his throat, welcomed them with the sign of the cross and addressed the congregation, reminding them of God's presence and his desire to bless Shane and Ava on their journey into married life. A quiet prayer followed, and the service, with its prayers, scripture readings, psalms, songs and reading from the Gospel According to Matthew 22:35–40 unfolded until, at last, their priest turned his questioning gaze toward them and began to ask their intentions toward one another. When it was Shane's turn to answer, Ava held her breath, absorbing the significance of the promises he was making to her before uttering her own. Then finally, Father Seamus said the words they were all desperately waiting to hear.

'On behalf of God and his church, I now pronounce you man and wife. You may kiss your spouse.'

The kiss had been included after some negotiation and a few free drams of the good stuff at the Shamrock, with the priest proclaiming nobody could ever say he wasn't open to the modern ways.

As it was, Ava wasn't sure she would be able to stop smiling long enough to kiss Shane, but as Grace stepped forward and took her bouquet from her, he moved toward her, slipping his arms around her waist. His fingers, as they pressed into the cool satin fabric skimming over her hips, were warm, and he pulled her to him so she could feel his heartbeat next to hers. Her arms wound around his neck, her fingers entwining in his hair as he dipped his head to meet her tilted mouth, his lips warm, soft and full of promise as they rested against hers.

The snow was still falling and looked to be settling on the ground when they exited the church to cheers, clapping and confetti. Ava had been presented with a lucky horseshoe by Sinead and Siobhan Molloy, which had delighted her, and between chatting to the familiar faces of the villagers who'd come out to see her and Shane wed, she sneaked kisses from her new husband, telling him this was the happiest day of her life.

Jeremy Jones was clicking away with the expensive camera he'd no doubt pilfered off his paper's photographer. The reporter had agreed to snap the complimentary photos in exchange for an exclusive on the Christmas Day wedding of Emerald Bay's miracle man. This time, Mrs Tattersall inadvertently photobombed the happy couple's first shot as man and wife as they exited the church.

'Toss the bouquet,' Freya called out, her blue hair a splash of colour against the white backdrop. Next to her, her fickle artist fella, Oisin, shifted from foot to foot warily.

Ava was happy to oblige and carefully stepped onto the icy path. Her back was to the crowd as the countdown chant began.

'Three, two, one!'

Ava threw her pretty flowers back as high over her head as she could and spun around in time to see Shannon nearly elbowing Isla Mullins in the eye as she leaped up, determined to catch it. There were claps of delight as Shannon, clasping the bouquet, gazed at James, her cheeks flushing pink as Eileen Carroll's less than dulcet tones rang out: 'You'll be next, Shannon.'

Meanwhile, Liam was being slapped on the back by Ollie Quigley, who was busy telling him he'd be putting his hand in his pocket for another wedding before he knew it.

'One more photograph of the Egan and Kelly families with their partners gathered together at the top of the stairs, and then we can all go home and enjoy our Christmas dinners.' Jeremy flapped them back up the steps and into position. Ava was sure he was beginning to think he was pretty good at this photography lark.

'Say cheese,' he commanded once satisfied that everyone was posed adequately.

'Cheese!' Shannon and James, Imogen and Ryan, Hannah, Grace, Nora and Liam, Kitty, Ava and Shane, Rory, Conor and Michael all grinned as the shutter clicked.

Rory kissed his new daughter-in-law on the cheek and welcomed her to the family. His sons followed suit, while Grace and Shane laughed about something.

Ava was filled with overwhelming joy. She was truly blessed, she thought, warm despite the cold.

It was then her attention was caught by a woman. She could be forgiven for thinking it was her mam standing on the periphery of the gathering, shrouded in a coat. She squinted into the gloaming, wondering if she was seeing things, and was about to call out when the woman turned abruptly, hurrying away.

Later, she'd hear talk of an American woman asking questions about the Kelly family, Nora in particular, but at that moment, she saw Shane. He was smiling at her and making a heart shape with his hands.

She made one back.

'C'mon with you now, Nora – leave the girls in peace. We've a handsome young American man waiting to chauffeur us to the church,' Kitty urged.

A sizzling sound could be heard, followed by Shannon shrieking, 'That better not be my hair you're after singing, Imogen!'

Nora and Kitty made their escape.

The nerves when they set in took Ava by surprise. They were down to Shannon's throwaway comment about the church being sure to be packed. Making excuses, she picked up her skirt and took herself off to the bathroom, where she stared at her reflection in the mirror. In a short while, she'd become Mrs Ava Kelly-Egan. It was what she wanted more than anything, but the thought of a church filled with people, all eyes on her, gave her palpations. Was Shane feeling the same way?

There was a tap on the door.

'Won't be a sec,' Ava sang out with false brightness, trying to relax her shoulders and breathe slowly. Her face was pale beneath her make-up.

'It's me, Aves. Let me in.'

'I'm grand, Grace.' Ava opened the door. 'Just a few jitters.'

'You've got this,' her twin said earnestly. 'You only need to remember three things as you walk up the aisle. One, you're the most beautiful bride Emerald Bay's ever seen. Two, you're about to marry the man you love, and three, myself, Shannon, Imo and Hannah have your back. OK?'

Ava's bottom lip quivered, and her voice held a dangerous wobble. 'I couldn't do this today if you weren't here with me.'

'Yes you could. You're you, and I'm me, but we'll always be together. I'm here for you whenever you need me.' Grace pulled her into an embrace. 'Don't ever forget that.'

'I love you, Grace,' Ava sniffed.

EPILOGUE

New York

The horizon swallowed the sun, leaving behind a skyline-streaked orange with tinges of dark purple around the edges. It slowly deepened, and the first lights in the iconic vista began twinkling. People were clapping at the goodnight spectacle the sun had put on for them. Ava clicked send on the cityscape bathed in gold she'd snapped before stuffing her phone back in her pocket. She smiled at Shane. 'I can't believe we're here.'

'Me neither.'

They'd arrived in New York two days ago. Shane already had an album of pictures on his phone sent through by Sinead and Siobhan of Jody settling in with the Molloy family. It had been hard to say goodbye to her, but at least he knew she would be well loved for however long their American adventure lasted.

And, speaking of adventures, here they were wedged between strangers on the eighty-sixth floor of the Empire State Building, staring out through the criss-cross of safety wires at a city that was familiar from having seen its skyline in so many movies and TV shows, and at the same time unfamiliar with its foreign sights and sounds. It was a view broken only by the Hudson River carving a watery path through the jagged urban sprawl below.

The overhead heaters tempered the stiff breeze whipping Ava's hair about her face where it peeked out from beneath the fur-lined trapper hat she'd pulled on. Close to where they were standing, a couple were posing for a photograph on either side of one of the many telescopes dotted around the 360-degree viewing deck.

Ava hauled out her phone again and opened the FaceTime app, waiting for Grace's face to loom back at her. She didn't have to wait long. 'We made it,' she squealed, panning the phone around. 'This is the view from the top of the Empire State Building!'

'Hey, Grace.' Shane waved as Ava aimed the phone camera his way.

'Hi there, brother-in-law!' Grace beamed at him. 'What do you think of the Big Apple, then?'

'It's amazing. How's London?'

'Pretty good, actually.' Grace looked coy but didn't elaborate.

Ava took charge of the conversation, filling her sister in on what they'd seen and done that day before signing off with an *I love you*.

Her twin echoed her words and blew them both a kiss. Then she was gone.

Ava stuffed her phone away then, standing on tiptoes, whispered in Shane's ear, 'I feel like we're in a film.'

'And if we were, what would we likely do next?' He grinned at her.

'Well, in this film, the hero would kiss the heroine, of course, and then they'd go and find a hotdog stand because the heroine's desperate to try a chilli dog.'

'A hot dog stand? I've never seen a couple share a big love

scene in the movies followed by them scoffing down hotdogs,' Shane protested.

'Shane Egan, this is my film.'

'Happy wife, happy life, sir,' the fully suited security guard standing close by interjected with a wink from under his peaked cap, making them both laugh.

'He's got a point, and I think I'd rather get that kiss in now than after the chilli dog.'

Ava laughed. 'Fair play to you.'

Shane placed his index finger beneath her chin and gently tilted her head upward. Ava rested her hands against the broad expanse of his chest, her eyelids fluttering closed as his lips pressed against hers.

The top of the Empire State Building was a long way from Emerald Bay, but Ava knew so long as Shane was by her side, she'd always be home.

A LETTER FROM MICHELLE VERNAL

Dear reader,

I want to say a huge thank you for choosing to read *A Christmas Wedding in the Little Irish Village*. If you did enjoy it, and want to keep up to date with all my latest releases, just sign up at the following link. Your email address will never be shared, and you can unsubscribe at any time.

www.bookouture.com/michelle-vernal

This story is predominantly a romance between Ava Kelly and Shane, but I so enjoyed writing about the relationship dynamics between Ava, Grace and Shane and spending more time getting to know Nora, too. I hope you found these aspects of the story interesting and that the love story at its core left you smiling. There's so much more to come with the Kellys, and I can't wait to share what happens next with you. I feel so lucky to spend my days writing about the Kelly family and the village folk who frequent the Shamrock Inn in the gorgeous setting of Emerald Bay, and I never forget it's down to you reading the stories that I do!

I hope you loved *A Christmas Miracle in the Little Irish Village*, and if you did, I would be very grateful if you could write a review. I'd love to hear what you think, and it makes such a difference helping new readers to discover one of my books for the first time.

I love hearing from my readers – you can get in touch through social media or my website.

Thanks,

Michelle Vernal

www.michellevernalbooks.com

facebook.com/michellevernalnovelist
twitter.com/MichelleVernal
goodreads.com/goodreadscommichellevernal

ACKNOWLEDGEMENTS

Thank you to my editor, Natalie Edwards, for her foresight in shaping this book into the best it could be, and for her enthusiasm, encouragement, understanding and love of this story. Thank you also to Natasha Harding for her watchful eye over my Little Irish Village stories.

Outside of the editorial, the fantastic Bookouture team work hard to send the best book package in all its formats out into the world. Thanks to Jess, Kim, Noelle and the team. Thanks to Jessica Regan – her delightful Irish accent and storytelling ability are perfect for narrating the Little Irish Village stories.

Thank you to the MRSC Valentia Irish Coastguards for sharing rescue protocol with me regarding a man overboard scenario.

Finally, I couldn't do what I do without my family cheering me on. I love you, Paul, Josh and Daniel. Oh, and I'd better not forget my trusty winter foot warmers, Humphrey and Savannah!

Made in the USA
Monee, IL
19 December 2023